MW01131306

HEART OF THE MAYA
MURDER FOR THE GODS

ERIC DOUGLAS

This is a Visibility Press original.
Copyright © 2014 Eric Douglas
All rights reserved.

ISBN: 1499544367
ISBN-13: 978-1499544367

DEDICATION

This book, like all before it, is dedicated to my family, for the unwavering support and encouragement they have given me over the years, even when they didn't quite understand what I was up to. Thank you, Beverly, Ashlin, Jamison and Kaitlin for tolerating me around the house...

CONTENTS

ACKNOWLEDGMENTS

A big thanks goes out to my readers and review committee: Beverly Douglas, Bonnie Blackwell, Rich Synowiec, Suzanne Garrett, Pam Collins, Elizabeth Gaucher, Leanne Stowers, Shelly Marsh Hodges and Kerry Collias. You each aided, abetted and inspired story lines and ideas in this book and I appreciate it more than you can know.

.

CHAPTER 1

"So that's how I ended up meeting the Castros. We solved the mystery behind the wreck of the *USS Huron*, found Spanish gold meant for Cuban revolutionaries and shined some light on *The Consortium* that was responsible for the whole thing.

"My degree in Journalism from Marshall University ended up taking me all over the world where I learned about many different world cultures. And I've loved every minute of it," Mike Scott said as he finished up his presentation at his alma mater. Because of his successes, culminating with the recent story of the *USS Huron*, he had been invited back to lecture as part of the University Artist Series. "In some ways, I feel like I've become an amateur archeologist, although sometimes I feel more like Indiana Jones than a real scientist. So, on that note, I'll take a couple questions."

Mike's presentation included photographs from many stories he had filed over the years and it had sufficiently wowed the students, faculty and general public alike. He explained how he had gotten his start and how luck, determination and skill had each played their parts in taking a small town boy from West Virginia around the world. As an international news photographer, Mike had won every major award available to him. After fielding questions for 20 minutes, he decided it was time to say good night.

"Thank you for these great questions, but I think they are about to turn out the lights on us. I'm going to wrap things up," Mike began, but he was interrupted as a student stood up and began talking.

"Mr. Scott, I'm sorry but I have one more question about your days here at Marshall. What do you remember about the archeological dig of the Adena mound when you were a student?" the young woman asked, nearly shouting

1

over the crowd as they had begun to applaud. The audience quieted, slowly, half-standing and unsure whether to leave or stay. For his part, Mike stood stock still. He hadn't thought about that incident in years.

"Wow, you've been doing some research," Mike said a little taken aback.

"Yes, sir, I write for *The Parthenon*, the school paper, and I decided to check to see if you were in the paper when you were a student. I found the final story you wrote about the incident really interesting," the student explained.

"Unfortunately, I don't remember much. After our graduate student advisor drowned in the cave, we were ordered to drop the project and most of us were too upset to do anything else. I can say without a doubt that incident encouraged me to learn to dive and to continue my pursuit of journalism. It probably piqued my curiosity for archeology as well. So, while I put that event behind me, it definitely shaped the rest of my career. Okay, well, thank you all for being such a wonderful audience. Good night!" Mike ended as he began picking up his notes from the podium. The crowd applauded and then began filing out of the Edwards Performing Arts Center.

As he finished up and spoke to the organizers of the speaking engagement, out of the corner of his eye Mike watched the young woman who had asked the last question. At 6'2", it was easy for Mike to see over most of the crowd. The girl hung around and looked like she wasn't quite finished. Mike was curious to see what else was on her mind. He was tired but he knew he wasn't likely to get any rest right now anyway.

Still, he waited for the girl to approach. He wasn't about to make it easy on her.

"Mr. Scott, do you have a minute? Can I ask you another question?"

"Technically you just did. But, sure. First, though, I get to ask two questions."

"What's that?" the student replied, slightly confused by his response.

"What's your name?"

"Sophia Cruz, sir."

"Okay, enough with the sirs. My name is Mike. Cruz? That was the last name of the grad student on the project. "

"Yes, sir, umm, I mean Mike. He was my uncle, or would have been. He died before I was born."

"Thanks for the reminder of how much older I am than you and just about everyone else on campus. So this meeting and your 'discovery' of the article wasn't an accident, was it?"

"Actually it was. I decided to check back in the archives to see what you had written about and was shocked when I saw you were writing about my uncle Erick. I knew his story, or at least the family version of it, but thought I would see if you knew anything different."

"Fair enough. Tell me what you know and I'll see if I can remember anything else."

"What was your second question?"

"Where can we get something to eat? When I was in school we would go to Hulio's, but when I drove into town I saw it wasn't there anymore," Mike said with a laugh. "I'm hungry. And don't worry, it's my treat. I remember being a broke college student."

CHAPTER 2

The restaurant was crowded and noisy, filled with students, faculty and townies, but Mike quickly drowned it all out as he slipped into his memory of a time 25 years before. The restaurant was in the same location as one of Mike's favorite haunts when he was a student, making it that much easier to forget the "here and now" and go to "then".

It was 1989. I was a sophomore and taking an anthropology class for a humanities credit. It was a little odd for me to get involved with a dig out in the field like that, but I was also writing for The Parthenon *and the professor in charge of the class said I could come along and do a story on it as well. It was great for me. I got credit for two classes at one time. The editor wasn't thrilled, but it all worked out. I, of course, had dreams of working for* National Geographic, *like every other journalism student, so I saw it as my big break. I didn't count on all of the hard work and digging, but that's how we learn, I guess.*

We were excavating an Adena burial mound that had recently been uncovered. There were several others in West Virginia, Ohio and Kentucky, but none this close to the Ohio River in West Virginia. It was a pretty exciting find. The farmer who owned the land thought it was just a natural land feature and had ignored it for a long time. He was digging an access road on his property and cut through part of the hillside with a bulldozer. He stopped when he saw bones sticking out of the ground.

He immediately called the police. Once they realized the bones were ancient, not evidence of a murder or an old cemetery, he called the university and rerouted his access road. And then we got involved.

Finding a new Adena burial mound in the late 20th century was pretty exciting for all of us. Most of the mounds had been excavated or destroyed long ago. The Adena themselves existed from about 1000 BC up to 200 AD and had left these burial mounds all over the

Ohio River valley as well as other places. They are viewed as a precursor civilization to many of the Native American populations that came along later. All things considered, they were pretty advanced for their time, too. They traded over the eastern United States from the Great Lakes down to the Gulf Coast.

So, we went out to the mound for weeks, slowly sifting through the dirt. We found several skeletons and then some burial beads and things. Whenever we would find something we would all gather around and 'ooh' and 'ahhh'. Your uncle, Erick, was heading up our daily activities and kept us going. He supervised the whole thing, under the watchful eyes of the professors, of course.

The most amazing day, though, was when we found the well. We were digging into the hill, excavating sideways into the mound. We hit a section of stone that had been buried at the base of the mound. You could tell it wasn't natural rock the way it was shaped. The stones were fitted together. We knew this was something really special.

Erick made us all slow down. He told me to get my camera and from then on, I was there to document everything they found. I shot rolls of film as the rest of the students dug around the stones. We eventually excavated a room inside the mound itself. There was this stone chimney on the floor a couple feet high. It was capped with another stone. The floor of the room was stone, too, so we knew we were down to bedrock. We decided the mound was probably built around this thing, whatever it was. Erick was careful, though, to not let us try to remove the capstone on the structure until we had the room dug out. They brought in some basic mining equipment to shore up the roof and the walls so we wouldn't get buried if the mound collapsed.

After the professors came out and looked over what we had done, they gave us permission to remove the cap stone. It ended up being the cover to an underground cave system. At first we lowered lights down inside, but we couldn't see much. We lowered a camera down the hole and found a big room with what looked like two more openings off to the side. On one side, there was water that came up from an underground spring. Of course, we were all convinced this was the greatest archeological find of the century.

Eventually, we got permission to climb down and look around in the caves below. They brought in Adena experts from all over. None of the students were the first to go down, but we did get down there eventually. Of course, we spent our time measuring and photographing everything. I was having a blast. I got to file several stories and was having dreams of going straight to National Geographic before I graduated.

We didn't find much in the caves at first. There were a few pieces of broken pottery and that sort of thing. There were paintings on the cave walls, too. It was interesting, but sort of fizzled out after a while. A lot of the experts speculated why the Adena had buried the caves under a mound, but it was mostly speculation.

And then Erick found something in the water. He was sitting at the edge of the pool taking a break when something caught his eye. It was just a straight edge, but Erick thought it might be important. He waded down into the water to get a closer look. It was a stone tablet with carvings on it, but it wouldn't budge. He ended up going home and getting a mask so he could look at the stone underwater.

After much examination and expert opinion, the professors all agreed that the Adena had made the carvings on the stone right where it was. The stone wasn't moveable. That meant the water level was lower at some point. No one knew if that meant the water had just been a few feet lower or if there was a larger cave system below.

After that, Erick became a little obsessive about it. He said he thought the carvings on the stone looked more Mayan than Adena, but that didn't make a lot of sense because while the Maya were around at the same time as the Adena, they didn't flourish and really excel at everything we know the Maya for until after the Adena had dispersed. He told everyone who would listen to him that the real discovery and the answer to all of the questions surrounding this mound would happen in the caves below. It was all he could talk about. He wanted to make a dive into the flooded part of the cave and see what was down there.

The university, on the other hand, wasn't thrilled about allowing anyone to dive into the cave to explore further. Everyone thought the risks were too high.

The rest is the hard part to discuss. We went back to the mound to continue the dig one morning. Your uncle told us to meet him there. When we got there, his car was already in the parking area we had set up. We looked all over the place for him, but couldn't find him. Until we looked down in the cave. We saw Erick floating face down in the water. He had scuba gear on, but he wasn't moving. He had decided to dive in the cave on his own and prove his theory.

After that, the university shut everything down. It was a big mess for a while. Promising graduate students weren't supposed to die on university-sponsored digs. The farmer who owned the land ended up putting a steel door over the opening and closing it off to further exploration.

We were all told to move on to other projects. I didn't end up learning to dive until I had graduated from college and then my career took off in other directions. To be honest, I never forgot about it, but I never thought about going back to the site after that.

CHAPTER 3

Mike and Sophia were sitting in Fat Patty's, a local burger joint adjacent to campus. Mike glanced around the room, thinking of his old days. He didn't feel like he had changed much in the 20-odd years since college, but his dark wavy hair was a little grayer now and things hurt more than they used to. He kept in good shape, mostly by staying active and on the go, rather than a significant exercise routine, but he didn't think he looked a lot different than he did back in school. Of course, that was what he told himself. He was sure the students in the restaurant thought he was a professor…and an older one at that.

After they ordered, Mike had started talking, walking through the story as he remembered it, surprising himself with just how much he could pull up. Sophia had the good sense to simply listen and let Mike talk.

When he was finished, they both looked down and realized they were finished eating, having done so almost on autopilot while Mike spoke.

"That's about all I remember," Mike said when he finished. He looked down and realized his beer glass was empty, too, so he signaled the waitress for another round—beer for him and Diet Coke for Sophia. He had spent the entire time talking and he knew Sophia would have questions.

"Thank you for taking the time to tell me about all of this. You've given me more than anyone else knew or could remember. It was a pretty rough time for my family and they don't like to talk about it much," Sophia said, sadness in her eyes.

"I'm sure it was. I can't imagine what it's like to lose a child like that, especially one with so much promise," Mike agreed. He had seen plenty of death on assignment, but some deaths were more memorable than others.

"I've always been curious about the whole situation and couldn't find out much until just recently. My granddad was cleaning out some boxes in his attic and found some of Erick's papers. After he died, the university boxed up everything in his office and sent it home. His parents, my grandparents, were so upset at the time, they never looked at any of it. Grandpa didn't want to look at it, but he said I could go through it if I wanted," Sophia explained. "Most of it was pretty typical stuff for a grad student. He was teaching a class and doing his own work toward his doctorate so he was pretty busy. And then there was all of the field work from the dig."

Sophia pulled some papers from his backpack and spread them out on the table.

"Of course, I was most interested in the notes from the dig to see if there was anything about what he planned to do. You're mentioned in there a couple times, by the way, and he had a picture of yours as well. It had your name on the back of the print. I hope you don't mind if I keep it," Sophia said, suddenly afraid Mike would want it back.

"I gave that to your uncle. It belongs to your family. Was there anything else in there?" Mike asked. "I'm guessing you wouldn't have brought all of this along if you hadn't found something interesting."

"Most of it is pretty mundane stuff. You could tell he was really excited about the dig. In the last couple days before he died, there are a couple of interesting things. He made a note on one page that he thought he was being followed. There is even a copy of a police report. He said he got run off the road on his way home from the dig site. He was in a university vehicle so he had to file a report even though there wasn't any damage," Sophia said, showing Mike the note on the report. "They didn't seem to take it very seriously, though."

"Pretty hard to prove. The campus police probably thought he was making it up to explain why he had a problem with the car. What else?"

"Whoever boxed everything up included a copy of the police report into his death, including the coroner's report. It had a note on it, addressed to my grandfather, saying he should read it. He never did," Sophia explained. "I didn't see much in it that seemed out of the ordinary. They declared the cause of death as drowning."

"That's pretty typical for dive accidents, especially when the medical examiner doesn't know much about scuba diving. They find traces of water in the diver's lungs and airway and rule it as drowning," Mike agreed. "And it's consistent with someone who made a dive and ran out of air underwater. He was back in a cave and couldn't make it back to the surface in time. He would have lost consciousness and then drowned. It's a terrible way to die."

"I thought that was the case and I did some research. I found out pretty much exactly what you just said. But here is what I don't understand. In the police report, someone checked out Uncle Erick's equipment. There's a note that he had 2800 psi in his air tank," Sophia said, pointing out the line in the report so Mike didn't have to search for it.

"A full tank only has about 3000 psi, so that tank is essentially full. That doesn't make sense. Someone could have made a mistake, I guess, but it's not really likely. If that's the case, he never made the dive. He died on the surface," Mike said, concern growing on his face.

"And that would mean someone killed him, wouldn't it?"

Mike was quiet for a few minutes while he looked through the accident report in greater detail. The police had called in a local dive instructor to consult on the incident. The diver had also noted that the equipment wasn't assembled correctly. Erick's regulator was on backwards and it was facing the wrong direction in the buoyancy jacket the grad student was wearing when he died.

"I never heard about any of this at the time. Not that I knew anything about diving yet, but it's strange no one reported this," Mike said, clearly puzzled by what he was reading.

"My family said Erick was an experienced diver. He had made more than 100 dives before the accident and been all over."

"I'm really confused by all of this and I don't like what I'm reading. Someone who has made that many dives wouldn't assemble their gear so poorly. It becomes second nature after a while. You just can't do it wrong. But the air thing has got me really concerned. We found his body floating on the surface and now I read he had a full air tank. He could have had a seizure or something, I guess, but really the only way that could happen is if he was unconscious when he got in the water and that means someone put him there. He was probably still breathing when he was pushed in the water and that was when he drowned."

"So you think he was murdered?"

"I'm not ready to go there yet, but something is weird. If its murder, whoever did it knocked him unconscious and then put him in his gear, putting it together wrong, and then put him in the water," Mike said, ticking off the points on his fingers.

"But you agree something is suspicious, right? I think we should go to the police. There's no statute of limitations on murder right?" Sophia said, standing as she said it.

"Hold on a second. First, it's late. Second, I've had a couple beers. The police are not going to want to see us right now," Mike said, motioning Sophia to take a seat. "Third, I want to read this a bit more closely and see if I can figure out what's going on. If we're going to get the police to reopen a 25-year-old case that was ruled an accidental drowning, we'll need to have more than this to go on. They will just write it off saying someone made a mistake about Erick having air in his tank. And we still don't have any proof that someone didn't make a mistake."

"I noticed you said 'we' several times. You'll help me figure out what happened?"

"I don't see how I can do anything but help. You've just told me there is a chance someone killed a friend of mine; someone I looked up to. I'm definitely going to get to the bottom of this," Mike said. "But remember, this won't be easy. The police aren't going to want to deal with this. That's no reflection on them. They have a lot of other things on their plate. We're going to have to give them more to go on than just our word."

"What do you want to do next?" Sophia asked.

"Well, it seems I have a little celebrity status as an alumnus 'who done good'. Let's see where that gets us. Let me take these papers and read through them. We'll meet on campus tomorrow and see if there is anyone still around who was here at the time and ask some questions."

CHAPTER 4

Mike didn't get much sleep after he dropped Sophia off at her dorm on campus and went back to his hotel. A trained and experienced journalist, when he was on the trail of a story, his mind went into overdrive. He started at the beginning, combing through Erick's notes and the dig journal. Instead of allowing himself to reminisce this time around, Mike read everything with a critical eye. He wanted to get inside his friend's mind and see what Erick was thinking in the days leading up to his death.

Done with that, Mike read every line in the coroner's report. The coroner had declared the cause of death "drowning while scuba diving". There was water present in Erick's lungs and airway. The coroner also noted some contusions and abrasions on Erick's face and hands, but didn't speculate what might have caused them except to note that it was likely Erick had probably panicked in the cave system below and hit his head on the rocks over his head while trying to find his way out. The injuries weren't thought to be directly related to the cause of death.

When Mike was done reading the reports, he decided to see who was still on campus. Searching through the university website, he discovered that the professor in charge of the dig was now the dean of the Anthropology Department, although a press release Mike found indicated the man, Dr. Dan Rowe, was about to retire.

Satisfied that he had a place to start, Mike tried to get some sleep, tossing and turning through dreams filled with memories of college life and the archeological dig.

The next morning, Mike met Sophia at 10:30 on the plaza outside the Memorial Student Center. The plaza included a large fountain to commemorate the deaths when 75 people died in a plane crash returning from a university football game against East Carolina, including 37 members of the football team, eight members of the coaching staff and local community supporters on November 14, 1970.

Mike was standing in front of the statue reading a plaque that included the names of those lost when Sophia approached him. His broad shoulders were slightly slumped as he thought about the tragic loss. And that reminded him of the loss that was closer to home for him; the one that Sophia's questions brought back to the fore.

"You weren't on campus when the crash happened, were you?" she asked quietly, trying not to startle Mike.

"No, I was here 20 years later. I didn't know anyone directly involved. It's just something we should never forget. College students aren't supposed to die," Mike answered as he turned and looked her in the eye. "Just like your uncle."

"Did you find anything in Erick's papers?"

"Not a whole lot more than what you told me last night, but I'm convinced something else was going on. It definitely looks suspicious," Mike said as he turned to face the young girl.

"What do you want to do next?" she asked.

"The professor in charge of the dig, Erick's graduate advisor, is still on campus. I want to talk to him and see what he remembers," Mike explained.

"Do you think he had anything to do with it?"

"Not really, no. Anything is possible, I guess, but I doubt it. I just want to see if he remembers anything from those days. But listen, I want you to leave this to me."

"Why?"

"Like I said last night, I have some credibility that you don't have yet. He may even remember me from when I was a student. I can talk to him about the 'old days' and get him to open up. If he thinks you're digging into your uncle's death, he might get defensive. Right now, I'm just trying to figure out what happened."

"Can I come along?"

"Sure. Absolutely. You started this whole thing. I'm not trying to take it over. I just think he'll talk more to me than he will to you," Mike said. "Okay?"

"Sure, that makes sense. And thank you," Sophia said.

"For what?"

"For taking this seriously and listening to me. You could have blown me off and gone on about your way when you were done last night, but you didn't. I appreciate it."

"Fair enough. You're welcome. Erick was my friend, too. I want to find out what happened to him. This isn't what I expected to get into today, but somehow I always seem to get involved with things like this. I've ended up stumbling across most of my best stories while I was looking for something else," Mike said. "I called ahead and checked. Dr. Rowe is in his office this morning. He's in Smith Hall. That's still over that way, right?"

"Yep, that's where I just came from. I was in a Journalism class, but the Anthropology Department is just upstairs," Sophia said. "Let's go."

As Mike walked across campus toward Smith Hall, where he took most of his own classes while studying Journalism so many years before, he found his mind wandering a bit, unconsciously searching the faces of students he passed for anyone he recognized, knowing that was unlikely.

Entering Smith Hall, Sophia immediately headed for the stairs, the quickest way to get anywhere in the building. By the time they reached the seventh floor, Mike was breathing hard, but the college student seemed unfazed.

She gave him a smile when they got to the correct floor.

"Remember, you do this every day," Mike said, returning the smile.

"Maybe you should stop taking 'vators."

"You're probably right about that. Now come on," Mike said with a laugh.

They walked down the hall, dodging students until they found the entrance to the Anthropology Department. A student was sitting at the reception desk reading from a text book.

"Hi," Mike said as he approached. "I'm Mike Scott. Is Dr. Rowe available? I'd like to see him for a few minutes."

"Do you have an appointment, Mr. ...ummm, Scott did you say?"

"Yes, Mike Scott. I'm sorry I don't have an appointment. I gave a presentation on campus last night and thought I would stop in to say Hello if Dr. Rowe has a moment," Mike continued.

"Madeline. Mr. Scott doesn't need an appointment. I've always got time to talk to a distinguished alumnus," Dr. Rowe said as he stepped outside of his office and gestured toward him with a big smile. "I saw you were on campus, but I couldn't believe it when I heard your voice. Come on in, Mike."

Rowe stood tall and straight, looking Mike directly in the eye, just as Mike remembered him. His hair was white now, and the close-cropped beard the man wore was almost the same color, but his eyes were still sharp and bright and the professor had moved from merely handsome, as Mike remembered him, to distinguished.

"Good to see you, Dr. Rowe," Mike said, easily slipping back into the professor/student relationship. "This is Sophia Cruz. I hope you don't mind me bringing her along."

"Not at all, Mike. I'm always happy to meet a friend of yours. Are you a student here?" Rowe said, turning to Sophia.

"Yes sir. I'm majoring in Journalism."

"So, she is one your protégés, I gather," Rowe said as he moved around behind his desk. "I would have thought you would be spending your time on campus talking to your old professors downstairs."

"I definitely plan on seeing what they've done down there and how *The Parthenon* has changed from when I was a student, but I wanted to stop in and say 'Hi' for a minute."

"It's great to see you, Mike. I've enjoyed reading about some of your exploits and I really enjoyed your talk last night. You're probably right, you're a little closer to Indiana Jones than what we teach here, but you've still made some important contributions nonetheless."

"Oh, you made it to talk last night?"

"Yes, I did and I have to admit I was startled by your young friend's question about Erick Cruz and the events surrounding his death," Dr. Rowe continued, nodding to Sophia. "Is that why you're here?"

"It is, Dr. Rowe. I'm sorry to bring up difficult memories, but I was wondering if there was anything you could remember from those days."

Before Dr. Rowe could answer the question, another professor stuck her head in the door and started talking.

"Hey Dan…Oh, excuse me, I didn't realize you had visitors," the stranger said as she entered the room.

"No problem, Dr. White. Come in," Dr. Rowe said as he motioned the woman into the relatively small office. "Mike, you remember Dr. White, although if I remember correctly, she didn't have a doctorate when you knew her."

Mike turned around to look at the woman who had entered the room. It took him a second to place the name and the face.

"Hi Alivia, err, excuse me, Dr. White," Mike said extending his hand. The woman took it with a forced smile.

Dressed as one would expect a college anthropology professor, in a simple blouse she bought on a field excursion into South America and slacks, Alivia White stood 5 '10" and wore her blonde hair in a pony tail. Mike remembered her as attractive, and that hadn't faded, but he also remembered Alivia as being a no-nonsense person who didn't seem to have time for fun or relationships when she was in school and that didn't seem to have changed either.

"Hi, Mike. Good to see you. And you don't have to call me doctor. I save that for the students," White said. "Call me Alivia."

"Alivia, Mike just asked me about the events around Erick Cruz's death. You were a grad student in the department when that all happened weren't you?" Rowe asked. "You probably knew Erick pretty well I guess."

"Yes, I was, Dr. Rowe. It was a terrible time, but honestly I didn't know Erick all that well," White replied. "We were going different directions at the time. He was really involved with the dig on the Adena mound and I was doing some different research. We had a few classes together and would see each other in the halls, but that was about it."

"Mike, I don't know if you've heard, but I'm about to retire. Dr. White is going to be taking over the Anthropology Department next semester when I'm gone," Rowe said.

"Good for you, Alivia. You've done very well for yourself," Mike said. "Do either of you remember anything unusual about Erick in those last few days before he died? Was he acting strange?"

"I don't," White said without hesitating.

"Mike, I really haven't thought about that incident in a while, and my memory has probably faded. It has been 25 years, of course. But I do seem to recall Erick coming to me with concerns about the dig and safety out there. He thought he saw some people watching the site. He was afraid of looters coming to steal items to sell on the black market. They...well, I guess you were out there so you know that nothing 'valuable' was ever found. There were some skeletons, of course, and some pottery shards and things. Items academics would find interesting, but not collectors."

"That's interesting, Dr. Rowe. Erick never said anything to the rest of us about security concerns, or at least not that I recall. It was a long time ago," Mike agreed. "Was anything ever published about the find? I assume the research into the artifacts went on after Erick died and the dig was shut down."

"Actually, several papers came out of the project. I'm sure you were credited in them. We probably used some of your photographs," Rowe said and then he turned to the other faculty member. "As a matter of fact, Dr. White ended up taking over the research after Erick died. That was what you used for your doctoral dissertation wasn't it?"

"Yes, I based my dissertation on the discoveries from the dig. It ended up going into several academic journals," White agreed.

"Would you mind loaning me some of those papers? I'd be interested to read them and see what came from it all," Mike said as he stood. "Now, I think we've taken up enough of your time. I do need to get downstairs and see what has become of the Journalism floor."

"Dr. White, would you ask the work-study student at the front desk to make copies of the various papers from the Adena mound project. They're all in the files," Dr. Rowe said as he stood to shake Mike's hand. "It is very good to see you Mike. I'm glad you've been so successful. It is always good to hear about the successes of a former student. Once Madeline has the papers copied, I'll have her bring them down to the Fourth Floor."

"Great to see you, too. Both of you," Mike said, acknowledging Dr. White still standing in the doorway. "Thank you."

Mike and Sophia walked outside and Sophia started to say something, but Mike shot her a look that told her to be quiet. They moved toward the steps at the end of the hall, before Mike said anything else.

"Well that was a bust," Sophia said as they entered the stairwell.

"Really? You think so?"

"We didn't find out anything."

"I disagree. We found out several things. Your uncle came to his advisor to question the security of the site. He wasn't a nervous or paranoid guy, so something made him uncomfortable. That confirms his police report. Also, we found out that Dr. White ended up profiting from Erick's death. She ended up taking over the research when Erick was gone, leading to several publications and her doctorate. She said she had been working on some other research, but she didn't say what it was. It must not have been very important if she dropped it and devoted herself to the Adena mound."

"Wow! Do you think Dr. White had something to do with it?" Sophia asked, excitement filling her voice.

"Who knows? But it's possible. She certainly ended up gaining from Erick's death and that is a motive. In the academic world, publishing is everything. I'll do some more checking, but I'll bet she did pretty well from it all. And, of course, professional jealousy is a huge motivation. I've seen people do a lot of things for a lot less."

"So that woman killed my uncle."

"Hold on. We have a long way to go before we make that case. I just said that to show you that there is more going on here than meets the eye. We definitely don't have enough to start making accusations."

"What do we do now?"

"Well, I do need to go talk to some people at the "J" School, and we'll wait on those papers. And then I'm going to see if I can get into the dig site. From what I've heard, it's been locked up since Erick's death. I want to see what it looks like."

"Do you really think that will tell us anything?"

"Maybe. Maybe not. This is one of those times when we don't know what we don't know. We won't find that out until we go look."

CHAPTER 5

Sophia had to go to her next class, and no matter how much she wanted to go along, Mike wasn't about to let her skip—even though they both knew she wouldn't really be concentrating. He promised to pick her up after he checked things out.

Being alone gave Mike some time to think about what he needed to do next. He wanted to look into the cave, just to confirm it had been left alone since Erick died. He wanted to get in the water and see if he could find what Erick was looking for and died for. His entire career he had spent investigating other people's mysteries and solving other people's problems. This time it was personal. He wasn't entirely sure how he felt about that.

To do what he wanted to do, Mike was going to need some dive gear. He hadn't planned on diving on this trip home, so he hadn't brought any dive gear with him. This was supposed to be a trip to his alma mater and a chance to see his family. So much for that. And then he needed access to the burial mound. It was on private property and it might be tricky to get the access he needed. A quick online search of local businesses gave Mike exactly what he was looking for, for the first problem, and a pleasant surprise at the same time.

Closer to the industrial side of town, along the Ohio River, Mike pulled into the parking lot of his destination, Scuba Adventures. Along with dive gear, he was going to need a dive buddy to help him out. As it turned out, he thought he could find one of those here, too.

Mike stepped into the store and looked around the place for a moment, waiting for someone to come out and greet him. The place was filled, almost to bursting, with dive gear and mementoes and pictures from dive trips all over the world. One wall was covered with a display of ancient shark's teeth, many as big as Mike's fist, from the Cooper River in South Carolina.

"Any divers in this place?" Mike called out after a minute when no one came. "I guess I'll have to leave."

"Hold on a second, I'll be right there. I'm up to my elbows in compressor oil," a man said as he entered the showroom from the back drying his hands on a towel, a dark smear showing on his forehead.

Mike simply stood there grinning, waiting on the other man to look at him. It only took a minute.

"Mike, is that you?"

The shop owner, Rich Synowiec, caught Mike up in a bear hug with much back slapping.

"Great to see you man! This is awesome!" Rich said. "What's it been? 20 years? You look great!"

"Good to see you too, Rich," Mike said, laughing at his old friend's reaction. "How's business?"

Rich stood 5'9" and had to look up to Mike's 6'2". His curly dark hair was showing hints of gray but had otherwise barely changed from their school days, Mike noted, and the shorter man still kept it under a ball cap to keep it under control. Rich was fit from his regular dives in the Ohio River as a commercial diver. Mike and Rich were roommates at Marshall with Rich studying business management and Mike doing time in the "J" school. For a couple of years, they had been inseparable, even though they didn't have many overlapping classes. After graduation, they had tried to keep in touch, but both had drifted apart as lives and families took their attention. It took them a few minutes to catch up.

"You don't know how happy it made me to see that this was your business. You talked about opening a dive shop in school. You wanted to go away to commercial diving school and then come back here and work just like your dad did. Looks like everything fell into place for you," Mike said.

"Let's just say it wasn't exactly a direct path, but I made it back full circle to where I started, and where I wanted to be," Rich agreed. "Is this a purely social visit, or do you need something?"

"I wish it was just a social visit, but I need a favor. I need to make a dive."

"It so happens that I can take care of you, Mike. Any excuse to go diving with you. When and where?"

"How about today?" Mike said and then he caught his old friend up on what he was talking about.

"You're really in luck today, my friend. At any other time it would have been difficult to get away on short notice. Let me make a couple of calls to get the shop covered and of course I'll go with you. I remember Erick and that whole mess. It was terrible," Rich said. "But the best part is I have a farm not far from the burial mound. I know the woman who owns the place now. Her father owned it back in the day and now she runs the place."

"That's great. Do you think she'll let us in?"

"It's been locked up tight since Erick died, but I can always ask and see what she says."

Rich left Mike for a few minutes to make a couple of phone calls. The current landowner was home and agreed after Rich explained what they wanted to do.

A commercial diver as well as a scuba diving instructor, Rich had a van full of equipment already loaded, including air compressors and full-face masks he and Mike could use to stay in contact. Rich didn't have an underwater housing for Mike's camera, but he had a smaller camera and housing they decided to take along. An hour later, they were geared up and ready to take off.

Mike called Sophia and caught her just as she was coming out of class. They picked her up in the van and headed to the farm and the site of the Adena Indian burial mound. When they arrived 20 minutes later, Rich jumped out of the van to get things ready. Mike and Sophia both moved a little slower.

"This is going to be sweet!" Rich said as he opened containers and began setting up gear. When he didn't get a response, Rich turned to check on his old roommate. "Mike, are you okay?"

"Yeah, Rich, I'm good. Sorry, this is just the first time I've been out here since the accident. I hadn't thought about what it would feel like to see it again. Lots of old memories," Mike said. He turned to look at Sophia and saw a troubled look on her face.

"This is where Erick died," she said simply. "It nearly destroyed my grandparents."

"Sophia, I'm sorry, I hadn't thought about how hard this might be for you. We can take you back to town," Mike said.

"No, Mike. I want to stay. I want to see it all, and I hope we find something that answers my questions," Sophia said, with a deep breath. "I'll be fine."

"All right, guys. Let's get things set up and see what we can see," Rich said. "Madeline, the farmer who owns this place, told me that she didn't have the key to the chain holding the door shut, but she told me to just go ahead and cut it off. I told her we would replace it," Rich explained.

"How about we go open things up and see what we've got to work with before we drag a bunch of dive gear out," Mike said.

"Awesome. I'll get the bolt cutters and let's go take a look."

The parking area that Mike remembered near the burial mound had returned to nature, but they had gotten the van as close as they could. From there, it was an easy walk down a gentle slope to the mound's entrance. They all slowed as they approached, each in turn thinking about what had happened inside. Rich moved forward to inspect the door and the chain holding it shut while the other two stayed back for a moment. Both the chain and the door were heavily rusted as if they hadn't been opened in years. Without a word, Rich sprayed some rust cutting solution on the hinges before picking up his bolt cutters to cut away the lock holding the chain in place.

The metal in the lock gave way easily and Rich pulled the chain away, dropping it to the ground with a clank. He tried the handle on the door, but it didn't budge. He pulled harder, grunting as he did. The sound of his old friend's exertion shook Mike from his stupor and he approached, sliding his fingers into the gap between the door and the frame that had been set into the side of the hill. The two men worked together, pulling and then releasing the door, until it started to move. They rocked the door back and forth, straining the rust in the hinges. With each effort, they got the door open a little bit wider. After a few minutes, they were able to pull it open far enough that they could slip inside. Turning on the flashlights Rich brought with them, they entered the excavated chamber inside the Adena burial mound.

"Wow," Sophia breathed as she slipped inside. She turned slowly to survey the excavations made by the students, under the direction of her uncle, 25 years before. "I've seen all the pictures, of course, but this…this is different."

"Looks just like I remember it," Mike said. "Everything we found and cataloged went back to Marshall, so there isn't much to see up here. We really just dug this area out to expose the entrance to the chamber below."

The Adena burial mound itself stood more than 50 feet tall above the gently sloping ground. The university excavation had cut a hole into the side of the hill approximately six feet tall and then had expanded the room further, hollowing the hill out. It was a man-made conical cave with smooth walls leading down to a rock floor with timbers placed inside the hollowed-out hill to support the roof and keep the researchers safe. The walls had darkened over the years, aging from red clay and topsoil to a uniform brown-black. The only feature remaining in the room was the "well". Built from local river stones, the Adena had built a short structure two feet high to protect the entrance to the natural caves below. It resembled a well from above, but it wasn't filled with water; at least not until you got down into the cave system.

Mike flashed his light beam at the raised platform in the middle of the room. He saw a plywood board covering the hole through the chimney rising out of the floor. Moisture and age had deteriorated the board so badly it broke apart in his hands when Mike tried to move it.

"Doesn't look like anyone has been in here in a long time," Rich said.

"They said it was closed up right after the accident," Sophia said.

"I know, I just wasn't sure that that was true," Rich said, looking around the room. "Dust on the floor and the rust on the door tells me it hasn't been opened up in a long, long time and quite likely 25 years."

"What we really came to see is down below. Let's get our gear and get down there. I want to photograph everything we see, too. Let's grab the ladder and some lights as well," Mike said.

It took them a few minutes, and a couple trips to bring down lights, a ladder and their dive gear, but they finally had it all assembled at the top of the well. Mike and Rich flipped on the larger lights they brought along and immediately illuminated the room. Before they climbed into the hole that led to the cave system below their feet, Mike quickly photographed everything he saw, including the three of them and their gear. Rich lowered the ladder through the opening into the room below and then strung a light on a rope and lowered it down as well.

"I want to see where I'm headed as we go down there," Rich said with a shrug.

"Afraid of what's below?" Mike asked with a grin.

"You know, I've seen enough horror movies in my day that I don't go blindly, backwards, into a dark room. And definitely not in a creepy burial mound," Rich said, half jokingly.

"That makes sense to me," Mike agreed.

"You're the only one here with any experience with this place. I guess you get to go down first," Rich said.

"I would argue with that, but you're probably right," Sophia spoke up, speaking for the first time. "I really want to see the area below, but I can wait on Mike to go down first."

"You're both chickens," Mike said with a laugh. "Come on. Let's go see what we can find."

Mike stepped over the short wall that formed the chimney on the floor, leading down into the cave and began climbing down the ladder Rich brought along. He carried a flashlight in one hand and had his camera slung over his shoulder. The light Rich lowered into the lower room lit up the floor near the ladder, but not much else. Not that he would have admitted it, but it was a little creepy for Mike—and he had been in the cave many times.

When he reached the bottom, about eight feet down, Mike slowly turned to look around the room, shining his own flashlight as he did so. It would have been an exciting moment for him, if it weren't for the memories being there stirred up. He had been one of the first people, with two others, to discover Erick's body floating in the water. They had jumped in the water to pull him out and try to save him. When they realized Erick was long dead, they left him beside the water and went to call the police. In an era before cell phones, they had to leave the burial mound, dripping wet, and drive to the farmhouse where the farmer who owned the land lived. The rest of the day was a blur as the police arrived and shortly afterward the people from the university.

Mike jumped slightly as Rich bumped into him, climbing down the ladder.

"See a ghost?" Rich asked.

"Sort of, I guess," Mike said. Over the years, Mike had seen more than his fair share of dead bodies, even those of friends, when working as a war photographer. But memories of Erick were different. That was the first dead body he had seen, outside of a funeral home, and it was a friend.

"Sorry man. Didn't mean it that way," Rich said.

"No worries. Let's just get to work," Mike agreed.

Sophia joined them a moment later and the three of them inspected the site. Mike pointed out the cave paintings on the ceiling and wall and then directed them to the water that still filled part of the cave.

"That's where Erick was sitting when he saw the straight-edged rock. It got him thinking and exploring. That was what made him want to dive the site," Mike said, pointing to an area on the right.

Having sat undisturbed for 25 years, the water was clear as glass although they could tell there was a fresh layer of silt across the bottom. Dust and rain had slowly brought more sediment into the flooded cave system. An underground spring supplied the water.

"I see where you're pointing out the straight edge. But what is that?" Sophia asked, pointing her light off to one side. "It looks like someone dragged something out there. See how the mud is bunched up on the sides and smooth in the middle."

"You're right. It looks like someone pulled something really heavy out of there," Rich said. "It's been a while. The scrape marks are covered in the fresh layer of sediment, but someone definitely pulled something out from under water."

"I skimmed through all of the papers Alivia White and Dr. Rowe published about this dig site. They never mentioned anything about coming back to the cave after the accident and definitely never mentioned any other recoveries or discoveries," Mike said.

"Something isn't adding up," Sophia said.

"I think it's time we get in the water and see what we can see," Mike said.

CHAPTER 6

Rather than bringing conventional dive gear, Mike and Rich had agreed on a setup more commonly found on a commercial dive site. Rich kept the gear packed and ready to go in two large plastic bins, each about five feet long. Each one was set up with everything a diver would need. It took the threesome about 15 minutes to lower the containers into the lower section of the cave and unpack everything.

They both planned to use full-face masks so they could speak to each other, rather than using hand signals to communicate under water. They were also going to use surface supplied air. Their tanks would remain on the surface and they would remain connected to them by an extra long air hose. Staying connected to the surface made the communications easier and also assured they would always be able to find their way back out of the cave. They weren't prepared for a long cave exploration and didn't know what they might reasonably find. They simply wanted to take a look around and see if "something" was missing. Although neither diver knew exactly what that "something" might be. Their communications cables were connected to a single box that Sophia could control. She would also be able to hear what they said and talk to them.

"How do you want to handle this?" Rich asked.

"Let's take it easy. I only have a couple of goals for this dive. I want to take a look at that tablet Erick found. We'll clean it off and photograph it. And then I want to see if we can figure out where those old drag marks came from and see if we can tell what came out of there. Lastly, I want to make it back to the surface alive," Mike said, without humor.

"Roger that. I'll be your wingman on this one. You just direct me where you want to go," Rich agreed.

"I really don't expect to be underwater too long, probably 15 or 20 minutes at the most. And we have a maximum of 100 feet, right?"

"That's right. We've each got a little more than 100 feet of air hose. I could get more if you want, though," Rich said.

"No, let's keep it simple. If the cave system goes on further than that, we'll leave that up to the professional cave explorers. We'd need a lot more equipment and support if we were going to do that," Mike said.

After a quick safety check of their equipment, Mike and Rich zipped up their DUI drysuits to protect them from the cool, spring-fed cave water and donned their facemasks. They confirmed they could hear each other and that Sophia could hear them as well. The moved to the far side of the pool of water and did their best to enter the water as gently as they could. They didn't want to stir up the sediment. There was no water flow and they had no way of knowing how long it would take the water to clear again if they stirred up a silt cloud. As soon as both men were floating on the surface of the water they agreed to submerge. Mike was carrying Rich's camera in the underwater housing and both men were carrying dive lights and backups as well.

The communications gear they were using made both divers sound as if they were talking inside of a tin can and they had to listen to each other inhale and exhale, but at least they could hear each other.

"This water looks great, Rich. It's like the freshwater springs in Florida," Mike said. "A bit colder, though."

"You're right about that. It's like swimming in air. One difference. Remember, there's no current. Keep your fins up off the bottom," Rich said.

"No doubt about that. Okay, come around me and let's look at the tablet first. I want to get a couple photographs of you cleaning it off and then I'll take some close ups of it."

Rich was much more comfortable diving in close, confined spaces like this and accomplishing a task. He did it every day. He easily moved around behind Mike and approached the outline of the submerged tablet where it rested just a few feet below the water. Mike marveled at the man's ability to glide through the water, barely appearing to move a muscle. Using a gloved hand, Rich pushed the accumulated silt off of the flat rock, being as careful as he could. He traced the outline of the mostly-square rock and then spent a little more time cleaning sediment out of the grooves carved into the stone.

"Mike I see a problem already. I can tell that this has been carved, but it looks like someone hit it with a hammer a few times. Some of the symbols are messed up."

"Can you tell if the damage is ancient, or it's been done more recently?"

"Just a guess, but I would say more recently. The grooves from the original carvings are pretty smooth, like they've been underwater for a long, long time. But when I run my fingers across where it looks like it was hit, the edges are a lot sharper."

"Someone tried to destroy it, or at least hide what it said. That tells me something is going on here."

"I wish I could see what you guys are seeing," Sophia said, startling both divers.

"Hey there kid. How're you doing up there? I almost forgot about you," Mike said.

"I'm fine. It's a little creepy up here all by myself, but I'm okay."

"Hang tight. We won't be too much longer," Mike said. "Rich, if you have it cleaned off, let me move in there and get some close ups. We might be able to tell something from the symbols that are left undamaged."

Rich backed away from the stone tablet and Mike moved in, photographing as he went. When he got close enough, he filled the camera frame with the tablet and took a few more images. Then he moved in even closer, thankful that the camera had a built-in close up feature, and took photographs of individual carvings as well.

"Now what?" Rich asked when Mike appeared to be finished.

"Let's follow the path of the drag marks."

"Roger that."

Just a few feet away, both men could easily see where two parallel mounds led down deeper into the submerged cave with an unnaturally flat spot between them.

"Put your hand in the middle of the mounds. I want to get some scale," Mike directed his old friend.

"Got it. Looks like it was about a foot wide," Rich said. "And pretty heavy, too."

"I agree. Whoever did it probably wrapped a rope around it and just pulled it up to the surface," Mike said.

Rich was slightly ahead of Mike as they followed their lights deeper into the cave when he suddenly stopped.

"What is it?"

"I found the end of the road," Rich said. "The trail stops here."

"Okay. Let me come around you," Mike said.

"That's good because you're almost out of hose up here," Sophia said.

"Roger that. We're only about 25 feet underwater, but we've moved horizontally back inside the cave," Rich said.

The two men hovered just above the bottom, barely breathing as they stared at the end of the line. They could clearly see where something used to sit, but it was long gone now.

"There is sediment built up on three sides. Whatever it was sat here for a long time," Mike said. "Maybe a statue or a carving of some sort."

"Someone discovered it and decided they wanted it for themselves," Rich agreed.

"I'm betting that tablet at the surface was some clue it was back here. Whoever took it didn't want anyone else to know what was down here. They couldn't pull it out so they tried to destroy it," Mike said.

"You think Erick was on to it? And someone decided they wanted it more than they wanted him to find it?" Rich asked.

"Sounds like a pretty reasonable explanation to me."

"But who?"

"If we knew the answer to that, we'd probably know who killed Erick in the first place," Mike said.

"No doubt in my mind that Erick was killed now," Rich said.

"Mine either," Mike said. "Let me get a few more photographs and then let's get out of here."

Mike covered the entire scene, thinking like a crime scene photographer instead of a photojournalist at the moment. He did his best to capture minute details and anything out of the ordinary, rather than worrying about telling a complete story with the photographs.

"All right. That'll do it. Sophia, we're coming up. Pull on the air hoses so they don't get tangled."

Both men were quiet for a moment, expecting the young girl to answer them, but they were met with silence.

"Sophia, are you there?"

Still nothing.

"Do you think she got scared and went outside?" Rich asked.

"I doubt it, Rich. She would want to be there when we got out. Let's get to the surface."

"I've got some more bad news for you," Rich said. "We're running out of air."

"How could that be? We haven't been down here that long," Mike said.

"It's getting harder to inhale. We've still got some air left in the hose, but there isn't as much pressure behind it. Let's get out of here," Rich said, his voice eerily calm in the face of an emergency.

CHAPTER 7

"Switch over to your backup pony bottle. It's attached to the BCD on your lower right. You'll have to ditch your full-face mask and we won't be able to talk anymore," Rich said.

"Got it, Rich," Mike said. "See you on the surface."

They had more than enough air in the tanks on the surface for the dive they were making. They should have been able to stay underwater for more than an hour and they had only been down about 20 minutes. Before they started the dive, Rich showed Sophia how to monitor the pressure gauges. She should have alerted them if they were getting low, but she wasn't answering either. Something had obviously gone wrong, and now Mike and Rich were on their own. They had to get out of the water before they could figure anything else out.

If it hadn't been for Rich recognizing the feeling of running out of air before it got critical, it might have been a bigger emergency than it was. If both men weren't experienced in the water, they might have panicked and bolted for the surface, rushing toward air and safety, and injuring themselves in the process. Rich's daily work as a commercial diver and dive instructor kept him calm in the face of a potential disaster. Mike wasn't in the water every day like his friend, but he had been diving for years and had seen his fair share of problems as well. They both handled the situation as well as anyone could.

Both divers removed their full-face masks and pulled the smaller "pony" bottle loose. They exhaled into the back-up regulator to clear the water from it and began swimming. The small emergency air tanks had enough air for them to swim for a few minutes, but that was it. They were only intended for a diver to make an ascent to the surface in an emergency. By removing their full-face masks, they couldn't see clearly, the water made everything blurry, but that couldn't be helped. They hadn't brought along backup masks. Mike and Rich followed their air hoses through the cave and back to where they started.

Just a few moments after they began making their exit, the divers saw the surface of the water shining above them in the reflection of their hand-held lights. It looked like a pool of quick-silver flowing back and forth over their heads. But the cave room above the pool wasn't lit up, even though they had left the lights on. As soon as they broke the surface, both men breathed deeply in the dark cave. Air had never tasted as sweet as when they thought they might be deprived of it.

"Sophia, are you here?" Mike called out after a couple breaths. "Sophia?"

Rich began crawling out of the pool, hauling his gear with him. He wasn't concerned about keeping the water clear this time.

"What happened to the lights? And our air supply?" Rich asked the walls.

Mike dropped his dive gear at the water's edge and climbed out of the pool as well. Shining their lights around, they saw their equipment was still in place. Rich flipped the switch on the side of the lights he had set up and they came right on. Mike checked the air control panel. When he turned the valves, the pressure gauges responded instantly. They had more than half of their air supply remaining.

"So, someone turned out the lights and turned off our air. I guess they left us for dead," Rich said. "I don't know how I feel about that."

"Unfortunately, this isn't the first time for me," Mike said with a humorless laugh. "But I don't like it at all."

"Do you think it was Sophia?" Rich asked.

"I just met her, but she doesn't seem the type. I mean she started this whole quest in the first place. Why sabotage it now?" Mike shook his head. "I'm guessing someone else did this. And that makes me worried about her. If they were willing to kill us, where is she and is she still alive?"

"Sounds like we need to stop standing around, then," Rich agreed. "Just leave this stuff. I'll call Madeline, the landowner, and let her know to keep an eye on it. I'll come back and get it later. No one will bother it. Let's get out of here."

"Hold off on calling Madeline for now. I don't know your friend, but for now we don't know who might be involved in this. It's time to call the local police and get them involved. We have a possible murder, attempted murder and kidnapping so far. And seems like someone stole antiquities as well," Mike said.

"Lot's going on here," Rich said. "Let's get to work."

CHAPTER 8

It took a while for Mike to get someone in charge to listen to him long enough to understand what was going on. There wasn't much cell signal at the mound so they tried calling from Mike's mobile phone on the way back to the town, but the signal kept breaking up. They really only got action when Rich called a friend who worked for the Huntington Police Department and got things started. He provided "recovery" services for them from time to time. Both men ended up giving statements to the police station and then were told to stay close. Investigators went back to the burial mound on their own to begin the investigation.

"What do we do now?" Rich asked back at his dive shop.

"I'm not one to sit on my hands," Mike said, staring at the wall thinking.

"Sorry, this whole attempted-murder thing is new to me," Rich said.

"Like I said, you sort of get used to it after a while," Mike said without smiling. "Okay, let's think this through. The police are working through normal channels and treating this like a disappearance of a college student. That's fine. But let's think about our own situation."

Mike went on to recap the events of the last 24 hours. They had strong evidence that Erick Cruz was murdered 25 years ago, but they still didn't know by whom. And now, while looking for more information, someone had tried to kill both of them and had taken Sophia.

"This came out of left field yesterday for all of us, so whoever is doing all of this is reacting. They haven't had a chance to plan any of it," Mike said. "So, who stood to gain from killing Erick Cruz? That's going to be the root of all of this."

"That makes sense. You said Alivia White ended up publishing a bunch of stuff after Erick died. Sounds like it really set her career off. Do you think she had anything to do with it?" Rich asked.

"She definitely benefitted from it," Mike agreed. "I wonder…"

Mike stood up and walked toward a Rich's desk without finishing his thoughts. He picked up the box of papers Sophia brought him just the day before and started going through them.

"You care to share what you 'wonder' about?" Rich asked after he watched Mike sort through the papers for a minute.

"I was just wondering if I missed something when I went through all of this stuff last night," Mike said. "There could have been something staring right at me, but I didn't know what it was last night."

"Like what?"

"For it to be someone like Alivia, there would have to be some connection to what Erick had found. She wasn't directly involved with the dig so it would be hard for her to just spontaneously decide to kill Erick and take over," Mike explained. "She had to realize there was more going on at the dig site than anyone else suspected."

Mike slowly sorted through Erick's notes from the dig looking for anything that he might have missed earlier. He paused when he opened a sketched drawing on a piece of note paper.

"You know what this is?" Mike asked.

"Looks like the tablet we found underwater, but without the damage to it," Rich said.

"I think that's exactly what it is. Erick was snorkeling in the water to get a closer look at the tablet. We know that. It's what set him off on the idea that he needed to dive in the cave. It must be a clue to something else down in the cave…whatever got stolen. If Erick showed this to someone like Alivia, and she recognized what it meant, it might have been the trigger that set all of this in motion," Mike said.

"Lots of 'ifs' in there," Rich said.

"You're right about that. Too many to take the police at the moment," Mike said. "But how about we talk to Alivia and see what she says?"

"You really think she'll tell us anything?"

"Probably not, but we'll see how she reacts. If she suddenly looks scared, we may have our man, so to speak," Mike said, grimly. "And that will get Sophia back. Whoever did this is probably pretty scared right now and that might make them act rashly."

"How do we find her?" Rich asked. "Most of the college professors keep their phone numbers and addresses unlisted so students can't find them when they go home."

"It's about 8 o'clock. Let's see if there is anything going on around the Anthropology Department. That's the great thing about a college campus. People don't work 9 to 5 here," Mike explained. "Even if she isn't around, there might be something that gives us her home phone number."

After a quick check to confirm that Alivia didn't have a listed phone number anywhere locally, Mike and Rich jumped in the car and headed to campus. Mike led the way this time, as Sophia had that morning, to the seventh floor of Smith Hall. As they left the stairwell and headed down the hall, they nearly ran into the woman they were looking for.

"Hello Mike," Alivia said, speaking first, looking tired, but not uncomfortable. "Odd to see you on campus this late at night. Can I do something for you?"

Mike looked at Alivia before he made a decision.

"Can you tell me where you were earlier today?"

"I've been here all day today. This is normally my longest day. I teach two classes today and then have office hours. I ended up picking up one of Dr. Rowe's night classes as well. He called to say he was feeling ill. That's the one I just finished as a matter of fact," White explained. "May I ask why?"

Mike quickly gave Alivia an overview of what had happened that day. He decided there was no point in hiding anything from her. White would have had to have been a tremendous actor to be so calm and cool in response to Mike's question and it obviously wasn't her who had kidnapped Sophia. She had plenty of witnesses to her whereabouts.

"That's a pretty amazing story, Mike. This sort of thing seems to follow you around, doesn't it?" Alivia asked. "But why did you immediately think I had anything to do with it?"

"You seemed to gain the most from Erick's death," Mike answered.

"Yes and no. I ended up having to drop all of my own research to take over the Adena mound dig. It worked out well for me, but it wasn't something I was looking for. Dr. Rowe came to me after Erick's death and asked me to do it. He said the university had put too much into it to not follow through on it," White explained. "I was actually pretty angry for a while that I didn't get to finish what I was working on. I never really set it completely aside and plan to pick it back up fulltime as soon as Dr. Rowe retires and I'm in charge of the department."

"So, if Erick Cruz had come to you with a drawing of something he found underwater, you wouldn't have been able to decipher what it said?" Rich asked.

"Now, probably. Back then, no. I didn't know much at all about the Adena and early American cultures back in those days. I wanted to study the isolated tribes in the Amazon," White answered.

"Sorry to suspect you, Alivia," Mike said. "But now we're back to square one."

Just then Mike's phone vibrated in his pocket. He pulled it out to find a text message from an unknown phone number. It said:

"Bring all notes to the cave and all your pics. Midnight. No police. The girl in exchange. Come alone."

"The plot gets thicker and thicker," Mike said with a grimace as he looked back up at Rich and Alivia. "They must have gotten my phone number from Sophia. Whoever it is knows I didn't die in the cave so they're bargaining to get all the evidence."

"I bet they didn't bargain on getting me in exchange," Rich said. "I owe them for trying to kill me in that mound."

"Me too," Alivia chimed in. "I don't know who's doing all of this, but Erick was a friend of mine. And I'm not going to let someone hurt that innocent girl either. That family has been through enough over this dig."

"Fair enough," Mike said. "Let's get started."

CHAPTER 9

Mike drove back to the Adena burial mound by himself. It was 11:45 pm. He was nervous, as he was every time he put himself in a situation like this. It truly did happen more often than he preferred, but the butterflies in his stomach didn't make him hesitate. He wasn't worried about his own safety, just Sophia's. He didn't know the girl well, obviously, but he felt responsible for getting her in trouble.

He parked just up the hill from the entrance to the mound and walked toward the steel door with a flashlight in his hand, although a nearly full moon in a cloudless sky gave off a bright light. When he reached the base of the mound, he found the door was still halfway open although the interior remained dark.

"That's strange. I would have thought the police would have locked it up tight when they were done," Mike said to himself out loud. He hadn't been sure if the exchange would happen inside the mound or outside, but he seemingly had his answer now. "Guess we're going to do this inside."

Mike entered the excavated room beneath the burial mound where they discovered the entrance to the cave system below 25 years before. He moved cautiously in the dark, scanning his flashlight methodically back and forth, looking for traps or things out of place. His beam found the entrance to the cave below and he instantly realized he wasn't alone.

He saw Sophia tied to a chair, leaning precariously against the stone chimney that served as the access to the lower chamber. She was on the far side of the chimney, facing the back wall. Her hands were taped together and she had duct tape over her mouth. Mike could see her eyes as she looked around at him and he could see the fear there. Her captor had positioned her so one wrong move would send her tumbling into the cave below, head first.

A bank of lights suddenly lit up the room came on off to Mike's side, nearly blinding him and throwing him off balance as if he was hit by a physical blast.

"Stop where you are, Mike" a muffled voice said from behind the lights. "That's far enough."

As Mike's eyes adjusted to the lights, he got a clearer picture of the situation. There was a rope tied to the back of Sophia's chair that led directly to the man standing behind the lights. With a sharp pull, the man could send Sophia crashing into the hole. It wasn't a deep drop, but she would probably land on her head or neck. If it didn't kill her she would surely be paralyzed.

"Sophia? Are you okay?" Mike asked.

Unable to speak, the young college student nodded her head, ever so slightly, afraid to disrupt her balance.

"She'll be fine if you do what I say. If not, she falls."

"What do you want?" Mike asked.

"I want all of Erick's notes," the voice said. "And I want the pictures you took on your dive."

"We didn't take any pictures…"

"Come now, Mike. I know you took photos. You wouldn't be stupid enough not to," the voice said. "Now give me the camera and all of the papers and notes."

"It's all here in this backpack," Mike said as he slipped the bag from his shoulder. He tossed it, letting it land a few feet short of the lights.

"We had a deal," Mike said. "Take it and get out of here."

"And have you follow me? Or stop me soon as I hit the door? I don't think so," the voice said. A pair of steel handcuffs arced through the air and landed at Mike's feet. "Handcuff yourself to the bolt on the stone chimney that held down the wooden cover. It's anchored into the rock. You won't get loose from that any time soon."

Mike picked up the handcuffs and moved slowly toward the chimney. Sophia's eyes watched him intently. With his back to their captor, Mike mouthed "It's gonna be fine," to Sophia. Mike snapped one end of the handcuffs to his wrist tightly and as he moved forward, he angled his body to obscure what he was about to do from the man behind the lights. He began to move downward in the direction of the well cover and then he lunged forward, snapping the other end of the cuffs to Sophia's chair. Mike couldn't pull Sophia off of the trap, but he could keep her from falling into the hole.

"Hey, what are you doing?" the muffled voice shouted. "That's not what I told you to do!"

"None of the rest of this was in the bargain either. Sometimes you don't get what you want," Mike said.

Before the voice could reply, they heard sounds of a scuffle just outside the door. A moment later, Rich came through the doorway with his hands up and blood running down the side of his face. Behind him was a woman in her mid 50s, holding a shotgun like she was versed in its use.

"I found this one outside," the woman said in the general direction of the lights.

"I thought I told you to come alone, Mike," the voice said.

Mike ignored the voice to talk to Rich.

"You okay, man?" Mike asked.

"Yeah. I'm fine. She hit me from behind as I moved toward the door. Must have been waiting on me. Mike, this is the landowner, Madeline, I told you about. Up until 30 seconds ago or so, I thought we were friends," Rich said and then he surveyed the situation and saw where Mike was. "Looks like you've been having fun yourself."

"Loads of laughs. It's been great in here," Mike said.

"Enough of this," the voice from behind the lights said. "Now, I guess it doesn't matter if you know who I am. You aren't getting out here alive. None of you are," the voice said, becoming clearer as the man stepped from behind the lights.

"Good evening, Dr. Rowe," Mike said. "I assumed you were the one behind this."

"In just a few weeks, I was set to retire and Madeline and I were going away. We were going to disappear and never see this place ever again," Rowe said.

"I assume your retirement nest egg was padded with money you made from selling artifacts from the caves below," Mike said. "So this was really all just about greed. Sad, really."

"Why I did it is none of your concern," Rowe said. "But now, instead of one young man dying 25 years ago, we'll have to add three more people to the list."

In the quiet of the moment, Mike detected a faint sound and began to smile. Sirens. The police were coming.

"What have you done?" Rowe asked, his face turning white.

"It wasn't him, Dr. Rowe. It was me. I called the police," a new voice said, as Alivia stepped into the hollowed out cave holding a handgun.

"What? Dr. White?" Rowe said. "What are you doing here?"

Taking the distraction as an opportunity, Rich whirled on the woman behind him, hitting her with his flashlight. She had hit him, but hadn't searched him. The light struck Madeline's arm and knocked the shotgun away. Rich tackled the farmer through the doorway, taking Alivia with them as they fell.

Mike moved as Rich did. He lunged forward, pulling Sophia away from the hole in the floor. They landed together in a heap beside the well.

"No, No. It can't be you. NO!" they all heard Rowe shout. Mike looked up to see Rowe looking toward the lights and stumbling backwards.

"You can't be real. No, it's not you. It can't be," Rowe shouted again. "Go away! Leave me alone!"

Without warning, the professor was gone. He stumbled backward and fell through the hole in the floor, landing headfirst on the hard rock cave floor below. Just like he had set Sophia up to do.

CHAPTER 10

While they waited on the police to arrive, Rich and Alivia tied Madeline up and Mike tended to Sophia, freeing her from the chair and checking her for injuries. When he was done, Mike shined his light into the well, looking at Dan Rowe's body below. It wasn't that far, but the man fell through the opening head first and backward. There was no way he could catch himself. His head was twisted at an awkward angle and he didn't appear to be breathing.

"I'll go check on him," Rich said as he came back into the cave. Mike started to protest for a moment and then gave in.

"Okay, but if he's dead, leave him exactly as he lies. Don't try to move him," Mike said.

"Got it," Rich said as he climbed down the ladder.

Explaining everything to the police took some time, although Alivia had given them an idea of what was going on. Still, having a distinguished university professor lying on the floor of an ancient cave system with a broken neck and a farmer tied up with ropes outside of the cave, on her own property, raised some eyebrows.

Mike, Rich, Alivia and Sophia each gave their statement to the police. Sophia's was the most interesting to the police as she recounted how she had been kidnapped and held at gunpoint in the farmhouse throughout the day until they met back up at the cave. There was one point the police detective couldn't quite understand, though.

"Both of you mentioned this," the detective said to Mike and Sophia after he was finished recording their statements. "The other two said they were outside and didn't hear anything, but you said Rowe said 'No, no. It can't be

41

you. No' or something like that and then said 'You can't be real'. What was he talking about or who was he was he talking to?"

"I have no clue. Maybe his conscience got to him," Mike said. "I didn't see anything myself. He just kept yelling that and kept backing up. And then he fell into the hole. He was looking back toward the lights in the corner."

"It was my uncle," Sophia said.

"You think it was who?" the detective asked.

"My uncle was Erick Cruz who died in this cave 25 years ago. Rowe killed him. I think he came back for his vengeance," Sophia said matter-of-factly. "And don't try to tell me I was stressed or anything else. Just after Rowe stepped forward in front of the lights I saw my uncle back there. I know what I saw. He smiled at me and I felt at peace. I knew nothing was going to happen to me. Mike, he looked at you and smiled, too. I think he recognized you."

"Sophia, my first reaction is to tell you that you didn't see Erick, that it wasn't real and that Rowe was just hallucinating; the guilt got to him. But you know what? I've seen an awful lot of things in this world I can't explain. We are standing underneath an ancient Adena burial mound and you and Rowe seemed to see the same thing. I think I'm just going to have to say I'm glad it all turned out like it did and leave it at that," Mike said with a laugh. "I'm supposed to be here visiting family and hanging out at my alma mater."

"I'd like to talk to you about that, Mike," Alivia said as he and Rich approached the others.

"What's on your mind, Alivia?"

"Rich was just telling me what you both saw on your dive into the water down below," Alivia said. "Dr. Rowe must have gotten wind of what Erick found and killed him so he could steal whatever he pulled out of here. But with him dead, we don't know what that was and where it went. Madeline says she doesn't know what it was and that Rowe never told her. I don't know if that's true or not, but for now I'll just have to believe it is."

"Makes sense to me. I'll be happy to share the photos we took down there. Actually I don't have to do anything. They're on Rich's camera. He can give them to you," Mike said.

"I know and I appreciate that, Mike. I'll definitely want to look at them, and I'd like to go back through your uncle's notes and journals, Sophia," Alivia said. "Here's the thing. I'm not a diver and have no interest in learning right now. I know the history and the archeology side, but I need some people I can trust to dive into the cave and help me understand what's down there. I need someone with experience on archeological digs and especially underwater ones, who can help me out here."

"I see where this is headed…" Mike said with a smile.

"I'd like you to consider staying around for a while to help us figure out what was down below and what was stolen," Alivia said.

"Alivia, I'll tell you what. It's about three in the morning. I know better than to agree to just about anything at this time in the morning when I'm this tired. Give me a couple days to think it over. I need to visit with my family while I'm in town," Mike said. "And I need to talk to my editor and see if I can take a little more leave time from my job."

"I understand, Mike. Take all the time you need. It will take us a few days to get this all sorted out and get permission to dive into the cave. That should be interesting since Madeline owns the land and was involved in everything, but give me a shout in a few days and let me know. You and Rich seem to make a pretty good team." Turning to Rich she said. "How would you like a contract to provide the equipment and do some exploring for the university?"

"If Mike's in, so am I!" Rich said, back to his normal exuberant self.

CHAPTER 11

Red Bird stared into the fire thinking about what had to happen next. For the good of the kingdom, for the good of his king, he had to complete the sacrificial rites. So much blood had spilled down the altar, running in rivers through the carved stone, but to no avail. Nothing had happened. Crops were still failing. His city was still dying. The commoners, where he often went to find sacrifices, were dying; sick and starving. His king, Feathered Warrior, demanded he do something. But what? The rains hadn't come in more than 10 moons. The kingdom to the north was raiding their lands to find food for their people. Nothing was going right for Feathered Warrior's people.

"High Priest Red Bird, I am sorry to disturb your meditation, but King Feathered Warrior requests you to come before him," the young acolyte said quietly behind Red Bird.

"He requests my presence, does he?" Red Bird said with a smirk. As things had gotten tougher and he failed to find solutions, his relationship with the king had also suffered. As Red Bird realized there was nothing he could do to solve their problems, he also realized that the Feathered Warrior might not be as divine as legend said he was.

"I am sorry sir, I do not understand your question," the acolyte asked, shaking in fear from the misunderstanding of his master. Red Bird was known for being one of the gentler priests, but he had also been a warrior in his youth and the acolyte had seen the older man remove the heads of too many prisoners without a moment's hesitation to think the priest didn't have a cruel side.

"It is nothing. Just my thoughts escaping," Red Bird said standing. "Please carry word to the great king that I will be there as quickly as I can."

"Yes, my lord," the acolyte said, relieved, as he backed out with his head bowed. "The messenger said the king was in his private chambers and wished to see you there."

I really shouldn't speak my mind in front of the boy. My troubled thoughts are too much for him to understand, Red Bird thought. The knowledge that Feathered Warrior wanted to see him in his private chambers only troubled Red Bird's thoughts that much more. While Red Bird had been to the private chambers before, it was an unusual request and it could only mean that Feathered Warrior wanted to say something to him that was not meant for the court as a whole.

Red Bird donned the ceremonial robes he wore to meet with Feathered Warrior and gathered the things he thought his ruler would want to see. He knew the man was expecting a sign from him that things would improve for their city, or that he had a plan to appease the gods and make the rain return. He had neither.

Under normal circumstances, Red Bird would take his acolytes and the younger priests with him, traveling as a group to meet the king. The court and the rituals of meeting with the king carried great weight and importance. But, for a more private meeting, as he was called to today, there was another way. Red Bird had a hidden way out of the temple where Red Bird had his residence that would allow him to visit with Feathered Warrior unseen. He pulled a plain cloak he kept around from his days as a warrior over top of his priestly robes and slipped out through the back. He knew his acolytes would think he had disappeared into thin air. He smiled at that thought. He might be a priest, but Red Bird knew he was as much of a man as the next one on the street, a thought the other leaders refused to accept.

Red Bird was one of the few in the kingdom who knew his way into the king's chambers. He slipped down the hidden pathway and then through the separation built into the stone wall. The walls were overlapped in such a way that even under close examination, it appeared to be solid. In reality, a normal man could easily pass through the opening. The craftsmen who built it were put to death as soon as they were finished with the task to hide the secret doorway. Red Bird stepped into the room from behind a tapestry so quietly that everyone in the room started at the sudden appearance of the high priest; all except for Feathered Warrior, of course. He knew how the man got there. The king's attendants and guards thought Red Bird had worked magic. It was a misconception both men were happy to continue.

"My lord, I have come as you commanded," Red Bird said with a bow. "I am here to obey."

It was a ritual opening, but one required of service to Feathered Warrior. While the king felt the aches and pains of life, he actually believed he was divine and infallible. He believed everyone should obey him without question.

"Red Bird, my high priest, I ask of you that you remind me of the story of the founding of our city. Tell it so my closest advisors here in my private chambers can hear and remember," Feathered Warrior said. Red Bird was taken aback to survey the small room to realize that in fact most of the king's highest advisors were present. Without looking at the small group seated on the floor in front of the king he had assumed they were simply servants. Now that he looked closer, he realized he knew every one of them. They were the warriors and princes that Feathered Warrior kept closest to him. And then Red Bird realized he was the last to be called. The others had been meeting for some time, it appeared. Even more interesting, Feathered Warrior hadn't asked Red Bird to take a seat with the others on the council. The king had left him standing and asked him to recite history.

As the high priest, Red Bird was the keeper of the legends of the city. One of the tasks of the priesthood was to tell and retell the stories, training the acolytes to remember them word by word, to carry them down to future generations. Red Bird had come to the priesthood later in life than most, having had a vision at the end of a battle that convinced him his days as a warrior were done, so he hadn't memorized the stories from childhood, but he knew them well enough that he was comfortable reciting the story the king asked of him.

"The founder of our city came from the north. He was a great man, a great leader," Red Bird began. "After traveling many cycles of the moon, beginning in a land where the air was sometimes cold beyond imagining, but water flowed freely down the mountains and the land was green. His name was Two Wolves, but we know him as First Father."

Red Bird continued recounting the story of the man who had journeyed to find this land, guided by visions from the gods. He had traveled for moons, always heading south, enduring many hardships. The gods told him he should make the journey to find a well in the earth connected to one in the home he had left behind. They told him the well was one of the many entrances into Xibalba, the underworld. He traveled with a special stone from his home. When he found the right place, it would glow and move with power as if it were alive. That was when he would know the gods were pleased and his travels were finished. Two Wolves discovered a cenote that opened up into the limestone and let sunlight into the cool, crystal clear waters below.

When Two Wolves found the Holy Cenote, and the stone reacted as the gods said it would, he blessed the place and promised them he would create a city to give them glory. A man of great stature, the local people revered him and made him their leader. He set them to work building a temple close to the Holy Cenote and from that temple blossomed an entire city. The city had lasted and grown for many generations, through more than a dozen kings. The first king after Two Wolves ordered a statue of Two Wolves be built. Rather than the life-size likenesses constructed of stone to memorialize present kings, the statue was made from jade and obsidian and gleamed brightly, always lit and always guarded in the Tempe Dios del Viento, the Temple of the Winds, built by Two Wolves himself. In the statue's chest, the king ordered the craftsmen to work in the holy stone that Two Wolves found. The statue brought glory to the city and it rose to great power. Everyone believed the statue and the holy stone were the keys to their success.

When Red Bird was finished retelling the story, he closed his eyes and bowed his head. The story of Two Wolves always spoke to him. It touched him deeply as if he had a direct connection to the man himself. Like Two Wolves, Red Bird was taller than the rest of the men and women in the city, including the king. He closely resembled the Two Wolves of legend as well, with his light brown flowing hair and blue eyes while the others in the city had raven black hair and eyes. The people often whispered that Red Bird was Two Wolves returned to lead them, something the king didn't approve of since it brought his own leadership into question. With the recent troubles, that whispering had grown louder.

"Thank you priest for reminding us of the story of the founder," Feathered Warrior said after a moment. "You have been unable to find the correct sacrifice that will appease the First Father and return our city to health and strength. We are set upon from the north and are dying from within, but you have not done what needs to be done to make our city right with the gods."

"My king, I am searching the heavens and beseeching the gods to show me…" Red Bird began but Feathered Warrior cut him off.

"Priest, I have not given you freedom to speak," the king said with a growl.

Rather than replying and arguing with the king, Red Bird lowered his head and looked at his feet. Inside he was seething, but it would not do any good to show that anger now.

"You have not done what I believe we need to do. The gods spoke to me directly last night and they have told me what we need to do to save our city and make it great once again," Feathered Warrior said, speaking to the advisors in the room as much as he was speaking to Red Bird.

"My advisors tell me the people think you, high priest, are First Father come to us again and they look for you to lead us even though they have a king," Feathered Warrior said. "That is evil and that very talk, that very challenge to the true king, is the root of our problems. The gods told me in my vision that the blackness at the heart of the priesthood is what is causing our city to be sick and set upon by our enemies."

"My lord, I never fostered those sayings!" Red Bird shouted, defending himself in spite of the king's order to remain quiet. His eyes blazed at the accusations directed at him.

"The First Father himself told me the sacrifice we need to make is not more prisoners or virgins, but they want one special sacrifice. They do not want more blood spilled on the steps of the temple," Feathered Warrior said, a ferocity in his eyes evident to all those in the room.

"My lord, please tell what sacrifice the gods have demanded and I will make it happen at once," Red Bird said.

"Priest, the gods have demanded your sacrifice. They want you to drown in the Holy Cenote. They have told me that is the only sacrifice that will appease them and convince them to return our city to its rightful glory," Feathered Warrior said and then he turned to the other men in the room. "Get the guards. Bind the priest and let us begin preparing him."

CHAPTER 12

Everyone knew Mike would be back to finish exploring the cave under the Adena mound when he left for a few days to visit his family in Charleston. The news of Dr. Rowe's death and the belief that he stole "something" after he killed Erick Cruz dominated the local news. Mike was well-known in the area and several former colleagues attempted to interview him about his role in uncovering the murder, but he deferred as much as he could back to the university. He wasn't interested in being part of that story at all.

As a journalist, Mike had traveled the world and seen some of the best, and the worst, in people. He knew no matter what happened there was usually a fairly simple explanation for it. Motivations usually came down to money, greed and jealousy or power; often all four.

Mike was, however, interested in getting to the bottom of what Rowe had stolen from the cave in the first place. He wanted to do that for Erick.

Mike checked in with his editor in New York to clear his schedule for a while and got a laugh from her when he told her about what had happened. "It never ceases to amaze me how you fall into these things everywhere you go," she told him. She wasn't interested in the story of the murder, but she told him if he did uncover something interesting in the cave to let her know. So, essentially, Mike was still working even though he wasn't on an assignment. There was a feeling of familiarity about that for him. It was nice to know he had the backing of his magazine.

That settled, Mike headed back down the interstate toward Huntington to see what he could find out. He drove around town for a few minutes to get a feel for how much had changed since he graduated so many years before. It brought up some bittersweet memories for him as he did, wondering what had happened to old friends and girlfriends. He hadn't planned to completely disappear after graduation, and in truth it wasn't like it had happened overnight, but within a few years, Mike was off on an adventure that had led him home 20 years later, finally coming full circle.

Mike pulled into the parking lot beside Rich's dive shop as the evening sun was beginning to set. He chuckled when he realized it was less than a week since he first saw Rich again for the first time in 20 years. They had been close in school and now they were working together again, in a way neither of them ever imagined.

"Hey buddy, what've I missed," Mike said as he walked into the store and saw Rich behind the counter.

"Oh, not much. You know. Just a typical week around here," Rich replied as he stepped around the counter and shook his friend's hand.

"If the last week is a typical one for you, I'm not sure I want to hang around," Mike said with a laugh.

"If the next week ends up being anything like the last one, I don't want to hang around here either. You're taking me wherever you go," Rich said.

With Madeline, the landowner, out of the way the university was able to work with the local government to set up permits to explore the Adena mound and the caves again. It was considered to be important to closing the case into Erick Cruz's murder and various other attempted murders and kidnappings. The main suspect had died, but they wanted to make sure there weren't others involved so Mike and Rich had been given unlimited access to the site, with the understanding that someone from the university should be present at all times.

"When do we start?" Mike asked.

"I've already been to the site setting up equipment and running better lighting systems and such in the cavern. All the dive gear is in place. Everything is pretty much ready and waiting for you to appear," Rich said.

"You haven't been back in the water?" Mike asked.

"Nope. I said I would do this with you or not at all," Rich said. "I knew you'd be back. You never were the kind of guy to let something like this go. And from what I've read of your career that's only intensified over the years."

"Fair enough," Mike said. "Sounds like we're ready to go."

"Yep, we just need to get someone from the university to come out there while we dive to examine anything we find," Rich said. "I've got a local commercial dive buddy of mine who will come out and be our surface support and function as a standby diver as well."

"You've covered all the bases haven't you?"

"You know the drill. You have to be thorough," Rich explained.

"Let's call Dr. White and see if she can send someone out tomorrow then. No reason to sit on our hands," Mike said.

"Sweet!"

CHAPTER 13

Mike and Rich had laid out a plan of attack over dinner that night and then agreed to meet at the Adena mound the next morning ready to get to work. The Adena had buried their revered dead in that mound and scores of others in the Ohio valley. There was speculation among archeologists that the mounds were also ceremonial sites, although they couldn't prove much of that. There just wasn't much evidence of an Adena belief system at all.

Mike approached the mound in his rental car on the old farm road and could already see his old friend's van parked outside the mound. Rich wasn't in sight so Mike guessed Rich was already inside getting things set up. Mike was 20 minutes early for the time they agreed to meet, thinking he would take a few minutes to make peace with everything that had happened there. The Adena mound had cost the life of one of Mike's college friends and he watched another man he respected die. Dr. Rowe had murdered Erick, something there was no forgiveness for, but he had also been an exemplary scientist and teacher. All of that was difficult for Mike to reconcile.

"Looks like I won't get any alone time here," Mike said to himself as he got out of the car and caught site of his friend. "Probably just as well. I've been thinking too much lately anyway. Time to get to work."

"Hey Mike, you're here early," Rich said as he came outside into the morning light.

"And you're here earlier," Mike replied.

"That's how I am. To be early is to be on time; to be on time is to be late," Rich said. "You know the drill."

"That I understand. So, what's going on?"

"I've got everything set up. Come on in and I'll show you," Rich said, motioning Mike into the Adena mound.

It was less than a week since Sophia had been kidnapped and Dr. Rowe had died, but what a difference those few days had made. The room created during the original excavation had been cleaned; swept clear of dirt, dust and cobwebs. The river stone wall around the opening in the floor that led to the cave and pool of water below had been reinforced and made more secure. The original stones that gave it a well-like look were still there, but they had been covered with a steel band to allow Mike and Rich to hang a ladder into the room below without worrying about damaging the ancient masonry.

Rich had set up lights in both of the rooms along with a generator and an air compressor in the upper room. He had a series of storage air tanks outside the mound that would hold an emergency air supply. They planned to explore the caves below using surface-supplied air, just as they had on the first dive, but this time they would be connected to the larger storage tanks. If something happened to the generator, there would still be plenty of air for them to finish whatever they were doing and ascend back to the surface slowly and safely. During the first dive, Dr. Rowe had turned off their air supply, but that wouldn't happen this time around as there would be at least two people on the surface monitoring the divers in the water at all times. One was a fellow diver and the other would be the university representative.

There was also a series of underwater lights that were connected to a surface power supply. They would set the lights at key locations around the submerged cave and use it to light everything up instead of relying solely on their hand-carried lights. Lastly, there was a closed-circuit video camera system that they would carry along with them to record everything they saw during the dive and allow the university representative to follow along while staying dry. They had even set up a small cellular phone tower just outside the mound to make sure they had a solid signal at all times.

Mike shook his head with appreciation after Rich showed him the preparations.

"This is pretty sweet. Should make this relatively easy," Mike said.

"I don't like to work any harder than I have to," Rich said with a boyish grin.

They both looked up when a man entered the low door into the mound.

"Mike, this is Gardner. He's my back up diver and will be our surface support," Rich explained.

"Nice to meet you, Gardner," Mike said. "Is that your first name?"

"Nah, but it's what everyone calls me," Gardner said.

"That works," Mike said. "The only person we're waiting on is the person from the anthropology department of the university."

"Then it's a good thing I'm here," Sophia said as she walked through the door.

"You're not who I expected to see," Mike said with a smile as he walked over and gave the young girl a hug. "Good to see you, though."

"I hope you're not disappointed it's me," Sophia said with a smile.

"Not at all," Mike said. "Just surprised."

"Well, it won't be me all the time, but I asked Dr. White and she agreed to let me come out some. If you guys find something, it'll be someone a lot more important than I am, but until then, it was pretty hard for them to tell me no."

"I'm glad you're here. If it weren't for you, none of this would have happened," Mike said. "Are you going to be writing something for *The Parthenon,* as well?"

"Not officially. Dr. White said I could come out because of my involvement so far, not because of the paper. But if something interesting happens, I will try to stay on in my capacity as a journalist," Sophia said.

"Well, if the university wants to send someone else out, I'll find you something to do. You are welcome on my dive site any time," Rich said.

"Thanks, Rich!" Sophia said. "I'm surprised you would say that after I left you guys to run out of air the last time."

"Can't really blame you for that, now can we?" Rich said smiling.

"Are you guys gonna dive, or just talk all day?" Gardner said gruffly, but with a twinkle in his eye. As he walked away, shaking his head, he mumbled "Someone told me you were divers…"

"And the divemaster has spoken," Mike said with a laugh. "Time to get to work."

The foursome made their way down the ladder and began setting up their equipment. Mike, Rich and Gardner each pulled on drysuits and readied dive gear. Gardner wasn't planning to dive, but he was going to be ready in case there was a problem down below and they needed his help. Otherwise, he would stay on the surface and monitor the air supply, compressors and other equipment.

Mike and Rich donned nearly the same equipment they had before with full-face masks that would allow them to communicate with the surface and with each other. This time, though, they each had a video camera attached to the top of their masks. They were also wearing helmets on their heads in case they bumped up against the cave walls. Rich had refilled their emergency pony bottles as well. Those backup tanks saved their lives on the first dive and even though they had a better support system for this dive, Rich wasn't taking any chanced.

"We ready to get this show on the road?" Gardner asked into the communication gear microphone as a way to test it.

"Ready to go here," Mike said.

"Everything is 5 by 5 for me, too," Rich said.

"Time to get wet then," Gardner agreed.

"Can I say something?" Sophia asked Gardner.

With a quick glance at Mike and Rich, Gardner nodded and handed the microphone to the young college student.

"Mike, this isn't about my uncle any more. This is about exploring and finding out what's down here. But I want to thank you, and you too, Rich, for everything you've done and thank you for letting me be part of it. This has meant so much to my family," Sophia said. "They all said that if there is any way we can repay you, please let them know."

"You're welcome," Mike said simply. "And tell your family thank you for the kind offer."

Mike and Rich both gave Sophia a diver's "OK" sign, forming their index finger and their thumb in the shape of a circle with their other fingers raised, and a nod, and then headed toward the water.

Rich had laid boards down in the water so they could ease themselves into the water without stirring up sediment. They spent the first few minutes of the dive carrying lights into the pool and positioning them where they thought they might need them at first although they knew they would end up moving them around if they discovered anything.

Once the lights were in place and on, Mike and Rich headed back for the spot where they had originally found the platform for whatever was now missing.

"This is where whatever it was stood," Mike said to Gardner and Sophia on the surface.

"Looks like something was dragged out of there, all right," Gardner agreed.

"Now we have to see if there is any clue as to what it might have been," Mike said.

"Let's swim around the perimeter of the cave," Rich said. "We'll get a lay of the land and then make our plan of attack from there."

"Sounds good," Mike agreed.

As a team, they moved to the right of the opening into the lower submerged cave and began following the wall. They both panned their heads back and forth slowly to make sure the video cameras captured everything they were seeing. The room was egg-shaped and relatively large. Clockwise, from the top of the egg, they had entered about the 7 o'clock position. The room extended back 50 feet and was at least 30 feet wide. The ceiling was nearly 10 feet off of the floor most of the way around sloping toward the stone floor. The walls were mostly smooth as if it had once been dry and had been hollowed out, or at least cleaned out, on purpose.

"Mike, is that an opening in the wall?" Sophia asked into the microphone.

"Sure is," Mike said, pointing his mask-camera at the dark opening at the 3 o'clock position. It began inches off the floor and ended about five feet above that. The lights they positioned at the far end of the cave didn't project light into the small opening. When Mike and Rich were in front of the opening, they shined their handheld lights into the hole and realized it went another seven or eight feet back into the wall.

"Everything down here is covered in silt," Rich said. "But I think this might be worth checking out later."

"No doubt about that," Mike agreed. "I've been to a couple of places where entire tribes made their homes in caves dug into the hillsides. This looks just like that to me."

"Except it is under an Adena burial mound, of course," Rich said.

"There is that. That stuff is for the scientists to figure out. I'm not here to figure out how it all happened and when the Indians did what. I'm hoping for some clues as to what Erick found down here and what happened to it."

"Then shouldn't you be looking at the pedestal where whatever it was stood?" Sophia said over the comm system, startling both divers.

"We will definitely check into it more, but I want to get a good grasp of what's down here. For all we knew before we started this dive, this could have been a cave system that stretched for miles, but it looks like it is an enclosed space," Mike said. "That's good. It means we have a limited area to search. But there could be clues to what it was anywhere in this room. We'll have to search through it all."

"About time for you guys to come back to the surface for a while. You've been down about an hour," Gardner said. "It's not all that deep and you have plenty of air, but whatever you're looking for isn't going anywhere, either. Let's do this in short easy dives."

"And once again, the divemaster has spoken," Rich said with a chuckle. "Heading back to the surface. Start pulling in the air hoses, please."

"Right behind you," Mike said. "I want to look over the video and see if we missed anything."

CHAPTER 14

Red Bird's world was spinning. The other priests, on Feathered Warrior's orders, had given him a potion that would incapacitate him. He had given the same potion to thousands of men who were slated to be sacrificed. It made them more agreeable and easier to handle. But this was the first time Red Bird had actually taken it. He didn't like how it made him feel. His eyes wouldn't focus and he felt like he was going to vomit. His body was no longer in his control.

On the other hand, Red Bird's mind was fully alert. He could hear everything down to the breath of his captors.

Did the gods demand my life? Red Bird asked himself. How have I failed them?

No answers came while the priests, men that Red Bird himself had trained, performed the ceremonies to prepare his body for the sacrifice. They drew symbols on his naked body, intoning words and sounds to prepare the way to Xibalba and the afterlife.

Some sacrifices were intended to appease bloodthirsty gods, Red Bird knew. The priests took the lives of hundreds of enemy warriors captured in battle. The men were brought forward, held down and their blood was released onto the temple stones. At the end of the day, the temple reeked of death and the copper smell of thickening blood.

This sacrifice would be different. The king said Red Bird was to drown in the Holy Cenote. Red Bird himself had offered his share of offerings into the Holy Cenote. He knew the process.

Once all was prepared, the priests would come and tie him to a board. They would drape him with flowers and lead a procession toward the Holy

Cenote. Feathered Warrior would even be there as well to participate in the ceremony, making it that much more special. He would tell the elite who attended that the gods themselves had ordered this sacrifice.

Red Bird wondered why the gods hadn't told him that directly as he was lifted into the air for the march through the streets. He could smell the tallow burning all around him and he could hear the sounds of the incantations, but the potion clouded his mind, blending them together.

Was this really ordained, or was Feathered Warrior just jealous and eliminating competition?

At the water's edge, Red Bird's eyes began to focus. As he expected, Feathered Warrior was there and he was speaking, commanding his people to obey and commanding nature to accept the offering. It was obvious to Red Bird, if no one else present, that the king was as afraid of the people as he was afraid of the elements and the gods. The clarity that came from the potion showed Red Bird that his former king, and friend, hoped this sacrifice would discourage the leading warriors and priests from rising up against him.

With a suddenness that caught Red Bird off guard, he was lifted into the air and then he felt his body falling. His arms were bound behind him, but his feet were free. His eyes were open as he fell.

Hitting the water was startling for Red Bird. He had never been in water over his head before. He didn't know how to swim and had no idea how long it would take for him to die. Red Bird noticed the water was warm and it felt good surrounding him. He felt at peace and at ease.

As he sank, his mouth closed and he held his breath, something it hadn't occurred to him to do before. Red Bird opened his eyes and looked upward. He could see the light from above and could just make out the bodies of the priests, warriors and the king standing around the edge of the cenote, watching him disappear.

Red Bird didn't know what happened when a living man was thrown in the Holy Cenote and he guessed no one else did either. He knew in his mind that the gods were there waiting on the sacrifice and would take the body away. He simply hoped it would be one of the kind and benevolent gods, not the violent and terrible ones. He hoped the gods would come quickly, ending his suffering.

The opening to the cenote seemed to move further and further away. Red Bird wondered if he was already dead and moving toward the nether world with the gods.

Red Bird's body began to scream at him through the potion-induced haze. He needed air and he needed to breathe. He realized he wasn't in the realm of the gods yet. He felt a fire in his chest and his vision turned red. He pulled on the ropes binding his hands and realized they were loosening. He knew, without thinking about what it might mean, that he didn't want to die. He didn't want to be a sacrifice to the gods. Somewhere in the back of his mind he wondered if all of the men he had put to death felt the same way.

It didn't matter what he wanted, though. The gods would surely come for him to receive their sacrifice. Another pull and twist and suddenly Red Bird's hands were free. His mind was starting to rage and his lungs felt like they were going to explode. Red Bird expected to burst into flames at any second.

The opening to the sky and the light where the king stood and ordered Red Bird cast into the water grew smaller and smaller as the water pulled him down. And then Red Bird noticed another light ahead of him. It began to grow larger.

The gods must be there. That is the opening to the underworld and the gods will receive me there as the sacrifice. Wanting the pain in his chest to end, Red Bird began to pull toward the light. He didn't know how to swim, but he reached out with both hands and pulled at the water. His head began to grow light. He was sure it was the gods pulling him in. He relaxed knowing the pain would be no more in just a moment. He found his arms couldn't move anymore; they were heavy. The light grew larger and Red Bird closed his eyes as he drifted toward the light.

The sacrifice was complete.

CHAPTER 15

"The Mayan people have been ignored for too long. We are the butt of jokes and people 'oooh' and 'aaah' at our abandoned cities throughout Central America, but then they go home and forget that the Maya live among us. We are real living, breathing people, not dusty relics in history books and we need to be recognized," Marcus Montero thundered from the podium at a meeting of the Confederation of Central American States. "We have lived in the shadows for too long. We are not Mexicans. We are more than that. We were Mexico before the Spanish came and sullied the blood of our people."

Montero was invited to speak to the group, hearing various speakers talk about the minority populations throughout Central America—like the Miskito Indians and the Garifuna—and how best to support them. He was by far the most frustrated of all the speakers.

"The other speakers today have made impressive cases for their peoples and I respect them and their efforts to support their cultures. We are truly brothers in the sense that we have been neglected in our home countries for far too long. However, where the Garifuna live together in a village in Honduras, preserving their language and their culture as best they can, and the Miskitos occupy the semi-autonomous region of the Moskito coast, overlapping Honduras and Nicaragua, and living off the sea like their fathers and their father's fathers did, the Maya are spread from the Yucatan to Guatemala and Honduras. We are everywhere," Montero continued, taking a more even tone. "In recent years, much was discussed about the calendar and what men who didn't know better called the Mayan End of the World and other things. None of that was true, or real. We have come to a time, though, that is the dawn of a new age. That time is coming and the Maya will rise up and lead the world. My people have origins older than any country in this world and older even than this world. We come from a world far away, across the galaxy. You can join with us and support us, or you can suffer the consequences and die. My people will not be silent any longer," Montero finished, glaring at the audience.

"Just what is it you want?" a voice shouted from the audience. Montero really wasn't expecting questions from the attendees, but he was prepared with an answer anyway. He had practiced it and said it many times before, but never to this big of an audience. He had only said what he was about to say to his ardent followers, the men and women he had rallied to his cause.

"We have neglected this world for too long. We have nearly destroyed it. We have fought wars. We have poisoned the air and the water. No more. The Maya will no longer stand for this. We will rise up and lead this world!" Montero said.

"A new Mayan renaissance…" a voice teased from the audience, full of sarcasm. "The poor and the uneducated will save us all. What if we don't want saved?"

"You will have no choice!" Montero barked back and then left the stage fuming.

Behind the curtain, Montero met Carlos. To call Carlos an assistant, was like calling a boa constrictor a good baby sitter for an infant, but Carlos served many purposes and Montero liked to keep him around.

"Carlos, we are not prepared today, but soon, very soon, we will have the power to destroy those fools who choose to mock me. I want to bring every one of them down. Did you see how they treated me?" Montero said as they left the building, walking quickly. "I will show them."

"Do you want me to have a discussion with them now?" Carlos asked, his expression bland, ready to do what he needed to do.

"Yes, I want you to…" Montero began to rage and then he stopped himself. No matter how much satisfaction it would bring him to release Carlos to "take care" of the fools who mocked him, he knew better.

Carlos, for his part, simply stood waiting. He knew his boss was struggling with his emotions and he would not react one way or the other until given a clear direction. He had learned not to try to anticipate Montero's thoughts. They were too mercurial.

And then Montero laughed. It broke the tension, even though the laugh had an edge to it that wasn't all about humor, either.

"You test me, my friend, and that is good. I know you would do whatever I ask and do it without hesitation. I value you for that. And I would not waste your talents on something as mundane as teaching a lesson to rude men of power. Soon, we will have the statue and the power that goes with it. That power will dwarf anything they can do today. From there, we will have the throne of the Maya and control of the world. Then, those same men will come crawling to me for forgiveness. I want them to live to see that day, Carlos. I want them to live to see that day. And then we will remind them how they mocked me and know in their hearts the mistake they made as I crush them under my heel."

Carlos didn't say anything. He simply looked into Montero's eyes and watched the manic glee cool as Montero found his self control.

Together they left the building to head home and put their final plans into action.

CHAPTER 16

"There are several places, I want to check out," Mike said as they finished reviewing the video from the first dive.

"I'm really intrigued by the small cave off to the side of the main one," Rich said. "It seems like a special room."

"Did you make a discovery?" Dr. Alivia White asked as she climbed down the ladder to the cave.

"Oh. Hi, Alivia," Mike said. "I didn't know you were coming all the way out here. We really don't have anything to report yet."

"I realize that, Mike. I know you just got started, but I wanted to check in on you. And the university wants to make sure the public knows what's going on as well," Alivia said, gesturing back toward the ladder as a woman's legs, in a skirt, came slowly down the ladder. She was immediately followed by a man, carrying a television news camera.

"Dr. White," Mike said, changing his tone for the journalists. "I'm not sure we have anything all that noteworthy to say to the public or the media."

"I understand your concern, Mike. Don't worry, we don't expect that you will have solved all the mysteries this cave contains, but with the death of Dr. Rowe and everything that happened last week, along with the reopening of the case about Erick Cruz, the public has a great amount of interest in what's going on here," Alivia explained, gesturing toward the reporter. "When the news director from WSAZ called to ask what was going on, the station jumped at a chance to observe the first dives into the cave and to interview you. They sent out a news crew immediately."

"That sounds good. We'll do whatever we can," Mike said, even though that was exactly the last thing he wanted to do. As a journalist himself, he felt sorry for the reporter and videographer. It wasn't their fault that they were thrown into the middle of the situation, so Mike wanted to help them out. But he really wanted to be working, not holding hands.

"We've done one dive already," Mike said, turning to the reporter. "We were just about to go back in and make a second one to check out some of the things we saw during the first dive."

"Oh, that's great Mr. Scott," the attractive young blonde said. "My name is Regina Hartley, by the way. This is Ken."

"Nice to meet both of you."

"Do you think we can interview you about all of this as well?" Regina asked, flashing Mike her best smile.

"Well, I was going to make the dive…" Mike began, glancing at Alivia. Mike didn't work for White and really didn't have any connection to the university so he didn't have to follow anyone's orders in this situation. He was there for himself and that was it, although his editor was keeping an eye on what was going in. Making people happy was not his top priority. But he really wanted to find out what happened. The only way to do that was to keep Alivia happy. And then Alivia interrupted his thoughts.

"Mike, can I speak to you for a moment?" she asked as she started to move across the room away from the reporters and the divers, assuming he would follow. She turned to face Mike as he stepped up behind her and then moved in close to him so they could speak quietly. "I know you really don't want to do the public relations side of this. You're a man of action and decision. I understand, but I need your help here," she said as she placed her hand on his chest and looked directly into his eyes. "Can you do this for me?"

Mike returned the look for a moment before responding. He wasn't sure if Alivia was manipulating him or being serious. Still, as they stood there for a moment, close enough to touch, he could smell he perfume and feel the heat of her hand through his t-shirt. He realized she was a very attractive woman who needed his help. Attractive or not, he had made a long career of helping people out of tight spots so this was no different. And he really did want to find out what was going on here. He made his decision. He smiled.

"Sure. I'll do anything I can to help you out. We are on the same side here."

Mike paused a moment to enjoy the sensation of being so close to Alivia. He looked at her again with new eyes. She really was an attractive woman, both physically and personally. She was intelligent and strong, both qualities that Mike looked for in women. Mike remembered entertaining asking her out when they were both students, but she was a couple years older than he was at the time and she was so focused on her career that she didn't seem to pay much attention to him. Maybe things really were coming full circle here. He chuckled as he patted her hand on his chest and then moved back toward the group.

"Miss, Hartley was it? Can you give me just a minute? Let me get things set up with the other divers. While you're waiting, let me introduce you to Sophia Cruz. Her uncle was Erick Cruz and she is here doing a story for *The Parthenon* and WMUL," Mike said as he pulled Sophia forward. Mike noticed Alivia's slight grimace in reaction to his bringing Sophia in as a reporter for the school paper, but he didn't worry about it.

Mike joined Rich and Gardner where they were doing their best to stay out of the way and out of the front of the camera.

"Gardner, you take this dive with Rich and I'll monitor things from up here," Mike said.

"Sure, Mike, no problem. I remember how you are. Doesn't surprise me you want to spend a little time with the cute little reporter," Rich said, teasing his old friend.

"Yeah, right. She is about half my age. No thanks. And you know exactly where I want to be, but what am I going to do? Leave her up her with Mr. Talkative?" Mike said, gesturing at Gardner with a grin. All he got was a grunt in reply.

"Okay, you handle the topside and we'll do our best to not screw up down there," Rich said.

"You better not. If you do, the whole state will know about it," Mike said.

Rich and Gardner suited up quickly while Mike explained what they were doing to the reporter and Alivia. He showed them some of the video they captured on the first dive as well, to give them a better idea of what to expect.

Once the divers were back inside the cave, Mike guided them where he wanted them to be, partly because he wanted to be making the dive and partly as a running commentary for their visitors.

"Guys, let's get some measurements of the pedestal that held whatever was dragged out of there," Mike said into the comm system microphone. He watched the television monitor connected to the video cameras the two divers wore.

"That looks good, guys," Mike said once the pair was done. "Now, head over to the small cave and let's take a closer look at the small mounds in the silt we saw on the video. It looks like something is buried in there."

"That's gonna stir up a lot of silt. Might make it a little harder to see," Gardner said, breaking his silence over the comms.

"I know, but we'll just have to deal with it," Mike said.

"You got it."

The side cave was small enough that the two divers quickly decided only one of them should enter it while the other positioned himself to show everyone topside what they saw with his helmet camera. Gardner got the honors of entering cave.

"Do your best to stay off of the cave floor," Mike said. "You don't want to stir up any more of that powder than you have to."

"Not my first rodeo, Mike," Gardner replied.

"Sorry man. I know it's not. I'm just saying out loud what I would be saying in my own head if I were the one going in," Mike agreed.

"Understood."

As Gardner entered the cave, he realized that while the silt covering the floor was uniform, it slowly got shallower toward the back of the cave. Where the silt settled gently over hundreds of years, there were a series of humps on the floor that indicated the floor itself wasn't flat. Or, if the floor was flat, there was something lying there, underneath the layer of fine powder.

"I'm going to go all the way in and work my way back toward the opening. I'm hoping that won't mess up the visibility too bad," Gardner said.

At the back of the cave, where the roof curved down to the meet the floor, Gardner gently poked his finger into the first pile of silt. His finger traveled two inches into the muck and then struck something solid. As slowly as he could, he brushed the silt away. A cloud bloomed upward in front of Gardner's camera.

"Damnitman."

"What is it?" Mike asked into the comms. "We can't see much up here. There's too much silt in the water. Rich, can you move closer to get us a shot of what Gardner found?"

The camera angle changed as Rich moved forward. The screen cleared as some of the silt fell away and both cameras showed the same scene from different angles.

A toothy grin showed on the monitor. Gardner had found a skull.

CHAPTER 17

Finding a skull at the bottom of the cave changed everything dramatically. Alivia quickly took charge of the operation for the university. After conferring with her colleagues, she decided to have the divers bring the skull to the surface, but leave everything else in place. They called the police, unsure if the skeleton was ancient or a more recent death. The uniform appearance of the silt made it unlikely that the body was modern, but they didn't want to take any chances. Officials from the university arrived and so did more news media. The story quickly switched from an interesting story in the second segment of the local evening news to the top story with regional and national interest.

Mike realized seconds after they discovered the skull that their progress would be halted for the rest of the day, if not longer. He switched mental gears and started thinking like the journalist he was. He pulled his camera from his bag and took some photographs of the setting. When Rich and Gardner surfaced, he took photographs of them holding up the skull and it being transferred into a plastic bin filled with water from the cave for transport back to the university for analysis. They didn't want to expose the probably ancient bones to the air or let it dry out, both of which could damage or destroy it. Preserving it in the water it has been exposed to for, possibly, thousands of years was the safest course of action.

Mike called his magazine editor to let her know what was developing and then helped Rich stow their dive gear for the day. Sophia went back to *The Parthenon* offices as well to file her own story. Mike promised to email her photographs for the school paper.

When everything settled down at the dive site, with express instructions from Alivia to not make any more dives until they had a plan in place to deal with any more bones or artifacts from the site, Mike, Rich and Gardner headed back into Huntington and ended up at Fat Patty's again for a beer and a burger.

"Pretty exciting day, huh?" Rich said once their pints of Bridge Brew Works ale had arrived.

"Interesting, but not my first body actually," Gardner said.

"Mine either," Rich agreed.

"That sounds really strange, guys, but it's not my first skull either," Mike agreed with a shake of his head. "Gardner, you first."

The three men spent the next few minutes swapping stories about their own experiences finding bodies, or parts of them, underwater. As commercial divers Gardner and Rich had both been called upon from time to time to search for bodies or evidence from crimes in the Ohio River or lakes in the area. Mike's personal experience was closer to today's than the grisly crime scenes the other two talked about. He had found part of a skeleton on a shipwreck near his home on the coast of North Carolina.

A television behind the bar showed the local news channel, but none of the men were watching it. They were more interested in their conversation, at least until someone walked up to their table after recognizing them from the story that had just aired—it was picked up by the national news.

"So the whole country just saw us find a skull?" Gardner asked.

"Don't worry, I don't think they heard you scream like a little girl when you pulled it out of the silt," Rich said.

"I didn't scream. I was frustrated with the silt. I couldn't see anything," Gardner said, shaking his head.

"Sure you were," Rich replied. "I just hope they got my store logo and website on camera."

Before he could answer, Mike's phone rang. It was Sophia.

"Hey kid, what's going on?" Mike said as he answered.

"I guess I have you to thank," Sophia said.

"For what?"

"For the magazine that just called and asked to run my story about what you found today," Sophia said over the phone.

"Oh, I might have mentioned to my editor that you were on the site so there was no point in me writing up anything about what happened," Mike said with a laugh. He knew it wouldn't hurt her to have a story published in front of a greater audience.

"Well, thank you," Sophia said. "One more thing, though. We've had several requests from national media come in this afternoon since the story broke. You guys are going to be famous. But several are sending their own reporters here. Dr. White asked me to tell you that she wants to hold a news conference tomorrow at the site and have you three diving as well."

Like trained dolphins diving for the crowd, Mike thought as he said "Lovely," the tone in his voice making it obvious that he felt that it was anything but.

"I didn't think you would be happy to hear that one," Sophia said, grinning.

"Not really, but we'll have to deal with it," Mike said. "Get some rest. Sounds like tomorrow is going to be a busy one."

Mike hung up his phone and explained to the two divers what was going on.

"Guess this is my last beer," Rich said.

"Probably best for all of us," Mike said, raising his hand to signal for the check.

After they paid up and were making their way out the door through the crowded restaurant adjacent to campus, Mike noticed a man staring at him. The man appeared to be Native American or Mexican, and was older than the rest of the crowd. He was well-dressed, but didn't really fit in with the university crowd. He was seated alone at the end of the bar. Before Mike got a chance to say something, the man turned away and Rich grabbed him by the arm.

"Come on man, just because this place is where Mycroft's was when we were in school doesn't mean you see someone you know. All of those girls moved on and got married," Rich said.

"Huh, what? Oh, yeah, I'm sure you're right," Mike said, not sure what to think about the look he received from the mysterious man at the end of the bar. It was piercing and angry, not the look of someone who recognized Mike from the television story at all.

CHAPTER 18

Images flashed through Red Bird's mind as he floated toward the light. He saw colors and sights he had never seen before. He saw himself facing the gods themselves. They were tall and broad shouldered. Their hair was long, but of many different colors and their skin was pale. Red Bird shook at the sight.

He saw himself rising up from the waters of the Holy Cenote, but it was a different place, the water was the same, but the opening to the water was different than before. He saw himself lifted gently from the water's edge and carried to a small village away from the great walled city. The people cared for him.

Red Bird saw himself standing in front of the ornate statue of the First Father, of Two Wolves. He had seen that statue many times before, but this time it looked different to him. It wasn't in its normal place.

Red Bird's perspective changed and he saw himself walking; only he didn't look like he did on the day he was sacrificed to the gods. He didn't look familiar to himself. His long, brown hair was cut short and it was gray. He looked thinner and his skin paler, too. Only his blue eyes looked unchanged. He was wrapped in robes. Some looked familiar and others looked like animal skins, although he had never seen animals that looked like anything that might have fur like that. He was stooped over and carried a heavy burden. The ground appeared covered in thick, white sand, only it wasn't sand. It was hard for him to walk in it. He had to pick up his feet and set them down to take each step.

Suddenly he was standing in front of the gods again. His skin glowed and he felt fresh and whole again. The gods faces shown down on him and his heart swelled with joy. He was at peace and the gods favored him. He felt as if he could spend eternity in that warmth and joy.

He couldn't tell how long he reveled in the glow, but it gradually faded away. Before he knew it, the warmth was gone. He felt cold. And he hurt all over. Red Bird heard voices in his head, but he couldn't make them out. They didn't make sense to him. There was a fog all around him and an intense pain in his back. He shivered.

Red Bird regained consciousness lying on his back on the smooth rocks at the edge of the water—the lower half of his body was still floating. His long hair was a tangled mess, wrapped around his head. His body was cold but his mind was on fire from the visions. He wasn't sure what to make of them all. The voices became louder, finally coming into focus as faces appeared in front of him.

"Who is he? Where did he come from? Have you seen him before?" the voices said.

Red Bird wiped the hair from his eyes and saw two young faces, an identical boy and a girl, about 12 years old.

"Help me," Red Bird croaked, his voice rough and his throat sore. Then he lost consciousness.

The next time Red Bird opened his eyes, he was on the floor in a small hut. It was dark outside. Before the sacrifice, the priests had stripped him of all of his jewels and markings. The villagers had no idea that up until a few hours before he was the high priest. At least it felt like it was a few hours before. He wasn't quite sure. Red Bird decided to play it safe and not say too much. He didn't want the villagers to be afraid of him, or to try and finish the job of the sacrifice.

Red Bird stood up. He was wearing a small covering from his waist to his knees, but that was it. He stretched for a minute to work out the kinks in his body and stepped outside to see where he was. A fire was burning and a small family was seated around it. They eyed him with caution; Red Bird was taller and broader shouldered than most of the other people of the palace, including the king. He was definitely larger than anyone from the villages.

"We do not have much to share, but eat from what we do have," the father said after sizing Red Bird up. "Tell us your name and how you came to be in the waters."

"Thank you, father," Red Bird said. "The gods of the ancient waters will be pleased with how you have treated me."

"The gods sent you?"

"Father, all I remember is being in the water and seeing the gods. They showed me things they wanted me to do and then I woke up to see your kind family," Red Bird said as he took his place near the fire. "The gods have put a path before me."

"You haven't told us your name."

"I have been called many things, but I think the name I like best is Two Wolves," Red Bird said. "Do you know my story?"

"If you are the ancient Two Wolves who came here from far away and created the city, I do," the father replied. "I have heard the priests tell the story many times on festival days. You certainly look like the Two Wolves in the stories they tell. You have not changed at all."

"I am that Two Wolves. And the gods have sent me back from the underworld with a task. I will start it tomorrow, but I thank you for helping me out today," Red Bird said. "You have earned great honor from the gods for your aid."

"Blessings on you, great Two Wolves," the father said bowing down in front of the stranger. "We will aid you however we can."

Red Bird gathered some of the prepared food from beside the fire and ate. He suddenly realized he was hungry, hungrier than he had been in years. It felt good to eat the food of the common people again…something he hadn't done since he was a warrior. The family left him alone and gave him space to think. He needed it. He needed to collect his thoughts from the visions he had after being sacrificed. He hadn't lied. He was sacrificed to the gods and they had given him visions and returned him to the earth. He wouldn't wait to act, but the morning would be soon enough. It seemed right to tell the family he was Two Wolves returned since he thought he knew what the gods expected him to do.

CHAPTER 19

Mike, Rich and Gardner were back at the dive site with the sun the next morning. They wanted to get a dive in before the press conference. They expected that the media circus, along with the presence of national media wanting their own special interviews, would end up ruining their chances of accomplishing much from that point forward. Of course, Alivia had told them no more diving, but he knew that right now was going to be his last chance for a while. And since he didn't work for the university, he wasn't concerned about the consequences. What could they do? Fire him?

Mike was torn, of course, because he was a member of the "national media" himself, although he had gotten to the point in his career that he was never called on to photograph press conferences and such. Still, he expected that he might know one or two of the out-of-town visitors, especially when the editors and producers at their respective home offices got wind of Mike being involved and on the other side of the camera for once. Winning a Pulitzer Prize for Photography had a way of creating a reputation.

"Mike, you want to get back in the water on this one?" Gardner asked as they were setting up their equipment. They were maintaining their need to have a safety diver on every dive, so one of them stayed on the surface, although fully suited up.

"I do want to get back in the water. Thanks. I want to get some higher resolution stills this time around," Mike said. He had asked his friends at his home on the Outer Banks of North Carolina to overnight his underwater camera housing to him after their first dive. It had arrived while they were making the dive the day before. He had opened it up and checked it out overnight at his hotel. This time, he wanted to photograph the scene with his professional grade digital camera. "Sorry. I guess I should have said something earlier."

"No worries, man," Gardner said in his usual laconic manner as he moved to set up the air controls and the communications system.

"I can stay dry this time. I've made two dives down there," Rich said. "Honestly, not much to see. Pretty empty except for the bones."

"Nah, you go on," Gardner said.

"Fair enough," Rich said, mimicking Mike.

With that Mike and Rich continued to prepare their equipment. After graduation and a few years in the local newspaper business, Mike worked as an underwater photo pro on Grand Cayman before deciding he preferred to photograph people. He still loved to take his camera underwater when he got a chance, but since he wasn't doing it every day, it took him a little longer than it would otherwise to get everything set up. Electronics and water don't get along very well, so it was extremely important to have the camera housing set up properly. The tiniest leak could ruin an expensive camera. Fresh water, like what filled the caves, wasn't as disastrous as salt water, but Mike didn't want to test it.

Rich stood over Mike's shoulder watching him work. He glanced back toward Gardner and then pitched his voice so only Mike could hear him.

"Do you think the skull spooked Gardner a little?"

"You know him better than I do," Mike said, following Rich's lead by keeping his voice low. "I've seen it happen though. Some guys can wade through blood and muck and then get upset when they see a puppy get hurt in a war zone. It's all about the situation."

"He just seemed happy to step aside and let us dive," Rich said.

"Seems like a solid guy to me. He wouldn't be the first person I met who didn't like the idea of being in a dark, closed in cave, with a body right below him…even if it is an old one," Mike said.

"Now that you put it that way…"

"Sorry, pal. You can't back out. I need you down there," Mike said. "And time's a-wasting. We better get in the water. Dr. White and the other people from the university will be here shortly to get set up for the press conference."

"Let's move then," Rich agreed.

It was only their third dive in the cave system, but they had already established a routine. They moved together, walking slowly down the boards that kept them from stirring up the silt and then floating out in the water once it got deep enough. When they were clear of the sides and less concerned about stirring up silt in the upper pool, they submerged and swam toward the lower cave. As they entered the chamber, Gardner turned on the lights to illuminate the room.

Mike took a minute to move a couple of the lights to cast shadows in different areas of the cave. He had portable flash units attached to his underwater camera, but he knew shadows cast by the lights might help them see things covered up by silt they would have otherwise missed—like they had with the skeleton in the small cave. They had agreed to leave the skeleton alone, to keep in line with the spirit of the orders from Alivia and the university to not dive, if not exactly the letter of law. Mike thought there might be other artifacts in the caves that would serve as clues to what was missing—which was their original mission, even though finding the skeleton had made things more sensational.

Mike glided into the smaller cave that extended off of the lower cave, what he had come to think of as the burial chamber, and photographed the scene. Using his widest angle lens, Mike pressed his back to the roof and was able to see the outline of the entire skeleton in the silt. The shadows revealed where each bone lay, presumably where the body was laid out, or where the "man" died. Mike drifted down closer to the floor and took close-ups of the various humps that made up the body parts. He was careful not to disturb the silt. He could already tell the water in the small cave was getting cloudier from their repeated visits. It might take days or weeks for the silt to completely settle out again.

Finished and not seeing anything else noteworthy in the burial chamber, Mike backed out of the small cave. Rich was hovering in the larger cave room waiting on him.

"You see anything else interesting?" Mike asked over the comm gear.

"I see some humps and bumps, but they may or may not be anything," Rich said. "Who knows?"

"You boys all right down there?" Gardner chimed in.

"We're fine. Just looking around to see if there's anything we've missed," Mike replied.

"Okay. Wanted you to know that Dr. White showed up with her crew. They are setting up a little stage outside," Gardner told them. "She wasn't thrilled that you were in the water."

"Fair enough, thanks for the heads up," Mike said. "She probably wants a dog and pony show. We can make another dive later if we have to, but I wanted to get a couple things done without people looking over my shoulder."

"Roger that."

"We'll be up in a minute."

Mike hovered in the middle of the room, slowly rotating to look at the entire cave room one more time before heading to the surface.

"Rich, do me a favor," Mike asked. "Move that floor light over there. Put it in the other corner. I want to see if my eyes are playing tricks on me."

"You got it."

Mike stared at one spot on the floor while Rich moved the light to the side.

"What do you see?"

"A straight line."

"Ummmmm, Mike?"

"I'm serious. I see a straight line on the floor a few feet away from the entrance to the small cave. Have you ever seen a straight line in nature?" Mike asked as he moved toward what he saw.

"Well, no, I guess not. What is it?"

"Remember, that was what tipped Erick off to the carving just below the water line up above us."

"You got me there."

Mike traced a line with his finger beside the line he saw on the cave floor. Whatever it was, it had a hard edge. He found a corner and then traced three more sides. The silt-covered square was approximately one foot square. It was a few feet away from where the missing item was dragged out.

"Looks like another statue base to me," Rich said, moving in closer.

"You're probably right, but I'm going to clean if off and get a better look," Mike said. "Take my camera and shoot some pictures while I clear it off."

Moving large amounts of the super fine silt could be dangerous. In different situations, silt could cloud up the water reducing visibility to zero. Divers had died in caves because of white-outs caused by silt. While that wasn't a concern for Mike and Rich—they were tied to the surface with their air hoses—but it could make it impossible to see anything in the cave. He moved cautiously and slowly to avoid problems.

Mike gently scraped the covering layer of silt to one side with the palm of his hand until he had the square uncovered. He was barely breathing as he cleaned it off. He quickly realized that while it looked like the stone square that had served as a base for a statue, probably, it appeared to be chiseled out, similar to the stone near the top of the cave, but this one hadn't been defaced.

"You think it's a tomb stone?" Rich asked.

"As in 'Here lies…'? Don't know. Maybe. Sure is interesting, though," Mike agreed. "Get a couple close ups on it and then I want to see if we can move it."

When Rich was done photographing the stone, Mike applied pressure to two opposite corners attempting to twist the stone in place, but it didn't budge.

"Do you have a dive tool on you?" Mike asked.

"Never leave home without it," Rich said. He handed Mike a blunt tipped knife that was used for digging, prying and cutting fishing line and ropes.

Mike wedged the tip under the stone and quickly rapped on the butt end of the knife with the palm of his hand. The stone moved.

"Just a little stuck," Mike said.

"Amazing what a little properly placed force will do," Rich quipped.

Mike slipped his fingers under the stone, careful to lift it straight up and keep it flat. A foot square and a couple inches thick, the stone was heavy.

"Okay, we're done. Gardner, we're headed up and bringing up a present," Mike said.

"Not another skull I hope," Gardner replied, his smirk obvious over the comm gear.

"Not this time," Mike said with a laugh. Gardner knew exactly what they were looking at since they were still wearing their closed-circuit video cameras as well, but it was still a funny line.

"What do you think Dr. White is going to say?"

"We'll find out in just a few minutes," Mike said, smiling behind his mask.

CHAPTER 20

If anyone knew how to get around the city without being noticed, it was the high priest. Especially since he was a ghost.

Red Bird woke up the morning after being sacrificed with a clarity he hadn't had in years. He knew exactly what he had to do and what needed to be done. Borrowing a knife from the family that rescued him from the water, he cut off his long hair. He wanted to leave his past behind him. The father gave Red Bird a simple cloak to put on over his broad shoulders and a hat for his head. That was all they had to spare.

"I am embarrassed to give you such poor and shameful things," the man said. "You should have a cloak of gold to return to the city."

"Father, you have given me the greatest present of all. Please do not be ashamed of your gifts. I have no need of gold or jewels. I promise you, I will repay your gifts many times over," Red Bird said, although he wasn't sure how he could deliver on that promise. He simply hoped the gods would smile on the family in the future.

For Red Bird, his path was clear. He was going to steal the statue of Two Wolves and take it away. He knew he would be successful. He had already seen himself doing it in his visions.

With nothing more than the few roughly made gifts from the family, Red Bird left for Tulum and his city. He had once been a leader and a man of immense power. As the chief priest, he could have men put to death for simply looking at him. He could have any woman he wanted. He had the best food and wore the finest robes, and he had the finest jewels for his fingers. Now he returned as a thief and he felt better about his actions than he ever felt before. He moved through the jungle with a clear mind and light steps like he had when he was a child.

The habits of the warrior he had been came back to him as he moved through the forest. He still liked to hunt so he had remained fit and strong. He found himself moving faster; smiling at the new freedom he had found. He had the gods behind him and a new mission directly from them, as compared to the things Feathered Warrior ordered him to do, saying it was decreed by the gods. As he ran through the woods, he began to doubt the king had ever heard from the gods at all.

Red Bird quickly realized he was closer to the city than he imagined. He thought the gods would have taken him far away when he was sacrificed. He reasoned they must have returned him close to where he started so he could fulfill the task they had set before him.

Red Bird quickly found the coast with its rocky precipices overlooking the warm, blue-green waters. Even before he got there, he could hear the gentle waves on the sandy shore below him and smell the salt air. He stood at the edge for a moment to enjoy the view before moving out on his quest. He hadn't expected to ever see the sea again. Now, he knew exactly where he was. He headed south toward the city.

Tulum stood on the cliffs high above the aquamarine waters of the Caribbean. Steps were carved into the rock face that allowed the people of the village to make their way to the water below to fish or cool off. Guards' outposts stood just away from the city itself, giving watchers a clear view of anyone approaching or leaving the city. The king had long since ordered the jungle to be cut back from the city walls, giving them a greater field of view. The ever-encroaching nature outside the city walls kept work crews busy hacking it back.

The city itself was guarded by a perimeter wall. Just to the outside of the wall, village huts made up most of the residences for the people. In case of war, the people were brought inside, but during times of peace, they spread out further. Inside the wall was a massive courtyard dotted with temples, fine gravel walkways and structures for the king, the priests and rituals that supported the daily life of the city.

Approaching the city's outer wall, Red Bird did his best to walk crouched over, without looking deformed, so he wouldn't stand out. He was taller than the rest of the men and women on the streets and he was worried his height would attract attention.

Red Bird knew it would be difficult to get near the statue of Two Wolves. He didn't know why the gods wanted him to take it away from the city, but he was certain that was what they expected him to do. The statue rested in a special ceremonial temple between the High Priest's temple—his former home—and the palace where the king lived. Red Bird was one of the few men in the city who knew how to get there from below. When they built the temples, a former high priest included a walkway that ran underground. It was better for the king and the priests to suddenly be seen standing at the top of a temple or of the palace, rather than to walk like a common man on the streets. He knew he was probably the only man alive, if he was still alive, that could actually pull off stealing the statue.

Moving along with the crowds entering the city through the gate, Red Bird noted the guards looking relaxed and casual. They were leaning against the walls with their spears resting beside them. They were talking amongst themselves and didn't seem to be paying attention to the people passing in front of them. Red Bird made a mental note to have the guards reprimanded...and then he grunted and smiled to himself. That was no longer his responsibility. Now, entering the city as a thief, he chuckled and thanked the gods that the men weren't taking their jobs more seriously.

Getting inside the city gates was just the first hurdle, however. He had to make it into the heart of the city and to the holiest of places. Common people were forbidden to even approach the main temple when there wasn't a ceremony and for one to make his way behind it was punishable by death at any time. But that was where he had to go. Red Bird knew the gods had set this task before him for a reason and he knew he couldn't fail. Or, if he did fail, it was by their decree as well. Turning back was not an option.

Red Bird approached the central market. He hadn't been in the market square since he was a young man and served his people as a warrior. Since he was elevated to priest, he had stayed in the holy areas and allowed his acolytes to serve him. He hadn't had the need to prepare his own food...something else he realized he would have to remember again now that he was beginning a new journey. For the moment, the food the family in the jungle served him was carrying him through. The excitement and apprehension of the moment made eating unnecessary. Afterward, he would manage.

Scanning the market for a moment, Red Bird allowed his senses to open. He hadn't used his warrior instincts in many years, but they were still there lying dormant. At first, all he saw was confusion and noise. Then things began to come into focus. He saw the patterns in the crowd. He could tell who had the best produce and who was struggling. He saw one man working his way through the crowd, acting suspicious. Red Bird marked him as a thief immediately. Another man strode through the crowd confidently, his head up and shoulders back. Red Bird didn't know the man so he obviously wasn't a noble or a high priest, but Red Bird guessed he was a leader among the warriors. He wanted to avoid catching the man's eye. It was possible the man would recognize him and that could spell disaster.

Looking closer at the market itself, Red Bird noted that it wasn't as big as he remembered from his youth. There weren't as many people present trading their goods. And what they had to offer didn't appear as good as what it had just a few years before. He knew the city was struggling, but this was a reality he didn't know about. He doubted the king did either, protected as they both had been by their servants and their belief in their own divinity. He laughed to himself. Hadn't he been born to a woman? Hadn't he had a mother? Hadn't he bled as a warrior just like the other warriors he saw and the men he himself sacrificed? Didn't his blood look just like theirs? How did he convince himself that he was immortal?

"I'll take your gold citizen," Red Bird heard uttered behind him. He started to turn, simply to see who had addressed him since what the man said hadn't fully registered with him. He felt the sharp point of a knife in his back and he froze. He was still on the fringes of the market. No one would notice what was happening to him.

"What is it? What did you say?" Red Bird asked, trying to focus on the situation behind him with the same instincts he had been using to assess the market.

"I said, I will take your gold," the man said more forcefully, emphasizing his demand with another thrust of the knife point. Red Bird felt the tip break the skin on his back, near his ribs. He could feel blood trickle from the tear in his skin. Regardless of what he thought about his own invincibility just a day before, that confirmed he was mortal now. Still, the gods had sent him on a quest and he wasn't about to let a common thief stop him.

"I'm not citizen. I'm just a poor farmer. I have no gold," Red Bird replied.

"You wear the hat and cloak of a farmer, but you have the bearing of a royal. You are trying to hide your height, but I can see it. And you have health like someone who has eaten every day while the rest of the city starves. You are a citizen. But that makes no difference to me. I will take your gold from you just the same," the thief said.

"You are very observant for a simple thief," Red Bird said.

"Maybe I was once like you. Proud and strong. But when you fall into disfavor with the king or the high priest, there's no saving you. I got away with my life…barely," the thief said. "Now enough talk. Give me your gold purse or I will empty your life on the streets here and take it from you anyway."

The man's voice didn't seem familiar to Red Bird, but he knew immediately the man was dangerous to him, not only because he held a knife to his back. If he had once been a noble or a warrior who had been scorned by the king, or worse by himself, and thrown down from his high place, the man would recognize him. He would immediately alert the guards and stir up trouble. If they didn't kill him on the spot as a devil come back from Xibalba, he would never be able to get to the statue and he would fail the gods. That was something he could not let happen.

"My friend," Red Bird began, "I have no gold as I said, but I do have something I think you might want."

Red Bird turned slightly to his side and reached inside his cloak as if to get something to give to the thief. At that moment, Red Bird allowed his warrior instincts to surge outward. When his finger tips brushed the hem of the cloak, he balled the cloth in his hand. As he rounded on his attacker, he wound the cloak around the knife and the man's hand, while he pulled the smaller man toward him. The knife wrapped in the folds of rough wool and was out of commission, Red Bird clamped his free hand on the smaller man's throat and began to squeeze. While he hadn't been a warrior in years, Red Bird had restrained many captives as he prepared to sacrifice them to the gods. He knew with just enough pressure on the man's neck that in a few short moments, the man would lose consciousness.

The fight was strangely quiet as neither one of them wanted to attract the attention of the guards. A thief running free in the market was one thing, but using a knife on a noble was something else entirely. The thief knew, even though he was being overpowered, the last thing he could do was yell for help or call out at all.

The thief's free hand flailed toward Red Bird but the larger man had him in a bad position. Red Bird moved the man around, pinning his knife hand behind his own back without ever letting up pressure on the man's neck. As the man's struggling slowed and grew weaker, Red Bird saw the man's eyes search out his own, trying to determine who had overpowered him. There was an instant of recognition as the thief realized who he had just attacked and who was going to kill him. Red Bird saw the man's eyes grow wide for a moment and then they began to lose focus. The man's eyes slowly dulled as he stopped struggling. After another moment, the thief was dead weight in Red Bird's arms. Red Bird dragged his assailant behind a stone building and laid him on the ground.

"I don't know who you are, but you seemed to recognize me," Red Bird said while he panted. The exertion of the silent fight mixed with the adrenaline that was flooding his veins to push Red Bird onto high alert. "For you, that means I cannot allow you to live. I don't know who or what you once were, but I have no sympathy for a lowly thief."

Without a moment's hesitation, Red Bird unwound the knife from the cloth of his cloak and looked at it for a moment. Knowing exactly what he had to do, Red Bird slit the man's throat just as he had done many times before on the ritual alter. He even mumbled the prayer he always said, asking the gods to accept the human sacrifice.

"Maybe you were sent to test my resolve to do this act the gods have set before me. Maybe you were supposed to be a sacrifice for this deed," Red Bird said, talking to the man while he wiped the blood from the blade on the man's cloak. "I will keep your knife in case I need it again."

Looking around to make sure he was still undiscovered, Red Bird dragged the man into a small building just off to the side of the market square. Had the market been fully operational, as it was in Red Bird's youth, that building would have been the outer boundary of the market itself. Now, in its reduced form, the building was off to one side and out of sight from the casual observer. Before he left the man, Red Bird searched him. He found some gold and then took the man's shoulder pack. He realized he would need it on his trip.

"I hope you find peace in the next world," Red Bird said as he left.

Back out in the open, Red Bird checked his cloak and adjusted the pack on his back. He took a moment to force himself to relax, feeling the adrenaline bleed out of his system. He started to shake, but quickly stilled himself and then began moving forward toward his goal. It was first time he had killed another man in anger since he had become a priest. He was glad his warrior blood hadn't thinned too far, but he took no satisfaction in the killing. He simply knew it was a test put in front of him by the gods. There would be others.

CHAPTER 21

"Thank you all for coming out this morning. We could have held this press conference anywhere, but I think you will appreciate what we have in store for you today," Dr. Alivia White said to the crowd of journalists, university people and local officials who were in attendance. She was dressed in her fashionable best, looking both professional and attractive at the same time. "As many of you have heard, we have made an astounding find in this Adena Indian burial mound. When the mound was originally excavated 25 years ago, we found several sets of skeletal remains from the Native Americans buried here. Dating the remains placed the building of this mound at the very end of the Adena period or the early part of the Hopewell Indian culture. We've still classified this mound as an Adena mound because the Hopewell culture was not known for mound building. Still, the mound itself raises many interesting questions. Those are mostly academic, though, and we all know that history is rarely as neat and clean as we academics would like it to be."

The crowd chuckled to themselves at the self-deprecating joke. Alivia had used the natural terrain surrounding the mound to her advantage. Rather than using the mound itself as a backdrop, she had placed her podium to one side of the mound, but slightly up hill from where the audience would stand. The natural bowl shape of the land immediately adjoining the mound made for a perfect amphitheater. The entrance to the mound was off to her right. Alivia was thoroughly enjoying herself and her performance. Over the years, she had spoken many times on various subjects, especially this burial mound and their findings there after she took the project over following Erick Cruz's death, but this was the first time she had been able to attract the attention of the national news media. The combination of Erick Cruz's murder, the attempted murder of his niece Sophia and the other drama from the last few days, along with finding the skull and presumably the rest of the skeleton at the bottom of the cave had fired the imaginations of scientists and the public alike. She had heard of several different "theories" already and a Facebook page dedicated to the remains of the space alien buried in the sunken cave. While that was amusing, she loved the attention. Alivia wanted everything to go perfectly, seeing this as her chance to hit the big time. She wanted the big publishing contract and she wanted the television interviews. She had even invited Sophia Cruz and her family to the press conference. She convinced Marshall University's president to dedicate the dig and the mound area to Erick Cruz and his family. A clause in the previous contract between the landowner and the university gave the university access and control to the site and it had never been withdrawn.

Mike, Rich and Gardner made their way through the doorway in the mound. No one had fixed the door hinges since Mike and Rich wedged the door open a week before. The three men were still in their dry suits; Mike and Rich were still wet. Before the threesome came outside, they spent a few minutes cleaning off the stone tablet Mike and Rich found on the dive. They wanted to see it for themselves and make sure it was authentic. Mike took a few more close-up images of it on the surface with the rest of the sediment washed from the etchings. It clearly depicted something with a series of small drawings carved into the tablet. The three divers had no idea, though, what it might say.

"Of course, the death of Erick Cruz in 1989 put an end to our excavations and investigations into the true meaning of this site. Thanks in large part to his niece, now a student at Marshall, we now know how Erick died and his murderer chose to end his own life rather than face the consequences," Alivia continued with a nod to Sophia and her family. "Because of that, we are dedicating our efforts here to Erick's memory and we are going to name a scholarship in the Anthropology Department in his honor."

There was a round of applause as everyone recognized the symbolism of that gesture. When Erick died, many in the university community thought Erick had broken the rules and died in the process. His reputation was sullied. Naming a scholarship after him was the first step to righting that wrong. The Cruz family learned about the plan a few minutes before the press conference and was still processing their emotions, but they appeared to be pleased with the announcement.

"The most exciting thing happened yesterday as we began exploring the rest of the cave that had been hidden away for so long. A team of divers discovered a skeleton and brought the skull to the surface. After taking it back to the university for further examination, experts were intrigued by the find. They have indicated to me that while the skeleton must predate the burying of the other Native Americans in the mound, there are some marked differences between the skulls of those and the new one we just found. Members of our team are consulting with experts on these Native American cultures from around the world and just about everyone is baffled about these differences," Alivia explained, relishing her role and her time in the spotlight. "Erick Cruz found a stone tablet in the cave before he was killed, but it was so badly damaged we don't know what it said or if it may have offered some answers to the mystery. We are re-examining that tablet now, but unfortunately we don't hold much hope that it will tell us anything."

"Ummmmm, excuse me, Dr. White," Mike said, raising his left hand to get Alivia's attention as he walked forward. "I have something you might want to see."

"Sure Mike, come on up here," Alivia said with a chipper voice, although the look on her face indicated that she was anything but happy about Mike's interruption. "Ladies and gentlemen, let me introduce Mike Scott to you. Mike is an award-winning photojournalist and helped solve the mystery behind Erick Cruz's death. He was also assisting the divers who brought up the skull. And, he is a Marshall alumnus, as well."

"I'm sorry to interrupt you, Dr. White, but we found something this morning that I think you might find interesting. Remember, you asked us to make a dive this morning to see if we found anything else that the media might be interested in seeing," Mike said with a smile.

"Oh yes, that's right, Mike," Alivia said, covering Mike's lie with a mixture of annoyance and gratitude. "Show us all what you found."

"We left the remainder of the skeleton undisturbed, like you told us to do. But just outside of the small cave, here," Mike said pointing at one of the drawings beside the podium showing the layout of the underwater caves, "we found another stone tablet. It looks very similar to me to the one that Erick found. This one has not been defaced, though." With that, he moved his other hand from around behind his back and held the square stone tablet up for everyone to see. The photographers and videographers immediately trained their cameras on the new discovery.

"Really? Let me see it," Alivia said, dropping all pretense of putting on a show for the audience. She was genuinely interested in the tablet.

Mike smiled and laid the tablet down on a table. The audience pushed forward to get closer and see what Mike had uncovered.

"Can you read it?" Mike said, talking to Alivia, rather than continuing the pretense of the show. She quickly forgot about the press as well, pulling a pair of reading glasses from her purse and bending down to examine the tablet. She gently brushed her fingers across the carved images.

"I need to get this back to the lab to decipher the rest of it, but I can make out a few things. Some of it appears to be typical of the Adena and Hopewell, but parts of it are symbols I've never seen here. I'm not sure what they mean," Alivia said, talking to herself as much as Mike and the press. "It seems to indicate a man, probably the man buried in the cave, and he came from a long way away. There appears to be a statue indicated here as well, although I'm not sure what that represents. This last line is probably his name, but I can't be sure. Just a rough guess, it seems to refer to Red Hawk or maybe just Red Bird."

"Dr. White, Dr. White," the press began shouting, trying to ask questions, but Alivia was no longer paying attention to them. Mike looked around the crowd for a minute, wondering if he did indeed know anyone from the national media who had come to town to cover the story when he noticed Sophia speaking to her grandfather. He shook his head when Sophia gestured toward the front. Mike moved toward them.

"Sophia, is something wrong? I'm sorry if this is a bit more chaotic than Dr. White planned, but I hate press conferences. I thought this would be more interesting anyway," Mike said with a smile.

"Mike, Grandfather Ernesto just told me something, but he doesn't want to share it with the crowd. He is nervous about his English in front of all the cameras," Sophia explained.

"What is it?"

"Before he immigrated to the United States in the 1960s, my grandfather was from the Yucatan Peninsula of Mexico, what many people call the Mayan Riviera. My family isn't Mayan, but my grandfather knew many Mayan people in the area," Sophia explained. "He just told me that there is a Mayan legend in Mexico about a priest named Red Bird who was sacrificed by drowning in a Holy Cenote. He came back to life as a giant bird and carried away a statue from the city. He disappeared and no one ever saw him or the statue again."

"Wow, that sounds really familiar," Mike said looking over his shoulder at Alivia as she continued to study the stone tablet. "I think it's time we wrapped up this press conference and talked about what is going on some more."

With that, Mike stepped back to the podium and took control.

"Ladies and gentlemen, let's leave Dr. White to her research. I apologize. I threw this curve ball at her this morning and we've gotten a bit off schedule. My fellow divers and I would like to invite you into the mound and to climb down into the cave below. We can show you video from our dives so far and we can even make copies of it available to you for your newscasts," Mike said gesturing toward Rich and Gardner. "Mr. Synowiec and Mr. Gardner are local expert divers and they will happily answer all of your questions."

The media members immediately turned their attention to the two commercial divers. Rich tripped over his tongue for just a second before finding his feet and began organizing the reporters into small groups to lead them to the lower cave. Gardner did his best to be invisible.

As the members of the press moved toward the entrance of the burial mound, Mike scanned the crowd still looking to see if he knew anyone. At the back, he saw a face he recognized, but not because of a professional relationship. It was the man who glared at him at the bar the night before. Dark skinned with black hair and eyes, Mike recognized the man as a Mayan. Mike met his gaze for a moment and he still saw nothing but anger there. Mike started to approach the man to see what was going on when a reporter from the front row shouted his name.

"Hey Mike! It's Ted from ABC News. Can we get an interview?"

Mike looked away from the Mayan man to see who had shouted his name. When he looked back, the man was gone.

"Hmmm. That's really strange," Mike said.

"Mike, did you hear me buddy?" Ted called again.

"Sorry, Ted. Sure, no problem. I'll be there in a second."

CHAPTER 22

Red Bird worked his way toward the path that would lead him to the back entrance to the Tempe Dios del Viento that housed the statue of Two Wolves. It was legend the city's founder was buried underneath the cornerstone of temple itself, but that happened many generations before Red Bird was born. Suddenly, he was unsure what was legend and what was real.

Wearing the rough shirt and hat the farmer gave him, he did his best to avoid attention. He didn't have a plan to get to the statue, or to get away, but he trusted the gods to help him. They had already provided him with clothes from the family and then provided him with a knife, some gold and a bag to carry the statue away. He knew if he trusted them, they would provide for him.

The sun was high in the sky; the heat beat down on Red Bird's shoulders. The rough cut stone that made up the temples and buildings in the holy part of the city were hot to the touch, nearly burning Red Bird's hands as he crept and skulked away from the main paths. He didn't want to be seen so he took his time and moved quietly. Often, that meant he had to lie down on the rocks or hide in cracks. His muscles were aching from the effort of not moving as he drew close to the rear entrance of the temple.

The Tempe Dios del Viento was built to one side of the main temple, near the water's edge. On holy days, or when the current king wanted to invoke the memory of Two Wolves for one purpose or another, the acolytes would bring the statue onto the temple grounds, parading it through the people and then carry it to the top stairs of the temple for the king and the high priest to bless, or be blessed by it.

When Red Bird finally reached the back steps of the temple, he let out the breath he had been unconsciously holding and straightened up. A smile crossed his face. This part of the city was quiet on normal days. No one would even watch the area behind the temples. The common people were in the fields, trying to bring in the harvest and feed the city or were in the market. The priests and royals were about their own business ruling or finding someone to blame for their misery.

Entering the temple, Red Bird took time to let his eyes adjust to the gloom inside the building. It was a small structure, built slightly above the rocks. Out the back steps, the Caribbean Sea slapped gently against the beach 40 feet below. It was square, 25 feet on each side, with a doorway on the front, facing the main courtyard, and one on the back, where Red Bird stood now. The structure wasn't nearly as ornately decorated as the main temple, but early artisans had decorated the top of the structure with scenes from Two Wolves' life. Openings in the temple roof allowed sunlight to enter the structure, while blocking out most of the rain.

Red Bird was struck, as he always was, by the site of the statue itself. Two Wolves was a tall man according to legend. There were stone statues around the city that portrayed the founder as at least 10 feet tall, although Red Bird doubted there was any truth to that. Fortunately for him, the statue in front of him was built on a much smaller scale.

In his travels and in the wars he fought with other cities as a warrior prince, he had never seen anything like this statue. Made from jade and obsidian around a stone base, the statue stood only three feet tall. Where many of the carvings and statues Red Bird's people made today were outlandish, portraying kings and priests as birds or animals, this one was carved to look like the man himself. Approaching the dias set in the middle of the structure, Red Bird felt as if the half-size statue was breathing and watching him. Sun from the openings in the roof caught the statue in such a way that it seemed to glow. Reaching the pedestal, Red Bird fell to his knees, overcome with the events of the last day. Had it really happened so quickly? His head spun and his mind was filled with visions from the day before where he carried the statue away from his city, heading to unknown lands.

After a few years, or mere moments, Red Bird opened his eyes, coming face to face with the statue.

"My lords, you have set me on a path I do not understand, but I do know that you require me to take this statue away from here, away from my people. I do not know what the city has done to give you displeasure after so many generations, but I do not question your wisdom. I only ask that you give me the strength and the wisdom to do your bidding. I do not have those things within myself. I know that. I will need your guiding hand upon me and your strength within me," Red Bird whispered to the statue. His hands gently touched its feet.

"Please forgive me for touching you and carrying you, but I know of no other way to make your visions come true. I saw myself carrying a heavy load, by myself, in a bag over my shoulder so you already know what I will have to do. I will not be able to carry your statue with the proper respect it deserves."

Red Bird took the bag he got from the thief in the market square from over his shoulder and opened the top, folding it down on itself. Returning to the statue, he gently rocked it backward and then lifted it off the stand it rested on. It was lighter than he imagined. Still, he knew carrying it for any length of time would be a burden.

As gently as he could, Red Bird sat the statue into the bottom of the bag and the pulled the bag up over the statue before closing it with the leather band weaved through the top. He said another silent prayer to Two Wolves as he did so, asking for his blessings.

Red Bird stood again and hefted the bag over his shoulder. He pulled his hat back down over his head and settled his rough shirt into place. He couldn't see himself, but he felt sure he looked like any common farmer with a heavy burden. If he could get out of the city, he was sure he could escape and begin his journey.

Getting out of the city was going to be the challenge.

Red Bird began retracing his footsteps, doing his best to move toward the city's main gates and freedom. He had been fortunate so far, but he wasn't sure how long that good fortune would last.

He made it away from Two Wolves' temple and quickly jogged through the open space between it and the high priest's temple; his home until just yesterday. He crouched down by the stone base of the temple and looked around to see if anyone was coming. As slowly as he could manage, he crawled forward, his hat low, holding his burden close to his body. He made his way to the corner of the temple and could clearly see the main gates ahead of him. That was his way out. There were other ways out of the city, through tunnels and hidden passages like he used to move from the high priest's temple to the king's private rooms, but there was too great of a chance that he would be recognized. At the very least, he would be caught and questioned as to why he was in that part of the city. No, his best way to escape was back through the front gates…back the way he came in. He just hoped the guards were as lax in their duties as they had been earlier. He surveyed the grounds ahead of him and planned his next move.

"You! Who are you? What are you doing there? This is the high priest's temple! This area is forbidden to you!" a voice shouted out. Red Bird had been looking out and around, but he had not looked up at the temple himself.

"You must go or I will call for the guards! You are not permitted here," the voice said again.

Red Bird realized the voice was young.

Keeping his head down, hoping the hat would cover enough of his face so he wouldn't be recognized, he stood, although he stayed bent over to disguise his height. "Priest, do not call the guards. I beg you. I only lost my way. I did not mean to trespass on these holy grounds. I am not from the city, but live in a village to the north. I came to ask the high priest for his help and was confused." Red Bird was mimicking one of the many requests he had regularly from the people outside the city. He had always liked to talk to the commoners and that experience helped him at this moment.

"I am not a priest and there is no high priest today. The king sacrificed him in the Holy Cenote yesterday. He is praying to the gods to name a replacement. Until that happens, there is no one who can hear your plea, farmer. Go home."

"I will do that young priest. Blessings on you for your understanding."

Red Bird began to relax as he moved away. He had no idea where the story he told the acolyte had come from and he said a quick prayer to thank the gods for putting it in his mind. He was certain he could have killed the boy if necessary, but he didn't want to kill anyone else if he didn't have to. He had seen too much killing in his life and he thought he recognized the boy's voice. It was probably one of his own servants.

"Halt! You there halt!" Red Bird heard the commanding voice behind him and feet trampling toward him. The acolyte hadn't alerted the guards but standing up and moving away from the temple had made him visible just the same. It had sealed his fate.

He looked around quickly at the men running toward him. There were six soldiers carrying spears. They appeared to be from the king's personal guard. It wasn't the boy's fault after all. These were not the city guards. The king was probably heading to the temple with a decision about the new high priest. In the back of his mind Red Bird wondered who would be taking his place.

In a flash, Red Bird knew what he had to do. Instead of running toward the front gates and trying to outdistance the soldiers, something he knew wasn't likely, he turned and ran toward the temple, taking the stone steps two at a time. He ran straight for the top.

As he ran, Red Bird's hat fell from his head. Priests from inside the temple came outside to see what the shouting was about and jumped backward when they saw Red Bird running straight at them. A few gasped as they recognized him, even with his hair cut short. Many of them had been part of the sacrificial ceremony the day before.

Red Bird ran to the top of the temple, more than 200 feet above the grounds of the city. He ducked inside the small structure on the top of the temple the king and the priest used to address the people. They would climb to the top of the temple from the inside and then appear to the city through the narrow doorway. The tiny structure was barely large enough to fit the two men.

Gasping to catch his breath from the run, Red Bird chanced a glance down the steps. The soldiers had hesitated halfway up the temple as the priests told them who they were chasing. He could see the fear in their eyes as they imagined him to be a spirit come back from the sacrifice. Red Bird closed his eyes and hung his head. Visions filled his mind and he made a decision. He was going to address his people one last time. He didn't know how he would make his escape afterward, but he was certain they wanted him to speak.

Taking off his shirt to match what he saw in his latest vision, and opening the bag he was using to carry the statue of Two Wolves, Red Bird stepped out of the small doorway that led to the courtyard in front of the temple. He was surprised by what he saw. The soldiers had moved back to the ground and people were crowding around the base of the temple. The courtyard was filled with priests and acolytes. Red Bird guessed the temple below him was nearly empty of people as they had all came out to see what was happening and see if the rumor that Red Bird had returned was true.

"My people!" he began, shouting. He raised one hand over his head, keeping his other hand on the top of the bag that held the statue resting on the ground beside him.

"Do not be afraid! I am not here to hurt you. I have only come to regain what is rightfully mine," Red Bird said. "The gods are not happy with this city and they sent me here to tell you. There must be a change. The city is corrupt and falling down. It is rotten from the inside. The king is not divine. He has failed to lead the people and provide for them, instead only caring about himself. You go hungry and children starve to death, while the king gets fat."

Red Bird heard grumbling from the people before him, but no one moved to stop him. In the distance, he saw the king himself leaving the palace and coming toward the temple.

"It is not right that the people should suffer like this and it is time for it to end. I am Two Wolves and until this city changes, I am taking away my support and allegiance."

"King Two Wolves, please do not abandon your people!" King Feathered Warrior said now that he arrived at the scene. The people at the base of the temple moved away from Feathered Warrior and his guards. Red Bird could tell Feathered Warrior was searching him, trying to see who he was and what was going on.

Red Bird decided to continue playing Two Wolves and say the things he had been holding inside for a long time.

"Feathered Warrior, you have led these people, my people, and they are starving. You eat the best of everything and sleep in the softest bed. You take your pick of the maidens, but you do not help your people. You do not love your people. You do not care for them. You believe yourself to be a deity, but I am here to say you are not. You are just a man. You only rule because the gods have given you their authority. You no longer have our blessing!"

Feathered Warrior fell to the ground, overcome with fear. The villagers and the royals around him on the ground mixed together, grumbling at what they had heard. Their king no longer had the blessings of the gods. They knew they were in trouble.

"People, listen to me. Sacrifices and bloodletting are not the way. The gods aren't bloodthirsty villains. They love you and want you to worship them, but they do not ask for the lives of your people. We do not need that. Those are lies told to you by evil men. It is time to change!"

With that, Red Bird lifted the statue from the bag over his head. The people amassed at the bottom of the temple gasped and fell down on the ground in fear.

Then things began to grow dark.

"Look at the sun! It is disappearing. The great snake god Kulkulkan is eating the sun and taking it away so it will no longer shine on your evil ways!"

Red Bird didn't know what was going on, and he hoped it wasn't permanent, but he took the opportunity of the solar eclipse to make his retreat.

"Until this city comes back to the true path, I will no longer bless this city!"

With that, Red Bird turned and ducked inside the temple. He didn't understand what was happening with the sun, he only knew it was the gods' will and it would give him a chance to escape through the corridors and tunnels in the temple and then outside the city without being seen. Everyone else would be outside watching the sun get eaten by the snake god. He was confident that this was the gods' way of helping him complete his journey to take the statue of Two Wolves away.

He knew his words, along with the consumption of the sun would leave the king in trouble, but that was one casualty he couldn't bring himself to be concerned about. The king had sacrificed him to the Holy Cenote without a second thought, looking for a scapegoat. Now he would have to deal with the consequences of his actions.

CHAPTER 23

It took hours for the crew to wind things up at the burial mound. Mike's surprise find of the underwater plaque turned the press conference on its head. Between the university officials getting excited about the unmarred carvings and the national press clamoring for "exclusive" interviews with the players involved, including Mike, the sun was setting before they got everyone out of there.

"Man, what a day," Gardner said, being more talkative than normal.

"You can say that again," Rich agreed. "I've spent more time underwater doing just about nothing today than at any other time in my career."

With Mike topside talking to reporters, Rich and Gardner made another dive to give the television crews something to shoot. They made digital copies of their own video footage available.

"My vote is we go get a burger and a beer after this one. My treat. And don't worry, I plan to expense this back to the university. Or my magazine. Or both," Mike said with a laugh. "You can even have two beers…"

"Ooooh, you big spender," Rich said as he stood to walk out the doorway of the burial mound. "It's almost creepy here now that we are alone again. Almost too quiet."

"You're just tired. Probably seeing reporters around every corner," Gardner said.

"It is definitely time to get out of here," Mike agreed and the threesome left the mound and walked toward their cars.

As Rich approached his truck, he started patting his pockets.

"Awww, man. I forgot my keys down below."

"Damnitman," Gardner said, using his favorite expression that meant a little bit of everything depending on his tone.

"Go get them. We'll wait on you," Mike said, laughing at Gardner.

"That's all right. You two go on and get a table at Fat Patty's. I'll catch up with you there. It'll just take a minute," Rich said.

Mike and Gardner agreed and Gardner jumped into Mike's rental car. Rich headed back down the hill toward the entrance to the burial mound. Mike and Gardner were quiet as they left the farm and turned onto the country road headed back toward town. A mile down the road, a car passed them going the other direction. The quickly fading light kept Mike from seeing into the other car, but he reasoned it was probably a local farmer heading home. Other than that, they were alone.

"You said this burial mound is about 2,000 years old, right? Makes me wonder what this place was like back then," Gardner said, staring out the window.

"Probably looked a lot like it does today, without the roads and fences, of course. I'm not an expert on the Adena, but I think they lived in fairly simple villages with wooden structures. They weren't savages. They had some structure, with chieftains, healers and that sort of thing. I've heard of a couple other digs on villages that had multiple buildings and wooden walls like a palisade around them," Mike said as he drove. "It's probably a little odd that this village was so far from the Ohio River, but there are streams and such for fresh water and the hunting was probably better in the hills that direction. I think they moved around some, as well. They may've had a place here and then one closer to the river, or even further south in the winter."

"Interesting," Gardner said, as they neared town. "You see Rich behind us anywhere? The way he drives, I thought he would catch us on the road into town."

"Not a sign of him, and you're right. I wasn't pushing it coming back, thinking he would be right behind us. You have his phone number in your cell? Call him and see where he is."

It took several rings for Rich to answer his phone and he sounded muffled as he did.

"Yeah?"

"You coming? We're almost to the restaurant. We're gonna start without you."

"That's okay. You guys go ahead and get started without me. I'm running late as usual. You know me. Can't be on time to save my life," Rich replied.

"Huh, okay. We'll see you when you get here," Gardner said and he punched the phone to break the connection. "That's strange."

"What's going on?" Mike asked as he turned onto Third Avenue.

"He said he was going to be late, "as usual" and then said something about not being on time to save his life."

"Rich said that? He's the most anal-retentive person I know about being on time. He couldn't be late to save his life."

"Maybe that's the point. He sounded muffled, too, like he was on speaker phone. He could have been driving, but it just doesn't add up."

"It adds up for me that something is wrong," Mike said as he whipped the car onto a side street and headed back toward the mound. "It may be nothing, but I think he was trying to tell you something. There are too many strange things going on around here. I'm not going to leave anything to chance."

"What's the plan?"

"We'll have to figure this out as we go. I have no idea."

Mike and Gardner were quiet as they headed back out toward the burial mound. They were worried about their friend and thinking their way through possible problems. Just before Mike turned off onto the farm road that would lead to the mound, he slowed down. Gardner looked at him and nodded, knowing what Mike expected without hesitation. Without waiting for the car to come to a full stop, Gardner jumped out of the passenger door of the car. He would make his way across the fields and approach the burial mound on foot.

Mike accelerated away and turned down onto the gravel road. There was no way he could approach without being seen. That was all right.

"Everything is probably okay and there is nothing going on, here," Mike said to himself. He often talked to himself when he was trying to work through problems. And then he saw Rich's van still parked just above the burial mound and another car was pulled in behind it, blocking the van's exit. *So much for that thought.*

Mike pulled in beside the van and got out of his car slowly, looking around for any signs of trouble. He grabbed a small flashlight he carried in his camera bag and then decided to pull out his external photo flash as well. He didn't have a gun or any other weapon with him, so his options were limited if there was a problem. He flipped the "On" switch on the powerful strobe and put it in his pocket. He had no idea how long it would take Gardner to get to the mound, so he tried to take his time. On the other hand, if Rich was in trouble, the longer he waited could spell disaster for his college buddy. Mike decided a direct approach would be the best option. The light spilling from the doorway to the burial mound was weak. Rich had probably only turned on a light or two when he went back in to get his keys.

"Hey Rich, you in there? Come on out here," Mike called out, standing 10 feet from the entrance to the mound. He didn't want to approach any closer unless he had to. He knew Rich would never stop giving him grief about it if everything was okay, but that was fine, too. "I got tired of waiting on you."

"Uh, yeah, Mike. I'll be out in a minute. Hold on," Rich answered from inside after a couple moments.

Rich came walking out of the burial mound with his hands held out from his sides. There was another man following close behind him. The last rays of sunlight didn't show Mike much detail, but he quickly guessed who the other man was.

"I saw you in the bar last night. You were watching us," Mike asked, speaking directly to Rich's captor. "What do you want? There isn't any treasure here if that's what you're looking for."

"I am searching for the treasure of my people. I have to have it!"

"You're Mayan aren't you? This is an Adena burial mound, not Mayan. I don't know what you think…"

"Silence!" the man shouted. "Your people have lied to us for too many years for me to believe you now. You call this an Adena mound, but you don't know that my people and the Adena are one. The Maya started here and returned here. The bones of that man in the cave that you disturbed, the skull you robbed, is from the burial of a Mayan priest who left his people long before your history began. He had something and it will go home with me. Now!"

"Look friend," Mike said, slowly moving forward, spreading his hand to his sides to show that he was unarmed. "I'm sorry you don't believe us and I am really sorry about disturbing the grave of one of your forbearers. It is an archeological site and we will return it all when it is done. I'm sure the university will be happy to consult with any First Peoples to discuss the best way to treat his remains with reverence. We are just trying to understand what happened here…2000 years ago and 25 years ago with the death of our friend."

Mike moved as close as he could to Rich and the man holding him. He wanted to see if the Mayan was holding a weapon or had just grabbed him. Mike didn't think Rich would let the man hold him without a fight, unless there was a gun pointed at him, but he didn't know what was going on. The man was stocky and short, with dark hair and skin common to the Mayan people. Most Central Americans were a mixture of the Mayan and the Spanish blood of the conquistadors, but Mayan blood ran truer in some than others. Some people who were raised in smaller villages further off the beaten path could trace their lineage directly to the Mayan civilization.

"You need to stop right there!" the man shouted at Mike as he jerked Rich around, putting him back between Mike and himself.

"Listen, you haven't done anything serious yet, but if someone gets hurt here, it will go badly for you. And that won't help your people at all. Talk to me and tell me what you're looking for and I will do everything I can to help, but you have to help me out, too. You need to let my friend go first or I can't help you. The police will be here any minute and then this whole thing will turn into a big mess."

"Legend says that the priest buried here was sacrificed in Mexico, but then he came back to life and took with him the heart of the Mayan people. There was a special stone crafted inside a statue. He disappeared and we have searched for thousands of years for that stone. It left my people defenseless when the Spanish came and destroyed our cities."

"So what are you doing here? We didn't find any statue in the mound," Mike explained, trying to figure out how to end this. He hadn't actually called the police, not knowing what was going on. They were on their own on this one.

"I don't believe you. The Master sent me here to get it from you at all costs. Without it, my people will continue to live as vagrants and second-class citizens in our own country. Your tourists will come and walk across our once-great cities. Without it, the world will end in a fiery death. With it, we will bring about the Fourth Age for all men. Senor Montero has told me so. Give it to me!"

"Stop what you are doing!" a deep, powerful voice boomed above them. It seemed to come from behind the burial mound.

"Who is that? Is that someone with you? Tell him to come around where I can see him or your friend gets it in the back," the Mayan yelled, a hint of the man's mental strings unraveling apparent in his tone.

"I have no idea who that it is, but please don't hurt my friend. If you do, it will be the end of your search," Mike replied, trying to calm the man down and appeal to his remaining reason.

"This is holy ground and you are defiling it with your anger. Cum Hau, the god of the Xibalba, of the underworld, will surely strike you down," the voice called out again, darker this time. "Stop what you are doing this instant!"

"Who is that? What is going on? I only take orders from my Master. He will bring about the Fourth Age and bring the Mayan world back to prominence! Cum Hau supports our work. My master has said so. " The Mayan's eyes darted around behind him, and Mike could tell he was starting to crack.

"Put down your gun!" the powerful, disembodied voice commanded. "You do not defile sacred ground and live. I will punish you for all eternity!"

Mike didn't know what was going on, but he decided to act anyway. Rich's captor was off-balance and Mike wanted him to be more so. When the man glanced over his shoulder, Mike pulled the external photo flash from his pocket. When the Mayan man looked back, Mike was pointing the flash directly at his eyes from just a few feet away. Their eyes were adjusted to the deepening gloom of evening and the bright light firing in the man's eyes hit him like a blow. He staggered backwards, unable to see anything other than bright lights and colors in front of him. Mike got the idea when Rowe turned on the lights in the mound a few days before. The concentrated light of the flash worked even better than the bank of lights.

Watching quietly from the shadows, Gardner leaped forward and knocked the gun away, tackling the man while Rich spun from his captor's grasp. The Mayan man tried to fight but Gardner held him tight on the ground, wrapped up in a wrestling hold. Rich picked up the gun and quietly pressed it to the man's forehead.

"I think it is time you stop, now," he said quietly.

The Mayan's eyes focused on the gun and slowly his muscles went slack. His eyes closed.

"Did he pass out?" Rich asked Gardner.

"No clue," Gardner replied. "I'm not letting go just yet."

"I'm on the phone with the cops. They are having trouble believing there is more trouble back out here, but they are sending cars. We are getting a bit of a reputation, I think," Mike said. "What is he doing?"

"Is he crying?"Gardner asked, still holding the man from behind.

"Sure looks like it to me," Rich said. "I can hear it lightly, too. Must have snapped. That would explain a lot."

"I think we need to get some security back out here if these sort of nut jobs are going to start showing up," Gardner agreed.

"Already on it. I'm on the phone with Dr. White from Marshall as well. She is mobilizing the university resources to get this place locked down," Mike said. "She sounds a bit exasperated, too, but not as much with us."

"That's good, I guess," Rich agreed. "I would hate for everyone to be mad at us. The ones who carry guns for a living is probably enough."

Gardner slowly released the Mayan man since he didn't appear to be any immediate threat and bound the man's hands together behind his back with his own belt and then stood up.

"How did you throw your voice like that, Mike? It was pretty cool," Gardner asked.

"What do you mean?"

"That big voice that sounded like it was coming from the mound. That was you, right?"

"Wasn't me. I thought it was you. I was just about to tell you that was pretty amazing. It really got the guy rattled," Mike said, his eyes searching Gardner's face to see if the man was messing with him.

"If it wasn't you, then who was it?" Gardner replied.

"It was me."

The threesome turned to stare at a large, bearded man with white hair and a beard, wearing coveralls and boots as he came walking out from behind the mound. He was carrying a shotgun hooked over his arm.

CHAPTER 24

Alone and afraid, tired and hungry, Red Bird made his way across the strange territory. He had seen so many new and different things on his trek he had lost count. How many moons had it been? He had no idea. Near starvation and pain had separated him from clear thought and focus. As he walked, he did his best to hunt and forage for food, but he didn't recognize any of the animals he saw now.

Moving ever northward, the great sun rising on his right every morning, Red Bird had long since left behind the sea with its blue water and the smell of salt air. Armed with only a knife when he left Tulum behind him, he had stolen food, hunted and fashioned a new spear…it was a walking stick, a hunting tool and for his own defense. He had to run and avoid warring tribes, hiding in cenotes and up trees to stay alive. Always, he felt the weight of Two Wolves' statue on his back. When he had first lifted it from the base in the temple, it was light and easy to carry. Now, it felt like the weight of the entire world was on his back. Still, he trudged on.

The air was growing colder and the trekking was getting harder for Red Bird. He found himself in mountains, something he had never seen before, and they were covered with great trees. There were hills and elevations above the water at his home, but nothing like this. The soil had long-since given up its sandy texture, becoming hard clay.

Every day was filled with moving forward, moving north. He did his best to stay on the tops of the mountains, following the ridgeline like the spine of a great monster in the earth. He hadn't seen many people since he moved into the mountains. Off in the distance, he saw smoke from fires—sometimes one fire, other times from many—but he avoided them. He didn't know if they were friendly and would help him or if they would kill him for his intrusion and take the statue from him. He could not allow that to happen. He had to trust the gods would show him a new vision; they would show him a sign to guide him where he needed to go. Until that time, he walked on.

Night was coming as Red Bird struggled to the top of the latest mountain. The last few days it had rained on and off all day but it had stopped for a few moments. A small clearing on top of the mountain gave him an unobstructed view ahead of him. He almost lost heart as he stared at the carpet of sameness in front of him. There were trees everywhere. In the distance to his left he could see a valley and the land seemed to get flatter and less mountainous. He noted a glint of light reflecting off of water that showed him there was a river there as well. He had passed, and camped along, many smaller rivers as he traveled but this one looked bigger. It would be difficult to cross.

He stood quietly catching his breath and attempting to decide his next move. Should he go down into the valley? Or stay along the ridges? A river that size was almost certain to attract people if there were any around. He hadn't seen any signs recently, but he knew that didn't mean much.

Without warning, he heard a twig snap behind him. He turned to look, but there was nothing there. To his right, he heard leaves rustle on the ground. They had started falling from the trees, something Red Bird had never seen before. He wondered if it signaled the end of the world, but he didn't have time to worry about that. He had to fulfill his vision and if the world ended afterward, that was the gods' choice, not his.

Moving slowly this time, Red Bird twisted his body to look at the spot where he heard the sound of rustling leaves muffled by the rain and damp ground. He could see one beady eye and the breath of an animal fogging the air. The wolf was mostly hidden behind a tree, but he could see enough to know he was in trouble.

A second wolf appeared in his peripheral vision 20 feet away. He had stumbled onto a pack and they were hunting him. Red Bird stood his ground, weighing his options in his mind. If he took off running, the pack would be on him in a moment. If he stayed to fight, they would wear him down and pounce on him from behind. Neither option sounded good and dying on this mountain didn't help him fulfill his vision. That was the only thing that mattered to him.

Red Bird turned in a slow circle, looking for a route to escape or something he could use to his advantage in a fight. He tightened the cord that held the statue to his back. Then he drew his knife with one hand and hefted his spear with his other.

He hadn't decided what he was going to do next when the first wolf decided it for him. Out of nowhere it came running toward him, from his left. Red Bird sensed the hungry animal before he saw it coming at him. The mangy animal had fire in its eyes as it bounded toward him. From 10 feet away, the wolf leaped at him, planning to take him down with a single strike.

On instinct, Red Bird dropped to one knee planted the butt of his spear in the ground, angling it toward the leaping wolf. The animal tried to dodge his defense, but it was already on its downward arc when it realized the danger. The spear point caught the gray wolf in the center of the chest, impaling it with barely a yelp.

The momentum of the wolf's leap propelled its nearly 100 pound body into Red Bird knocking him to the ground. All breath left his body from the force of the collision and he lay on the ground for a moment wondering if he was dead. His head swirled and he nearly lost consciousness. The blow would have been difficult for him to handle at his peak, but now after months of traveling, alone and on foot, he didn't know if he could fend off another attack.

Energy coursed through his body and he knew his only chance was to run. Some instinct told him to run down the hill in front of him, toward the water. He didn't know if it was the gods or fear that was directing him at this point and he didn't care. He rolled the dead weight of the wolf off of his chest and wrenched his spear free from its body. As he stepped into motion, he checked the bag on his shoulder and picked up his knife from the ground before he took off running.

The dead wolf provided enough of a distraction to give him a momentary head start. The other wolves from the pack converged on the dead animal before they broke away to chase after him.

Red Bird ran as quickly as he could down the side of the mountain in his weakened condition, stumbling and nearly falling as he caught himself on trees in his path. He lunged forward again as he heard the yelps and barks from the wolf pack grow angrier. They turned in his direction.

He dodged in and out of trees simply questing to go downhill, not worrying about where he was heading. He turned quickly to his right as he came to a deep ravine in front of him. He could hear the sound of water running below him. He made for the stream that coursed down the steep hill, hoping it would give him a clearer path. Red Bird tripped as he made it to the water's edge, falling headlong into the rain swollen creek. He was immediately pulled underwater by the rapidly flowing current. He bobbed to the surface to see the wolves arrive at the creek, but they stopped and didn't jump into the water. He heard them howl in frustration before the current dragged him back down. He hadn't had a chance to catch his breath before he went under and he began scrabbling to find anything to pull his way back to the surface.

Roots and limbs scratched his face and hands as the stream began pulling him down the hill faster. He was suddenly out of control as the water speed doubled, tripled. Even underwater, he sensed the sound around him multiply just as quickly, building to a roaring tumult. He grabbed for whatever he could find and suddenly he was flying through the air, hurtled over the edge of a waterfall coursing down the hill. The fall and winter rainy season had pushed the creek to its limit and he could only hang on.

The roots and limbs he grabbed before falling over the edge of the waterfall swung him back toward the rocks and he landed in a small cave behind the curtain of water. Out of breath, bruised and battered, Red Bird felt for the bag on his shoulder and the weight of the statue. It was still there. He dragged his body deeper, as deep into the cave as he could, and lost consciousness.

CHAPTER 25

"And who are you exactly?" Mike asked as the stranger approached them, eyeing the shotgun nervously. Rich was still holding the Mayan's pistol but the last thing Mike wanted was a stand-off between armed men. He had seen that in his travels covering wars and it never ended well.

Before the mountain man could answer, the police arrived, lights flashing. Dr. Alivia White and several cars from the university were right behind them. The police approached, guns drawn when they saw the stranger with his shotgun, but Mike, Rich and Gardner all quickly redirected them toward the man bound on the ground. The Mayan hadn't said a word since Gardner hogtied him.

Mike explained what happened to the police lieutenant, while Alivia listened intently.

"Dr. White, are we going to have some sort of on-going situation out here? If so, I need to know about it right now so we can get the proper security on this site. I would hope the university could help us out with that, too, or we might have to completely shut this area down for the time being," the lieutenant said, as he imagined his departmental overtime budget disappearing while his men stood guard on a dark hole in the ground.

"Honestly, lieutenant, I don't know. This is all pretty surprising. The things Mike just told us don't even make sense. The timing is way off on several things. The Adena were around at the same time as the Maya, but the end of the Maya happened more than 1000 years after the Adena moved on. This mound long-predates the end of the Mayan civilization as well. He is either delusional or someone wound him up with a bunch of lies and half truths and sent him this direction," Alivia said.

"You're right, Alivia," the stranger with the shotgun said from his perch on the hood of a police car a few feet away. "But I think there may be a little truth to his story as well."

Mike turned to look at the man for the first time since the police arrived. He hadn't had a chance to get back to him yet.

"You two know each other?" Mike asked.

"I am the Assistant De, er…, I'm the Dean of the Anthropology Department. Of course I know Mr. Blackwell. He is a bit of a local legend himself when it comes to legends and folklore," Alivia said.

"Is that all I am to you, Alivia?" Blackwell asked, his sharp eyes boring into Alivia, but smiling at the same time.

"Well, that is what he is now. Mr. Theophilus Blackwell, he goes by Anvil now, lives up on the mountain and collects local mountain lore, along with stray dogs at his cabin. When I was a graduate student, I did my thesis on Mr. Blackwell as well. He was doing some really interesting work in the 1980s into local native cultures and their connections to other indigenous groups around the world. This scary-looking bear of a man has a Ph.D. in Meso-American cultures. He came here in the early '70s to study the early people here and decided to go back to nature. What do you know about this, Anvil?" `

"There is a legend about a Mayan priest who was sacrificed in a Holy Cenote who came back the next day and stole a statue. That part is true, or as true as legends ever are. The story goes on that he disappeared back into the Holy Cenote and was never seen again," Anvil explained.

"Any idea if there was anything special about the statue? Did it hold a special stone, like the Mayan said? Mr. Blackwell?" Mike asked.

"Call me Anvil. Theophilus or Mr. is way too much of a name for a man like me these days. I do a little amateur blacksmithing. There's no way to know if there was anything special about the statue. And no way to connect it to this site, if that is what was stolen from the cave. The legend comes from difficult time in the Mayan world. It was a bad time for the city; when the priest was sacrificed, there was a drought for a few years, and it struggled for a while before regaining glory and growing with the rest of the Mayan culture. Right up until the Spanish invasion, of course," Anvil said. "Hard to know if the disappearance of the statue had anything to do with that or not. If memory serves, the king lost his head not long afterward, too. The people were scared after the priest came back from the sacrifice and stole the statue."

"So there is some truth to the story, anyway," Mike said. "I mean, this guy wasn't totally making things up. There is at least a legend that fits what we found."

"That's the problem with legends, Mike. They are fairly vague and can be twisted to fit a lot of situations. Whether that legend has anything to do with this location is tough to say and it is pretty far-fetched. The Adena traded with other tribes from all over the eastern seaboard all the way down to the Gulf of Mexico, but getting into Mexico somewhere is another leap entirely. For someone to walk all the way here from Mexico or somewhere else in the Mayan world would be nearly super-human," Alivia said. "I don't want you to get too excited about this."

"Mr. Blackwell, um, I mean, Anvil, what city is this legend from?" Mike asked.

"It began in Tulum."

"I know that area. On the Mayan Riviera on the Yucatan Peninsula. South of Cancun, right?"

"That's right, Mike."

"If someone were trying to pull legends back together and unite the people, like our friend suggested, it would make sense to bring the statue back to Tulum, then," Mike said, thinking through the situation.

"The Mayan fellow said something about Montero, right? A friend of mine in the area has mentioned a man named Montero. He is an organizer, trying to be king of the Maya. He is stirring things up in the Yucatan, especially in Quintana Roo around the Mayan Riviera," Anvil said.

"I have some family there, Mike," a voice said from behind the group. They all turned to see Sophia Cruz standing there. The only one person who didn't seem surprised to see her was Anvil.

"I heard the call on the police scanner. I keep it playing on my computer when I'm studying. It makes great background noise and every once-in-a-while I hear something interesting. Like tonight. I heard them mention the mound and knew something was going on," she said. "You remember I told you my grandfather knew the same legend."Anvil and Sophia exchanged a glance for a moment before the older man returned to his story.

"That whole area is full of cenotes and sacred wells," Anvil explained. "That high priest was sacrificed by drowning in a cenote. There are also some major and minor Mayan ruins in the area. It was definitely a major location for Mayan civilization."

"I'm sorry, what are cenotes?" Gardner asked.

"Freshwater springs that seep up through the limestone. Over thousands of years they form huge underwater cave systems. The water is beautiful, too. It is extremely clear and warm. I've dived in a couple different cenotes over the years," Mike explained. "Sophia, do you know anything else about this legend?"

"My grandfather has mentioned it when he talked about the old country," Sophia said. "My family came here a long time ago, before Erick was born, and settled here. My grandparents were university professors in Mexico. My grandfather studied a lot of Mexican literature and ancient cultures."

"That would also explain some of Erick's interest in this when we were in school," Mike agreed. "He was literally raised on it."

"My connections have been putting out feelers ever since this story broke. There are rumors that the statue is back in Mexico. I can't prove anything yet, but it looks like Dr. Rowe stole it a few months after he killed Erick. He let things die down and then he and Madeline took it from the caves and then sold it to a black-market collector there. I've also heard rumors that there is a Mayan who is trying to organize his people, in this same area of the Mayan Riviera, to bring them back to their former glory. I don't know if it is the same person or not," Anvil explained, lecturing like the professor he used to be and indicating he had been paying close attention to the unfolding story.

"Doesn't seem likely. I'm guessing this guy," Mike said, gesturing to the trussed Mayan the police were moving into a cruiser to take to the city and forming air quotes around the last part, "works for that Mayan organizer. From what he said to us, he is trying to stir things up and bring his people back to 'their former glory'."

"It sounds like the answers to this mystery are in Mexico," Anvil said, looking at no one in particular.

"What are you thinking about, Mike?" Alivia asked.

"Sophia, you said you have family in the Mayan Riviera?"

"Yes, I have an aunt and uncle in Playa del Carmen. It is right in the middle of the Mayan Riviera. I can take you to meet them."

"You're not going anywhere. You have classes to finish and this might just be a wild good chase. No, a phone number and an introduction would be great, though. I've been there, but it has been a while. Someone who knows the lay of the land would be great," Mike said, already planning in his head what he needed. "And it could be dangerous for someone sniffing around in the area about the statue. Look at what that guy did."

"But Mike…" Sophia started to argue, but with a simple nod from Anvil, she grew quiet.

Mike started to question that, not that he wanted to argue with Sophia, but he was curious what their connection was, when Alivia spoke up.

"You're right, Mike. Sophia shouldn't go with you. But since this is connected to the university I'll be going with you," Alivia said. Her tone suggested there wouldn't be an argument.

Mike looked at her for a moment before he replied. Everyone else held their breath.

"Good. The university can pay for our flights. I was wondering how I was going to get my magazine to pay for it," Mike said.

CHAPTER 26

The crowd outside Marcus Montero's home was growing restless waiting on the man to appear on the balcony. When he returned from his "exile" he had begun simply, stepping out on the balcony overlooking the street and talking to his few supporters. At the time he wanted to let people know he was back.

In the year since he made that first appearance, his regular appearances had grown to become events. One of the first things Montero did when he came back to the small mountain-side town in central Mexico was to begin distributing money; not as gifts, but by hiring people to work for him, buying produce from the local farmers and supporting the local economy. He also built a school and ordered new books and playground equipment for the children. Montero knew that he had to win the hearts of his neighbors before he could branch out to the Mayan people around the world. His influence was beginning to grow. They knew he was fighting for them. *That's all anyone wants, someone to fight for them,* Montero thought as he stepped outside.

"My friends, thank you for coming to see me today. I missed you while I was away," Montero said, his voice booming through speakers he had installed beneath the balcony. He wore a tiny lapel microphone in his shirt connected wirelessly to the sound system so he could gesture with both hands. The crowd was larger than it had ever been, numbering in the hundreds, and Montero spread his hands wide to welcome them all to his family.

"As you know I have just returned from speaking to the members of the Confederation of Central American States. They asked me to come and talk to them about the Mayan people and wanted to hear my thoughts on how to restore glory to the Mayan people. Or at least that is what they said they wanted me to talk about. When I got there, it wasn't so. They lied to me," Montero said, pausing for effect. The crowd booed and grumbled showing their disapproval. He knew he had them where he wanted them. They were his people.

"No, they didn't want to talk about giving the Mayan people, my people, my friends, a place at the table and equal rights. They talked about giving us handouts and government support. When it came down to it, all they talked about was keeping us down like we are some poor, disadvantaged group incapable of caring for ourselves. Those arrogant corrupt politicians, all they wanted to do was to keep us poor, dirty and disorganized so we couldn't be a threat to them. Those mixed blood "Latins"; they think they are so superior. They share some of our blood, but they don't understand who and what we are as a people. We built magnificent cities and ruled this land when their European fathers were still rubbing sticks together and covering themselves with animal skins. When the Spanish came, they didn't outsmart our people, or dominate them. They killed us with disease. They spread it intentionally. It was germ warfare and they used weapons of mass destruction to kill us off and enslave us.

"Not long ago, misguided people around the world said our calendar indicated the world would come to an end. They said our calendar that had been accurate for thousands of years ended. Without ever asking a Mayan what that meant, they simply guessed. You know as well as I do what that end of that calendar meant. It meant the end of one age and the beginning of the next. It was never the end of the world. It signaled the start of the Fourth Age. Is it any surprise that I came home to you on the very day the last age ended?"

The crowd outside Montero's home was seething, angry at the slights their people had received at the Confederation of Central American States meeting, and the murder caused by the Spanish hundreds of years before that. They were angry and Montero smiled inwardly. Yes these people, and thousands more throughout Central America would follow him because he offered something different. They shouted at the injustice and cheered for Montero at the same time.

"The time is nearly here that we will take our rightful place. We won't be pushed to the back of the room and given scraps. We will sit at the head of the table and lead!" Montero paused again, letting the people cheer. He loved to work with their emotions, and build them up, nearly into a frenzy. When the sound died down, he began again, quietly, pulling the crowd closer to him.

He was making each and every one of them feel as if he was speaking directly to them.

"There is just one thing I need, that we need, to make this all happen. You know the legend of Two Wolves and the heart stone he brought to our people. It was the very strength and power that Two Wolves used to build a great city and expand his reach throughout the Mayan world. And then, disaster. The heart stone was taken from the people and the Maya failed. Legend says that a priest took the stone away because the people had become corrupt. He took it away to hide it and keep it safe. I think that is only partially true. It was taken away from us by evil men who wanted us to fail and suffer and die. But I will soon have the heart stone back in my hands. I don't have it yet, but my people have spread around the world looking for it and they will soon bring it to me. And with that heart stone, the power it bestows will help us lead again and prosper and rule. The rest of the world will have to listen to us and give us the respect we deserve or they will suffer and die at our hands!"

The crowd was cheering and screaming for Montero. He knew that if he asked them to riot or jump from a cliff, they would not hesitate. He offered the poorest and weakest among them one thing they did not have; hope.

"Stay strong…"

Montero began to speak again, but he was interrupted by a new voice.

"Tell the truth Montero. You weren't exiled. You were in prison. Tell the truth, you don't want to lead these poor people so they can regain their former glory, you want them to make you rich," the voice yelled from the edge of the crowd. "You just want to take over my business and take my money, but you don't want to give these people anything. You just want to take from them."

The villagers turned to look at the man who was questioning Montero. They saw the local drug dealer and several of his soldiers. Montero turned to face him, choosing to look at his adversary, while he continued to address the villagers.

"My friends, my people. You all know this man who questions me now. If you don't, his name is Juan Miguel and he is a drug dealer and a gang leader. He brings drugs and death and poverty to you, but has he ever brought you anything good? Has he given food to your grandmothers or school books to your children? Or does he only take? That is all I have seen him do, he and the men who follow him around, showing off their guns and acting tough, scaring innocents while they keep their boot heels on your necks."

"I provide a service these people want. I provide them the release from their existence," Juan Miguel said. "I do not force anyone to take my drugs. I give them what they ask for. How is that different from you, Montero? Tell your people why you were in prison for the last 12 years. Tell them how you maintained your operation even from prison and how you still do it today."

"This drug dealer, this animal, is correct. I spent 12 years in prison. Back then, when I was put away, I was selling drugs. I do not dispute that and you all know that history. I was serving punishment brought by the Mayan Lords. While I was in prison, I listened to their words and I learned. Prison changed me for the good. He is also correct; I still make drugs and sell them. I am turning the tables on the world, though. Instead of taking the world's handouts, I am selling the drugs to the Latins and to the Americans and using that money to feed and support my people. I do not sell my drugs here among the Mayans. I only sell it to the mixed-blood races and the whites. That is my first step in undermining those people. They are evil and they have killed us for hundreds of years and now it is our turn. We are going to take back control by making them weaker and making us stronger. Like the disease they brought to us, I give them poison. In this case, it is poison they ask for."

"Don't believe a word he says, people. He just wants to use you. At least I don't lie to you. I tell you like it is. I have a product and I make it available to you," Juan Miguel said.

"And that is why you came here with your men and their guns, ready to threaten these people into supporting you. I tell you right now it won't happen anymore, it won't happen again."

While Montero spoke to Juan Miguel, the people on the street had moved around the drug dealer and his men, pinning them in. Two of the drug dealer's men drew their guns and one got off a shot, but the fight was over almost before it began. The Mayan men had come in from the fields to hear Montero speak and they still carried their machetes with them. Montero watched the scene for a moment before he turned and headed back inside. Another of his rivals was out of the way and this time he hadn't even had to do anything. Juan Miguel had come to him. He made a mental note to send his men out to take over the gang leader's operation and absorb it into his own.

The people were ready. His network was ready. As soon as he found the statue, Montero knew he would have everything in place to make his move.

CHAPTER 27

Alone, cold and malnourished, Red Bird crawled as far to the back of the small cave behind the waterfall and lay there shivering. He didn't have the energy to try to build a fire, or even to stand up. He huddled against the earthen wall and tried to keep his eyes open. If the wolf pack found him, he wanted to see them coming. As the sun set outside, the cave got darker and the droning sound of the water cascading down the side of the mountain was his only company.

Still staring forward, Red Bird noticed the middle of the curtain of water was a little lighter than the rest of it. It slowly grew brighter and brighter. After a few minutes, Red Bird was shielding his eyes. He sat up and continued to stare at the light, even though it hurt to look. He clutched the statue tighter to his chest, unsure of what was happening.

Fingers from one hand began to part the water. A second hand reached through. In an instant Red Bird was no longer alone in the cave. He knew the man who stood before him.

"Two Wolves? Is that you?" Red Bird said, speaking out loud for the first time in days. His own voice surprised him, both from the fact that he hadn't heard it in a while, and in its tremulousness.

"My child, it is I. I have come to be with you in this darkest hour."

"Thank you, Lord Two Wolves. I was about to lose hope, but seeing you restores me. I have traveled so far and am so far from my home. I didn't know if I was on the right track. I even doubted you were real or that I was doing what you wished."

"Your journey is nearly complete. You have done exactly as I have wished and you will soon be able to rest."

"Will you bring me home to be with you?"

"No child, not yet. This is not to be your end. It will be many years before you join me in Xibalba, the underworld. Still I am very pleased with you and you have done well."

"Father Two Wolves, can you tell me why you commanded me to take the statue and bring it away from Tulum? And why I had to bring it these many months away? I would do whatever you wish, but it has been a terrible hardship and I feel as if I will never recover from it. Now you tell me I am not done yet."

"I cannot explain all to you yet. Just understand you have done me a great service. There is something inside the statue that could betray our people. It needed to be taken away from the hands of those who would use it for their own gain."

"Do you mean jade and obsidian? There is much more of value in the palace than is on the statue."

"Something much more important than obsidian. When our artisans forged the statue, they included a heart stone at its core. That stone is much more valuable than all of the gold and silver in the palace and in the temple combined."

"What should I do with the statue and the heart stone in it?"

"Nothing my child. Nothing. Just protect it and keep it with you. When you die, have them bury it with you. The world is not yet ready for the heart stone to come into the hands of men."

"Why did you have me bring the statue here so far away from our people?"

"Because this is where the stone itself came from. It is from these lands and our people here will understand it and will know how to protect it."

"You have been here?"

"Many generations ago, yes I was here. I found the stone and brought it to our people and used it to found our city. When I went to Xibalba, the fathers of the city protected it with the statue and kept it holy. Now it is up to you to do the same."

"I will Two Wolves. I will."

"Now, be strong my child. Take heart. Your journey is even now at an end and the men you will meet are here to help you. They will care for you and guide you."

Two Wolves began to glide backward and grew hazy as he moved toward the water from the waterfall. Red Bird's body ached and he was shivering. He was stiff and sore and cold. He realized he was awake and in the cave alone, but he was unsure if what he saw was a dream or a vision. He knew for the moment, though, he needed to move or he would die.

Red Bird rolled to his hands and knees and crawled toward the front of the cave. While he had spoken with Two Wolves, he had felt warm and content. Reality was much different. He hurt everywhere and his stomach growled with the lack of food. At the front of the cave, Red Bird stood and looked at his surroundings.

It was light outside, and Red Bird sensed it was morning. He had slept through the night. The water seemed to have slowed as well, and there was an opening in the falling screen of water to his left. He could step out from behind the waterfall without soaking himself again.

Red Bird moved the bag that held the statue back to his shoulder and straightened up to his full height. Two Wolves said he was about to meet men from a new city. He didn't know how soon that would come. He didn't know if that meant two minutes or two years, but he felt he should be prepared regardless. Moving gingerly to his side, Red Bird stepped out from behind the waterfall and surveyed the land before him.

Just a little further down the hill it appeared as if the land leveled out. There were trees on all sides from him and the stream that he had fallen into continued coursing through the creek bed. The first rays of sun peeked through the remaining leaves on the trees and it appeared as if the clouds were breaking up overhead. He could see blue sky. Red Bird listened intently to see if the wolf pack was still chasing him, but he didn't hear anything around him except for the calls of the birds and the babble of the stream.

Without warning four men appeared on the edge of Red Bird's vision. Were these the men Two Wolves told him he would meet? They were all carrying spears. One man called up the hill and two more men appeared. They were carrying the wolf that Red Bird had killed the night before at the top of the hill. Red Bird held his hands out from his sides to appear peaceful. He had lost his spear and his knife in the stream so he was defenseless anyway.

One of the men spoke to him, and it sounded familiar, but Red Bird didn't understand what he said. It seemed like they were speaking the same language, but the sounds and pronunciations were different. He shook his head slowly and answered back in his own tongue. The men stared at him. One of the two men carrying the dead wolf gestured toward him and spoke. When Red Bird turned to look, the man pointed at Red Bird with his own spear and then at the wolf. He seemed to be asking a question. Red Bird nodded in agreement. *Yes, he had killed the wolf.* He didn't know if that admission would get him killed. For all he knew, the wolves were sacred to the men around him. The man holding his spear nodded and smiled. He gestured for Red Bird to follow them down the hill.

CHAPTER 28

Mike and Alivia's plane touched down at the Cancun International Airport just south of the city itself with only a slight bump to let the passengers know they were on the ground. Cancun is in the state of Quintana Roo, on the Yucatan Peninsula at the northernmost end of what is known as the Riviera Maya, for its collection of sandy beaches and resorts facing the warm Caribbean and the Mayan ruins that dot the area.

Both travelers had been to the Riviera Maya before; Mike on stories about life above and below the water and Alivia on research trips. Cancun wasn't their final destination; it was just the location of the closest international airport. They planned to head south to meet up with Sophia's family in Playa del Carmen. The ruins of the Mayan city of Tulum were an hour further south of Playa along the Chetumal-Cancun highway that follows the coastline.

Stepping outside the airport to pick up their rental car, they were both greeted by a blast of heat from the Mexican sun. At just over 21 degrees north of the equator, and solidly inside the Tropic of Cancer, the air remained hot year round.

"What do you think we're going to find here, Mike?" Alivia asked once they were in their rental car with the air conditioner blowing. Mike had the most experience driving in foreign countries so he was behind the wheel. Until that point in the trip, the two had, by silent agreement, kept their talk to simple logistics and catching up with each other's lives. They had both wanted to take a break from everything that was going on and the burgeoning conspiracy they had stumbled into. Now that they were on the ground in Mexico and were heading closer to the place where the story began, however many thousands of years ago, they were back to work.

"I really don't know. I'd like to get a better sense for what happened here and what the missing statue looked like. I'd like to rely on dumb-luck and stumble on some clue about who stole the statue and why. If we do that, maybe we would understand what drove Dr. Rowe to kill Erick in the first place. A real bonus would be to find the statue and bring it back home," Mike said.

"I'm glad you don't have high expectations for this trip," Alivia said with a smirk.

"I know I'm reaching for a lot, but you would be surprised at the things I have stumbled into over the years. You just never know what is going to happen until you're on the ground."

They were quiet for a minute as Alivia stared out of the passenger window at the desert and scrubby trees passing inland. The land surrounding them was mostly flat with a few rolling hills. The limestone under layer just below the rocky/sandy soil was formed over millions of years by layers of marine animals dying in the ocean. Geologic changes raised them above the water level, but didn't leave a lot of topsoil.

"Did you check out somewhere?" Mike asked.

"Oh, lots of things going through my mind. As an anthropologist, I always find myself trying to imagine what this land looked like in the days of the Mayans. If it weren't for the freshwater springs that fill the cenotes, this would be a difficult place to live. It was wetter back then, but I doubt that made it much easier," Alivia said. "I was thinking about the legend of the priest who took the statue, too. Why did he do that, really, not according to the legend. And lastly, was it worth Erick's life?"

"Fair enough," Mike agreed. "To your last thought, no, it wasn't worth Erick's life. Rowe thought so, of course, but no, it wasn't. For the rest of it, this is unforgiving land; there is no question about that. The part of the legend that really intrigues me is how did someone start out here and end up in West Virginia, if that is what happened. I'm worn out and we flew here. Imagine walking the whole way."

"The simple explanation for that, if it did happen, is that people were a lot tougher back then. Or you could turn it around and say we are a lot wimpier today."

"I don't want to acknowledge that one because we're here," Mike said, as he turned down a side street in the resort area of Playa del Carmen.

Cancun was a playground for Americans who wanted a quick get-away and access to the beach for a few days. Playa del Carmen was a sleepier, less commercial resort town. There were a few big hotels, but most of the visitors stayed in smaller boutique hotels or vacation houses. It also attracted a fair number of Europeans and others from Latin America as well. It didn't have easy access to the rest of the world, but for most of the visitors there, that was okay.

Mike consulted the directions Sophia gave them before they left. She called ahead and made arrangements with her uncle and aunt to serve as guides for Mike and Alivia. They turned left onto Calle 2 Norte and made their way toward the water. Sophia's uncle and aunt owned a small boutique hotel, walled off from the street with a courtyard in the middle. Mike quickly found their destination and they went inside.

"Hi," Mike said as he approached the front desk. "I'm…"

"You are Michael and this beautiful woman must be Alivia, welcome to Playa del Carmen," the woman behind the counter said with a smile. She was about Mike's age, and reminded him of an older Sophia with long, dark hair tied in a pony tail. She wore a sun dress that showed off her sun-drenched skin. "We've been expecting you."

"Wow," Mike said. "I didn't expect this sort of reception."

"Dear Sophia described you perfectly. I am Loretta, Sophia's aunt. I am so happy to have you here."

"Es un placer conocerte," Mike said. "It is my pleasure to meet you. Unfortunately, that is just about the limit of my Spanish."

"That is not a problema, Michael. My husband and I speak fluent English. We run a hotel that caters to tourists so we have to be. I lived in the states for many years as well, before I decided to return and run this hotel with Hector. Sophia tells me that you knew my cousin Erick."

"We both did. Erick was an advisor to me in school."

"I was a student with Erick. We were both graduate students when he died," Alivia said.

"Two friends of Erick's are certainly welcome here. Sophia also told us how you rescued her, Michael. We are forever in your debt," Loretta said. "But I am sure you are very tired. Let me show you to your rooms. I hope you will both agree to join Hector and me for dinner this evening. We will happily tell you everything we know and get you started on your quest."

"That sounds perfect, Loretta. Gracias. We will look forward to dinner tonight."

After Loretta dropped Mike and Alivia off at their rooms, they discovered the rooms were connected by an internal door. Mike knocked and waited for Alivia to open it.

"Already making a house call? We just got here," Alivia said with a devilish smile when she opened the door.

"Umm, hmmm, that wasn't the reception I expected," Mike replied with a grin.

"I'm full of surprises, Michael," Alivia said with a slight accent on his name the way Loretta said it.

"I'm sure you are," Mike agreed, taking stock of Alivia in a different way than he had these last few days. They were on a quest together, according to Loretta. And she was an attractive, intelligent woman. Hmmm. Of course, they had started to connect in West Virginia, but this was their first chance away from everything else and away from people with expectations. Mike knew Alivia was conscious of being seen as serious. Flirting was not on the list of acceptable activities for a new university dean.

"Did you want something, Mike?"

"Oh, sorry, yes," Mike stumbled again, coming back to the moment. "I just wanted to say that it sounds like Sophia has filled Loretta and Hector in on everything that happened in West Virginia, so I don't see any need to hold anything back this evening. This is a fairly small town and everyone in this area knows everyone else. They may have some valuable information for us."

"I agree, Mike. If they don't know who we're looking for, they might know someone who does."

"Okay, well, that's it. I think I'm gonna stretch out for a bit and probably shower up before dinner."

"I'll see you in a few hours, Mike," Alivia said, "Unless…"

"Yes?"

"We'll talk about it later. After you've had a shower…" With that, Alivia closed the door between their rooms.

"Isn't that interesting?" Mike said to himself as he walked toward his bed. The nap he was planning on was a little slower coming than he had originally expected.

CHAPTER 29

"Michael, are you awake?" Mike heard at the door to his hotel room along with a gentle tapping. He had just finished getting dressed and he moved to open the door. A short nap and a long, hot shower did wonders for the inevitable jet lag of the trip. While they had only moved west one time zone, getting up early to head to the airport, along with plane changes and waits in airports always left him a little strung out. When he opened the door, Loretta was there waiting on him with a big smile.

"Buenos dias, Michael. I hope you feel better after your rest. Miss Alivia is waiting on you in the courtyard and dinner is ready if you are," Loretta said.

"That sounds great, Loretta," Mike said as he stepped out into the evening sun, the light filtering through the leaves in the courtyard. A small fountain in the pond emitted the only sounds Mike heard. Alivia was sitting at a small table sipping a drink when he saw her. She immediately smiled at him as he walked up.

"Hi. I trust you got some rest."

"I nodded off eventually. It took a little while, though. Someone put some strange ideas in my head."

"Isn't that interesting? I hope it wasn't me," Alivia said, her eyes twinkling. "We'll have to discuss your ideas later this evening."

"I'm sure we will."

"Buenos dias, Mike, my name is Hector. I am Loretta's husband," a slender man said as he walked up, carrying serving plates of food. "We will eat here in the courtyard if you don't mind."

"This is perfect, Hector. Thank you," Alivia said.

"Did you cook all this food?" Mike asked as he pulled up a chair beside Alivia.

"No, no. Not me. My wife is the cook in the family. I am just here to carry it all for her."

Loretta and Hector began setting out a spread of food. They began with ceviche, a mixture of fish, shrimp, onions, tomatoes and peppers in lime juice, and then local snapper baked on banana leaves, along with rice, beans and hand-made tortillas.

"Mike, Alivia is having my world-famous margarita, but Sophia told us that you liked to try beers from places you visit. I bought something special for you. It is Miel from the Cerveceria Real in Puerto Morelos, not far from here. They use organic honey in the brewing that they get from local Mayan communities. I thought that would be appropriate," Hector said with an easy smile.

"That sounds fantastic," Mike agreed. "Sophia is very observant to remember that. I mentioned it when we first met."

"She will be a good journalist, no?"

"There is no question," Mike agreed.

Without any hesitation, Mike, Alivia and their hosts began eating. They saved their heavier conversation until the meal was done. Once the dishes were cleared away and everyone had a fresh drink, Mike broke the ice by asking the questions that were really on his mind.

"Hector, can you tell me more about the legend of Red Bird? Sophia told us that you would be able to help us. You already know that we are looking for the lost statue. We think it was stolen from a burial site in West Virginia and brought back to Mexico."

"Si, si, Sophia told us about what has happened. I will help however I can," Hector began. "This legend has changed over the years of course, but most of the experts believe that it began in Tulum, just down the highway. The city was going through a bad phase. Other Mayan cities were attacking them, because the entire region was suffering from a drought. The king needed something to make his people believe in him again. He ordered the sacrifice of the high priest, called Red Bird. Rather than the usual sacrifice, though, he ordered that they drown Red Bird in the Holy Cenote. You know what cenotes, are, yes?"

"Yes, I do. They are sinkholes filled with freshwater from the springs or ground water. Some connect to the ocean through their network of caves," Mike said.

126

"Si, that is correct Mike. The legend is that Red Bird was sacrificed, but the gods brought him back to life and told him to take the statue away from the city and the king," Hector continued. "The king didn't live long after the statue disappeared."

"What is so special about this statue?" Alivia asked. "Many different statues were made and lost over the years. I've seen other statues torn down to make room for kings that came after them."

"Many Mayan kings made great stone statues of themselves and their forefathers, of course. This one was different. It was only about three feet tall, but it was very well made from jade and obsidian, with beautiful details. There is another legend about Two Wolves, who was the subject of the statue. It is said he had a magic stone. It was pink with veins of red throughout it. And the stone was always warm. Even if you placed the stone in the water of the Holy Cenote, it didn't cool down. That legend says the ancient ancestors gave the stone to Two Wolves and he used it to found the city. It had great power and its presence made the fields fertile and the wind and rains cooperate so they could build and plant. When he was dying, he ordered the stone to be made into the statue. The makers were unable to craft the stone itself, but they placed it inside a small box and crafted the statue around it. That stone is the key. When it was taken away from Tulum, the city failed. The people believed that the ancestors had turned their back on Tulum and the city collapsed."

"So, the statue is really just a box for this stone?"

"That is correct. In Spanish it is called 'del corazón de piedra'. That means the stone heart."

"Interesting. Do you have any idea where the statue is now?" Mike asked. "I know Sophia told you about something that was stolen from an Adena burial mound about 25 years ago and sold to a collector. We have no way of knowing what was stolen, of course, but there is a good circumstantial case building that it was your statue."

"Not my statue, Mike. I have never seen it. It has been missing for many years."

"Sorry, just a figure of speech. It seems like what we are looking for could be the statue you're talking about."

"I have heard rumors of people searching for the 'del corazón de piedra' recently and over the years I have also heard of a collector who has bought many Mayan treasures for his private collection. People say he has a great many black market items that he cannot show to the public. He keeps them for himself," Hector explained. "He lives not far from here. If anyone would know where the statue is, if it even still exists, he would."

"He might even have it in his private collection. Whatever was taken from the burial mound in West Virginia was sold illegally," Mike said.

"I do not know this collector myself, but I know a man who does know him. He is a Great Father in the Mayan community. He could take you to meet the collector," Hector said. "I will call him and have him meet you. In the mean time, would you like to dive in the Holy Cenote where Red Bird was sacrificed? It is an hour's drive from here, very close to the ruins of Tulum. Sophia told me you are a diver."

"That would be great, Hector, but I didn't bring any dive gear with me," Mike said.

"No problema. There is a dive business close to the entrance of the cenote that leads trips. They can supply you with anything you need. It might help you have a greater understanding of what happened to Red Bird. It will take a little while for me to contact the Great Father. He does not have a phone of his own. It will give you something to do in the mean time."

"That sounds good, Hector. Tomorrow, of course. I am too tired tonight, and I'm interested in having another beer."

"Tomorrow of course. We say mañana."

"Mañana, it is then."

CHAPTER 30

Years passed after Red Bird first met the tribe in the hills above their village. They renamed him Wolf Master after his kill, although he didn't learn that for a while. It took him some time to understand their language. There were some similarities between the two languages, but it was still rough going. He learned over time that the people from the village traded with other groups from all over the region he had just crossed, from the sea to the mountains. They were used to seeing strangers pass through, so he wasn't an unusual sight.

Red Bird thought his new Adena tribal name was appropriate considering his resemblance to Two Wolves from his own land. Now that he was older, his name had shifted again. The younger members of the tribe simply called him Father Wolf—none of them were around when he had first arrived.

Oddly, at least to him, his height wasn't out of the ordinary compared to the people of the village. Where Red Bird had towered over many of the people of Tulum, he looked many of the men, and a few of the women, in the eye. They quickly accepted him into their tribe, understanding that he was where he needed to be. They gave him a place to stay and he did his best to learn their ways so he could contribute. It felt good for Red Bird to work with his hands and to help the tribe. He had imagined during his journey that if he met people, they would either try to kill him and take the statue, or they would see him as a god-like figure and revere him. Neither happened.

But those days were behind him, too. Now, he was an old man and nearing the end of his days.

"Father Wolf?" a voice called into the small cave Red Bird had established as his own. Most of the villagers lived in wood huts but he had discovered a small cave not long after coming to live in the village. He had worked on it to clear it and prepare it and made it his home. He had grown up in warmer climes and the harsh winters of the north chilled him to his bones.

"I'm here, Quansa," Red Bird replied.

"Father Wolf, you know that is not my name," the adolescent boy said with a grin.

"I know but you remind me of someone from long ago. It makes me smile to think of him."

"Who was he, Father?"

"A great warrior. We fought alongside each other from our youth. He was my best friend and companion. He died much too soon in a battle with another city. I grieved for many days. And I slew many warriors from the other army in vengeance for him before I was done."

"Then I consider it a great honor that you have named me after him, Father."

Red Bird simply smiled as he went about tidying his small cave home.

"Father Wolf, why do you live in this cave? Some of the people say you come from the depths of the earth and are trying to return there."

"Is that what they say, Quansa?" Red Bird asked smiling. He had heard that whisper before.

"Yes, Father."

"The land I left was sunnier than this one. And hotter. Sometimes we would climb into the cenotes to cool off in the water or to get out of the sun, but no, I didn't live below ground. This place just seems right for me. My gods have shown me this is where I should be and I am content with it."

"I don't know what you mean when you speak of your gods."

"I've tried to explain it before but your people see things differently. For now, just imagine a being greater than all of us who watches over you and provides for you. That is enough. Your people respect nature and the seasons and the sun and the moon. My people's beliefs are much the same. We just see a "person" in the place of the sun and the moon."

"I think I understand, Father. Do you speak to them? Your gods I mean. Do you speak to your gods? My father told me that once, when I was young, you warned the village of an attack and our men were able to turn the invaders away without losing anyone. He said your god warned you of the attack."

"Sometimes I speak to them, but they don't often speak to me. I see things in my dreams that tell me what they want. They send me visions."

"I don't remember my dreams."

"I wish I could forget some of my dreams, Quansa. Sometimes I see my old home and the wars we fought. I see the men I sacrificed because the king commanded me to do so," Red Bird said, fire filling his eyes and a look of anger on his face. "My gods tell me now that they never asked for the tribute that the king demanded, but I killed those men anyway. Those visions are what fill my dreams these days.

After a few uncomfortable moments, the youth cleared his throat and spoke again.

"Did you need something? Shawnar told me you wanted to see me," Quansa said, getting to the point. He often talked with Red Bird and knew he had to be patient before getting to the purpose of the visit.

"Yes, Quansa. Your father is the leader, the chief of this tribe and he has been a good friend to me, too. Your people have been welcoming. Unfortunately, your father does not understand my speech as well as you do, so I wish for you to take him a message."

"I understand, Father Wolf. I will tell my father whatever you wish."

"Thank you, Quansa. Just please tell him that when I die, I wish to be buried in this cave. Leave my body where it is and fill in the front of it. Once I am done with my body, it is no longer important."

"I understand Father Wolf. I will tell my father your wish. It is a simple one. Surely it will be many moons before you are done with your body, though."

"I do not know. In the mornings when I rise it seems like that day is coming soon. Also, please, ask your father to bury the statue with me when I am gone. My gods have told me it should stay with me through eternity. I am certain my soul will not rest if that is not done."

Red Bird was certain of no such thing, in fact he wasn't certain of much anymore, but some of his more troubling visions included seeing himself as a specter roaming the planet, a much different one than the one he knew, in search of the statue.

In his visions, Red Bird knew the gods were pleased with him. The heart stone was back where it belonged and where it had originated so many years before. Red Bird himself was back where he belonged, too. He was, in fact, a direct descendent of Two Wolves and now he was living with his own ancestors although none of them realized that, either.

CHAPTER 31

Hector and Loretta cleaned up after dinner, leaving Mike and Alivia to themselves in the courtyard of the small hotel. A few safety lights along the walk ways and three candles provided the illumination since the sun had set. The fountain still gurgled, but the birds had gone to their nests for the night, leaving them in relative quiet. For a while, they sat lost in their own thoughts until Alivia broke the stillness.

"Thanks for letting me come along on this, Mike," she said, reaching out to touch his arm in the low light. "It will mean a lot to me to finish this up and make sure the work that Erick started gets finished."

"It's good to have you here. This is pretty far from my area of expertise. I'm used to investigating things and chasing all over the world, but the intricacies of Mayan culture and history, along with the 'heart of the Maya' are beyond me. It's really convenient to have my own expert with me, rather than trying to find one on my own."

"I'm glad I could make things convenient for you."

"Ummm, hmmm. I get the feeling I just missed something…" Mike said, shifting in his seat to make eye contact with Alivia. Her hand had not moved from his arm and her fingers felt warm to the touch.

"We'll see if you can redeem yourself."

"Interesting," Mike said with a smile, the scent of bougainvillea filling the air. "I've always enjoyed a challenge. So, what do you think we're going to discover down here?"

Alivia looked Mike in the eyes, trying to decide if Mike's question was literal, or if there was a hidden question inside it.

"Honestly, I don't know. It will be interesting to see what happens. We might stumble onto something really amazing. Or it might be a bust and all come to nothing. We'll have to wait and see I guess."

"That's true. There's a lot that is out of our control," Mike agreed. "I don't think we should wait too long, though. I want to get started as soon as possible."

"It sounds like we're going to have an early morning, then. We should probably get to bed," Alivia said, standing.

Mike's eyebrows rose slightly, wondering if their flirting had just taken a serious turn or if Alivia was just heading off to bed, ready for an early start in the morning. He decided the latter was the more likely scenario. She had said a few things to him that made him curious if there was some attraction there, but she hadn't said anything that overt.

"Then off to bed we go," Mike said as he stood. Alivia slid her arm through his as they followed the walkway toward their rooms. They came to Mike's room first and Alivia dropped her arm and fished her room key from the pocket of her shorts.

"Thanks again for bringing me along. This is pretty exciting. I'm sure we're going to get to the bottom of what happened," Alivia said with a smile. "See you in the morning."

"Okay, Alivia. See you in the morning," Mike said with a smile. "Good night."

Entering his room, Mike slowly got ready for bed, laughing to himself as he thought back through their conversation. Other than the familiar touch, nothing Alivia said really signaled anything other than professional curiosity. Mike quickly realized he had been reading things into her comments.

"I've been on the road too long. I need to settle down. It's been a while since I've even had anything close to a serious relationship," Mike said out loud with a laugh. "Probably Frankie in Italy is the closest to it and that was far from normal."

Dr. Francesca DeMarco, Frankie to her friends, was a beautiful archeologist in Italy that Mike met on a story. They became close for a while, but the inevitable happened. Mike's career took him off in other directions and Frankie's work kept her on the Adriatic Coast of Italy. Or, she was out touring and speaking about her discovery, the revelations of a religious artifact that had changed the religious and Jewish history worlds. They had parted as friends, and Mike heard from her from time to time, but he hadn't seen her in a while.

Mike finished brushing his teeth and was about to turn out the light in his room on the way to his bed when he heard a knock at the door between his room and Alivia's. He opened the door to see Alivia standing there, wearing a t-shirt. From his quick glance, he didn't think she was wearing much else. Mike was only wearing a pair of loose fitting shorts he liked to sleep in.

"Is something wrong?"

"No. Nothing is wrong," Alivia said as she pushed past Mike into his room with a smile. "I think you're right, though. I think we should get started as soon as possible."

CHAPTER 32

The boy called Quansa crept into the outer cave area and approached the smaller side cave Red Bird slept in. He could see the man inside the cave sleeping, his feet just inside the opening.

"Father Wolf? Are you still asleep? My father asked me to check on you."

No response.

The youth stood still, staring at the man's feet. He could only see part of the older man's body from where he stood. He moved forward, slowly, afraid of what he was about to find. This would not be the first elder that Quansa had seen pass on, but he liked the old man and enjoyed listening to his stories from the far away land he came from.

Quansa reached forward and touched Red Bird's foot. There was no reaction. Quansa lowered his head for a moment, sadness at losing his friend passing over him. Red Bird was not born into their tribe, but he would be missed. He had been a loyal member, refusing to become the tribal leader when the position was offered to him, but never refusing to work and support the tribe whenever he could.

Quansa left the outer cave without disturbing Red Bird any further. He needed to let his father, and the rest of the tribal elders know. He wanted to remind them of the old man's wishes to be buried in the cave with his statue.

*****

Quansa's father, Chief Argona respected Red Bird's wishes, but he wanted to honor the older man as well. Later that day, after the tribal healer confirmed Red Bird had left his body behind to go to the spirit world, he called the tribe together.

"Friends, Father Wolf has left us. I was there on the first day we met him stepping out from the cave behind the waterfall in the season of the rains. He stood tall and strong, and tired and worn at the same time. You could see the honor and strength in his eyes. I was afraid of him at first, believing he would enter our tribe and become the leader. It was a foolish fear of the young. I know now that he would have made a great leader. I offered him the position many times, and he always declined. He said he had been a leader and knew the temptations all too well.

"In the last years, we called him Father Wolf. When he first joined us, we called him Wolf Master for the wolf he killed on his way to be with us. He told me he had another name where he came from, too, but he liked what we called him better. He said it reminded him of his god.

"Father Wolf had one request. He wanted us to bury him in his cave. We will honor this request, but I wish to give him more honor than simply throwing dirt on his head. We will begin today building a burial mound over top of his cave. I have asked the healer to make me two stones. One we will place outside of his sleeping cave with his name, the name he came to us with, and the likeness of the statue he carried. The statue will stand guard outside of his cave until the world ends. The second stone will go at the entrance to the main cave. We will cover the entrance to the outer cave with stone and then begin building the mound," the chief said, drawing a picture of his intentions in the dirt. This was more elaborate than any of the other mounds their people had built—smaller but with more layers than any before this.

"With this work, our tribe will pay our respects to a great man, a great warrior, a great leader and a friend. He has become part of our tribe and he has made it stronger. From today on, he will serve as the foundation for the mound and our tribe."

CHAPTER 33

Heading down the Chetumal-Cancun Highway in Hector's truck the next morning, everything seemed right with the world for Mike. He was on another adventure. This one had a personal connection and he felt like they had a good shot at solving the mystery of the missing statue. He thought Erick would appreciate that. He sat in the front seat of the truck beside Hector. Alivia was in the back seat. Waking up beside her had been pleasant, too. Mike always thought she was attractive, but since they had arrived in Mexico, she had let her hair down, figuratively and literally, and seemed a lot more relaxed. He reasoned that in West Virginia she felt like she had to be professional and in-charge. Now that they were in the field, she could be herself. She had smiled a lot as they got ready and had breakfast that morning, but her manner toward him hadn't changed much, which was a relief.

The air was bright and sunny as Mike hung his arm out the passenger window, feeling the wind in his face. Mexico Highway 307, known as the Chetumal-Cancun Highway was mostly flat, following the coast to Mike's left. The road was on a bluff above the beach so they could often see the turquoise-colored water of the Gulf of Mexico. To his right, the land was desert with scrub, cactus and patches of trees usually located around cenotes that brought water near the surface.

Over millions of years, corals in the ocean grew and the ocean itself receded, leaving behind limestone piled high out of the ocean. Rain water and underground streams leached through the limestone, eroding weaker spots, forming a network of underground rivers, springs and caves. Cenotes are sink holes giving humans and animals access to the freshwater streams from above. In many cases, the sinkholes drop 30 or 40 feet to the water below. At times when the water level was lower, or when the caves themselves were dry, stalactites and stalagmites formed, animals fell in to be trapped and die and humans—the Mayans—explored them or offered sacrifices into them, believing they opened up to the underworld. Divers and swimmers still occasionally found bones or remnants of fires well back inside the caves.

Throughout the drive, Hector gave Mike and Alivia a running tour of the area. They had both been there before, in Mike's case several times, but he was impressed by Hector's knowledge of local history, lore and geography. After about an hour, Hector pulled his truck off the main road to the right and away from the ocean. He headed up a small dirt and gravel road toward their destination.

"How did you know where to turn off the road?" Alivia asked. "I didn't see any sign or anything back there."

"I have been here many times," was all Hector said.

"Is this site visited often? You said there was a dive shop out here where I could get some gear, right? I don't have anything with me," Mike said.

"The cenote we go to visit is not dived often and is not available to the general public. This road leads to a small shop that serves several cenotes and the divers who want to explore them. They cater to divers who know their business and don't want to deal with the average tourists, so they don't have a sign by the road. It helps them keep their business a bit more exclusive," Hector explained as he pulled into a small parking area carved out from the jungle that grew up around the cenotes. "I called ahead for you this morning to make sure the ladies had the gear you needed. You are bigger than the average tourist and I wanted to make sure they had a wetsuit to fit you."

"You got that right," Alivia said with a laugh. "He'll need one with lots of room for his...shoulders."

Mike knew better than respond to that crack, so he got out of the truck and walked toward the shop. He chuckled when he read the sign above the small dive shop, really barely more than a shack in the wilderness: Tres Chicas Dive Adventures.

"Is that the name of one of the cenotes here?" Mike asked.

"Nope, it just refers to the proprietors," a woman's voice said as she came out of the shack. "Buenos dias, Hector. It is very good to see you." The woman came out and hugged the Mexican man and kissed him on the cheek and then turned to Mike.

"You must be Mike. I'm Beverly. I own this place with my friends Shelly and Kerry. We came down here on Spring Break about, well, a while ago, and we never left," she said with an easy smile. Beverly was about Mike's age, pretty, fit and tanned from her time living in Mexico with brown curly hair and an easy manner.

"And I'm Alivia," Alivia said, interjecting herself into the conversation and stepping between Mike and Beverly.

"Nice to meet you, too," Beverly said. "So you need some dive gear, right? Is it just you or are you going diving too, Alivia?"

"It's just me," Mike said. "Hector is going to show me the cenote. Alivia will have to hang out on the surface."

"That's too bad for you, Alivia. The cenote you're going to visit is beautiful," Beverly said as she turned and headed back into the shop. "Let's get you everything you need."

Fifteen minutes later, Mike was sweating from trying on wetsuits and getting his gear ready for the dive into the cenote, but true to their word, Tres Chicas had everything he needed and they were ready to go. Loading the gear in the back of Hector's truck, another truck pulled up and two women got out. They came over and greeted Hector.

"Michael, these are the other two ladies who own this dive shop with Beverly," Hector said.

Mike approached the two ladies and smiled. He knew the visiting divers must enjoy working with this dive shop. Kerry and Shelly were both taller than Beverly, both nearly six feet tall. Kerry had long, straight black hair pulled back in a pony tail and Shelly had dirty blonde hair, cut short. They were all three good looking, but Mike could tell they knew their business as well.

"Nice to meet you, ladies. Any tips about the cenote we're going to see today?" Mike asked to make conversation. He was confident in Hector as a guide, but he thought they might have been there more recently and have something to add. He was surprised by their answer.

"Sorry, Mike. Neither of us has ever been in that cenote. The Mayans call them The Twins and they consider it sacred. We have agreed, along with the local dive community, to stay out of that one if there isn't a good reason to dive in it," Kerry explained. "Bev is the only one of us that has been in that cenote."

"Don't the Mayans consider most of the cenotes holy?" Alivia asked, making sure the two new ladies didn't miss her.

"That's true, they do," Shelly agreed. "This one is special, though. The Grandfather asked us to keep that one off-limits and out of respect for him

ERIC DOUGLAS

we've done that. It's not a big deal. There are so many places to dive around here, staying out of one cenote is not hard to do. We don't even mention it to tourists. Only people with special connections, like you guys, even hear about it."

"Hector, is that true? Do we need to get permission to dive in this cenote?" Mike asked.

"It is all fine, Michael. I have taken care of it with the Grandfather," Hector said.

"There you go," Kerry said with a laugh. "You're in good company there."

"Thank you, Hector. I had no idea," Mike said.

"It is no problem, Michael. We believe in what you are doing. The Grandfather is very interested in your search and wants to support it however he can," Hector said. "But now we must be going. It is time to make our dive. We don't want to be late."

"Sure, Hector. You're in charge," Mike agreed, moving toward the truck. "Thank you, ladies, for your help. We'll bring everything right back when we are done with it."

"You're welcome," Beverly said as she walked over to join her partners. "Come back any time."

CHAPTER 34

Mike and Hector geared up by Hector's truck and then walked toward the entrance of the cenote making their way toward the water. They followed ancient steps cut into the limestone years before. There was no telling how old the steps actually were or who cut them.

The entrance to the cenote was shaped like an amphitheater. When the roof collapsed, it fell in stages. The first opening was a relatively small hole in the ground, allowing light into the cavern below. That opening grew until it was approximately 20 feet across, hovering directly above the pool of water below when Red Bird was sacrificed to the gods of the underworld. Between Red Bird's time and modern day, one side of the cavern had collapsed into the cave, revealing the spectacle of the caves and the crystal-clear water below. Before the collapse, to enter the cenote and get to the water below, they would have had to have rappelled down ropes through the opening. The hike in their dive gear wasn't without challenge or obstacle, but it wasn't nearly as difficult as entering through the roof would have been.

Standing at the top of the steps, Mike surveyed the cenote. He had dived in Mexican cenotes before, along with freshwater caves in Florida. They each presented their own challenges and weren't for the novice diver, but Mike knew the rewards inside could be tremendous. Facing the pool of water 30 feet below him, Mike was struck by the jungle that grew up around the underground streams. Everything was bright green. At the same time, it felt close and oppressive. The air didn't seem to move at all.

"It almost feels like the cenote is waiting for us," Mike said to no one in particular.

"You might just be right, Michael," Hector said. "The Mayans believe these cenotes connect our world to Xibalba."

"Let's hope they aren't right. That means, roughly, 'the place of fear' and it is the underworld or world of death for the Mayans," Alivia said. "The 12 Lords of Death rule there."

"Well, isn't that a cheery thought," Mike replied and then he changed the subject. "How do you want to handle this dive, Hector? You're leading. I'm here to follow you."

Mike was a certified cave diver and, according to the ladies at Tres Chicas, Hector had been diving in the local cenotes since he was a teen, so Mike was confident they weren't going to get in trouble. Still, diving in a water-filled cave wasn't as easy as diving on a coral reef. They had to carry lights and backup lights, they would run a line to help them find their way back to the surface if they decided to explore outside of the light zone afforded to them from the Mexican sun above them. Some of the nearby cenotes were so well known and so open inside, local guides regularly took tourist divers inside without the additional training necessary to let them experience the caves. This was not one of those, however. It would be easy to get lost and die in a cenote like this.

Mike and Hector planned to make a simple dive so Mike could see the cenote that figured so prominently in the story of Red Bird and his sacrifice to the gods of the underworld, along with his return to the land of the living. Hector was not going to take him on a deep exploration and they had no plans to break new ground or find new passageways. They were simply going to look around and see the tunnels and corridors that Hector had dived many times before.

At the bottom of the steps, Mike and Hector stepped out into the cool water and floated while they donned their masks and fins and made sure everything was ready and in place for the dive. Alivia followed the divers to the water's edge and took off her shorts and t-shirt, revealing a two-piece swimsuit. She had borrowed a mask, snorkel and fins from the dive shop and planned to snorkel on the surface in the cenote while Mike and Hector made their dive. Mike gave her an appraising look as she dived into the cool water.

She surfaced and smiled at Mike. "What are you looking at?" she said with a wink. Alivia was in her early 40s, but took good care of her body and it showed. She didn't have much of a tan, especially compared to the women from the dive shop, but she felt she held her own anyway.

"Oh, just appreciating the scenery," Mike said, smiling back. "It sure is beautiful here."

"You better say that."

"Are you ready to begin our dive, Michael?" Hector said without realizing he was interrupting some pleasant flirting.

"Sure am. Let's get this started. The water looks fantastic."

The freshwater that filled the cenotes and the underground rivers percolated through miles and miles of limestone, filtering out impurities and leaving it so clear the divers almost felt like they were floating in air. The water was 77 degrees and felt refreshing in the steamy Mexican jungle that surrounded the opening to the cenote.

"Don't go anywhere, Alivia. We'll be back in a half hour or so."

"Be careful. I'll be waiting."

After a quick nod to each other, Mike and Hector placed their regulators in their mouths and let air out of their buoyancy compensation jackets as they descended below the surface and entered the waters of the Holy Cenote.

Mike was immediately struck by the silence of the waters. Years before, Jacques Cousteau dubbed diving in the ocean "The Silent World" but this dive was quieter than most. There were no boat sounds, no creaking docks or anchor chains, no cars on roads or even people talking. There was no background sound at all. All Mike could hear was the sound of his own breathing. He exhaled and bubbles flowed past his ears and then the metallic click as the valve switched positions and he inhaled, giving off a high-pitched whine.

Hector allowed Mike to get his bearings underwater before attempting to show him the special features of the cenote. Mike descended about 20 feet in the gin-clear water. As he approached the bottom, he could see a rubble pile of mostly limestone rocks from where the roof of the cenote had collapsed. Mike looked at the rock pile for a moment and quickly determined the rock fall had happened hundreds if not thousands of years ago. It was a solid mass of algae, sediment and rock now.

Moving out to the side, Mike could see that the main pool of the cenote was nearly round. As he moved from the sun-drenched center of the cenote, he had to pause for a moment and allow his eyes to adjust to the shadowy world underneath the overhanging rock.

At time when the cave was dry, water leached through the limestone, carrying trace amounts of rock with it as it traveled. Before it fell from the roof, it often left those minerals behind forming stalactites. Mike smiled as he remembered a professor in college telling him how to remember the difference between stalactites and stalagmites. Stalactites held "tight" to the roof. He never forgot that lesson. It gave the caves the jagged look of teeth as if the underworld was a mouth ready to swallow divers whole. Judging from their size, this section of the cenote had been out of the water for hundreds of years. There were rock formations above him and below him.

Mike shook his head and chuckled. No wonder the early Mayans thought of the cenotes as the door to the underworld. He was already doing it himself and he knew better. What was it like for those ancient men and women more than 2,000 years ago when they saw those gaping holes covered with fangs?

Hector moved up beside him and smiled, realizing from the look on Mike's face Mike's imagination had taken him. He gestured for Mike to swim around the curve of the cenote. They weren't in a hurry, but Hector seemed like he had something he wanted Mike to see. Mike nodded and moved slowly in the direction the older man indicated.

Both divers used slow, gentle movements and were careful to keep their fins up off the bottom of the cenote. They were still well within the cavern-zone and could easily ascend to the surface at any time if they got in trouble, but they wanted to avoid stirring up silt. Unlike in the cave dive in West Virginia, they didn't have their surface-supplied air hoses to follow to the surface.

Hector continued the tour, pointing out some of the more unusual features in the cenote for a few minutes and then he stopped in front of a dark passageway. He signaled for Mike to hover in the water and Mike adjusted his buoyancy so he neither sank nor floated in the water column. He was perfectly still except for a slight rise and fall as he inhaled and exhaled.

Hector took a reel filled with a thin, lightweight, but strong, line from his gear and tied it off on a large rock resting on the bottom. When he was ready, Hector gestured for Mike to follow him. Mike knew what to do and fell into line behind Hector. Hector played out the line and both men used their lights to illuminate the walls on either side of them. Unable to speak to each other, they used hand signals to indicate directions.

They followed a narrow hallway under the ground. Again, stalactites and stalagmites were evident all around. It made Mike think about the entrance to the underworld again. He imagined he was swimming down a monster's throat like Jonah and the whale. The walls got closer together and Mike forced himself to put aside his imagination and concentrate on where he was at that moment. He wasn't scared, but he knew enough to respect the situation.

Just as things started to close in even further with the walls almost touching Mike's shoulders, he was free. Thirty feet down the tunnel, Mike realized they were entering a larger room.

Hector gestured for Mike to kneel on the bottom and relax for a moment and then he checked his watch and nodded. He descended to the bottom of the chamber and stilled himself as well. When they were both settled, Hector checked his watch again and then turned off his dive light. Surprised at the move, Mike hesitated for a second and then turned off his as well.

After their eyes adjusted, Mike realized light was coming into the chamber from several sources. He could see a faint light back the way they came, signaling the sun in the main pool of the cenote. Glancing around the small room, Mike could see an equally dim light coming from a hall on the other side of the room. Lastly, he saw a light above them.

He could just make out Hector's face when he realized the older man was smiling and looking up with a calm, happy expression. Mike looked up and was nearly blinded as the sun came through a small pinhole opening in the roof above their heads. It illuminated the room in a dazzling display as light beams danced around the room. An air pocket at the top of the room caused the light to filter through the water's surface, refracting it like a mirror ball on the ceiling. Hector's expression never changed. He appeared to be nearly praying as he kneeled underwater. The lights bounced off of him, touching him with silent caresses.

In all, the display lasted five minutes and was gone.

Mike sat still in the gloom for a minute taking in what he just saw. It was obvious Hector brought him there to show him that display. He wondered, though, why the man didn't tell him about it. For some reason, Hector wanted him to see it unprepared. It was truly beautiful. It must only happen when the sun was directly overhead, he reasoned.

After another minute, Hector stirred and smiled as he turned on his light. Mike flipped his light on, too. Mike gestured back toward the way they came, asking the silent question if they were going back to the cenote. Hector shook his head to say no and pointed toward the other tunnel. Mike checked his air supply and realized they were only about 20 feet deep and he had only used about a third of his air supply. He nodded his head and gestured for Hector to lead on. It left Mike wondering what else Hector wanted him to see.

The second tunnel was similar to the first, with rock formations on either side. This time, Mike could feel the flowing water from the spring pushing them along through the tunnel. Mike realized they were quickly approaching another open area. Hector went through the portal first and Mike quickly followed him. Momentarily overwhelmed by the bright sunlight filtering through the water, Mike knew they had entered another cenote opening. Even though he was never worried about being underground while underwater, there was an almost primal reaction to seeing the sun again and knowing he could surface at any time. He smiled behind his regulator.

Hector left the reel connected to the guide line on a rock just outside the opening to the tunnel and began swimming toward the far side of the cenote 30 feet away. The bottom slowly began rising up in front of them, ending in a beach at the water's edge. They broke the surface in four feet of water.

Mike glanced around to get a better grasp on where they were. The opening in the earth came out of the side of a small rise and it appeared the water from the cenote fed a small stream. Pulling off his mask, Mike focused on the beach and realized there was a small man, in sandals, rough wool pants and a white Guayabera sitting on the beach. If he hadn't stirred and waved to Hector, Mike would have thought the man a statue.

"Michael, I want to introduce you to the Grandfather of the Mayans. He will answer all of your questions," Hector said.

CHAPTER 35

The divers pulled off their fins and made their way out of the water, heading toward a small picnic table to set their gear down. As Mike walked, he kept an eye on the old man. When the man stood, he picked up a woven blanket and gently folded it over his arm as he walked noiselessly following them toward the table.

The Grandfather remained silent as the divers dropped their equipment on the table and stretched for a moment. He was small and had the dark hair and skin of the Maya although his hair was streaked with gray and his skin was wrinkled from long years in the Mexican sun. Before the invasions of the Spanish, the peoples of the New World all looked like the Grandfather. Over the years of intermarriage, the people of Mexico and Central America took on the taller, lighter skin and European features of the Spanish. There were still some, though, who had blood true to their Mayan roots. The Mayan civilization might have disappeared with the arrival of the Spanish, but the Mayan people had not.

Mike turned and made eye contact with the old Mayan before he spoke. Mike sensed the depth of the man. Mike could feel the man's holiness…if that was the right word for it. He immediately felt that he should respect the man. Not because the man required it, but because he deserved it.

"Ola, Tata," Mike said with a slight bow out of respect. "Hello, Grandfather. It is my honor to meet you."

"It is very nice to meet you, too, Michael," his English nearly without an accent.

"Hector said you would answer my questions, but do you know the nature of my questions?"

"I knew of your coming and I have looked into the things you seek to know about," the Grandfather said.

"You knew of my coming?"

"I heard of it through the ether and learned about your mission."

"You heard about my coming through the ether?" Mike allowed the words to hang; neither a question nor a statement. Maybe both.

Years of traveling had exposed Mike to things he didn't understand. He had seen the unexplainable. Things that could only be ascribed to God, or angels or the great beyond. Whatever you wanted to call it. But he had never had anyone tell him of something in that category pertaining to him directly. He immediately got suspicious.

"When did you get this message?" Mike asked. He had only decided to visit Mexico a few days before in West Virginia.

"I got an email two days ago from Anvil Blackwell saying you were coming this way and that I should expect you. Does that surprise you?" the man said, his eyes twinkling at the joke.

"You know that big mountain man in West Virginia? Are you serious?"

"We met at a conference on alternative cultures years ago and have stayed in touch through the internet and email. That is communication through the ether, isn't it? Seems very magical to me," the old man said grinning.

"I think I've been punked," Mike said. "Are you really a Mayan?"

"Michael, the Grandfather's sense of humor is legendary but he is also a legend in the Mayan community and is the spiritual leader of the people," Hector threw in, still chuckling as well.

"Yes, Michael, I am truly a Mayan and the people look to me for guidance, although I see myself as a simple man," Grandfather said. "And you can call me Grandfather, or Tata as you greeted me, if you prefer. Most Anglos struggle with the pronunciation of my given name."

"Thank you, Grandfather," Mike said.

"What did you think of the trip through the cenote?" Grandfather asked.

"Your being here distracted me when we surfaced but I meant to ask Hector about that. That room with the lights was pretty amazing. I was sad to see it stop," Mike said. "And Hector you seemed almost worshipful down there. Is that room significant? I guess that's why you didn't want to be late."

"Do you know the legend of the Mayan priest, Red Bird?" Grandfather asked.

"Anvil Blackwell mentioned it and Hector told me some as well, but I'm guessing you know more of the story."

"Red Bird was a warrior/high priest of the Mayan city of Tulum, just to the south of here. The city was suffering and the king had Red Bird offered as a sacrifice to appease the Mayan gods. Instead of killing him and spilling his blood like most sacrifices, they bound him and threw him into a cenote to deliver him directly to Xibalba, the underworld, but he didn't drown. He got free and was saved by twins who took him home and cared for him. While he was still underwater and on the verge of dying, he had a vision from the Mayan Lords that told him what they wanted him to do," Grandfather explained. "That cenote is the same one used to sacrifice Red Bird and the room where you saw the lights was the same spot where Red Bird had his vision."

"So you believe that Red Bird's vision was inspired by the sunlight coming in through the roof of the cave?"

"No, Michael, you are looking at it the wrong way. We believe Red Bird had his vision from the Lords in the cenote and the residual effect of being in the presence of the Lords left the holes in the ceiling of the cenote that let the light of the sun through to this day," Grandfather explained patiently. "I do understand your skepticism and I'm not offended by it. But you must understand we didn't even know the room existed until recently and the light show only happens when the situation is just right. Hector told me about it and took videos of it for me. I am far too old to visit the room myself."

"With the blessing of the Grandfather, I have dived in this cenote many times. I wanted to find some evidence that Red Bird's story is true. Tradition has always said this is the Holy Cenote used for his sacrifice, but we couldn't be sure. I was attempting to retrace his journey through the water, for probably the 20th time, and saw the lights. It only happens for a few minutes every day when the sun is directly overhead. Until that day, no one knew it happened," Hector explained.

Mike could think of any number of reasons that someone would have known about the light and the room could have entered into legend and the story of Red Bird. There were obviously times when the water level was lower and locals could have explored it at that time. Still, Mike knew there were plenty of things in the world that he didn't understand and that had no logical explanation, even if Grandfather's "ether" was the Ethernet. Rather than questioning a matter of faith, Mike moved on.

"And this Red Bird is the one who took the statue away from Tulum? And that statue was the heart of the Maya?"

"Not exactly. In his vision, the Lords ordered Red Bird to take the statue away from Tulum as a punishment for the city. The heart stone is in the statue, but it is not the entire statue. The statue itself is made of jade and other precious materials. It is significant because it is a unique piece of art and would be very valuable to the world, but the heart stone itself is the most important element and it is priceless in the world of the Maya. It contains power over water and crops, life and death itself."

"If Anvil told you why I was coming, he must have told you of the possible connection between the skeleton we found in West Virginia and the legend of Red Bird and his statue. Is it possible that statue is back in Mexico?"

"Anything is possible, but I have not heard of it being here. Twenty-five years ago, I had several strong visions about the statue. Red Bird appeared to me in a dream and told me the statue was returning to the Mayan world, but I have seen nothing since then," Grandfather said.

"That's interesting, Grandfather. That was about the time we discovered the burial chamber underneath the Adena mound and Erick Cruz was murdered to cover up the theft of the statue," Mike agreed.

Journalists are natural skeptics, and Mike was no exception. He struggled to process the mystic explanations. Of course, even if the Grandfather heard about the death of Hector's nephew 25 years before, there was no reason for the man to connect it to the legend of Red Bird and the statue. No one had made that connection until he and Rich dived into the chamber.

"I know of a collector in Mayan artifacts. We have spoken many times. He operates a local museum and does much good work protecting artifacts and our history. I have heard, though, that he also has a private collection of priceless items that he doesn't share with the public. I have no proof of that, so I have not taken the information to the authorities. If he does have items, I know they are safe and that is good enough for me for now," Grandfather said. "My people don't need to be blinded by the money outsiders might pay for a piece of our history, our beliefs. I am working to restore us as a people."

"Could you introduce us to this collector?" Mike asked. "Even if he doesn't have the statue, maybe he will have heard something about it being on the black market."

"We can go see him this afternoon if you are interested. I know he is in town. I will call him and ask for an appointment," Grandfather said. "You said, 'introduce us'. Do you mean the three of us?"

"And Alivia. Oh no!" Mike said. "Alivia is still waiting for us back at the opening to the first cenote. I totally forgot about her. She must be getting worried. We need to get back. Now!"

The Grandfather had an old truck parked nearby. Because swimming back through the tunnel would take too long, they quickly gathered up the dive gear and piled it in the back. Hector promised he would retrieve the line he tied off in the cave later.

The three men jumped into the truck, with Mike in the truck bed with the equipment. Hector jumped into the cab and they bounced along the rough road back to the main entrance. The locals kept the Holy Cenote secret by doing as little for the road as possible while keeping it passable. Grandfather made his best time, but it was still slow going.

The old truck finally lurched to a stop beside Hector's truck. As they pulled up, Mike saw Alivia pacing back and forth at the water's edge. When the truck arrived, she came running toward them.

"Help! I need your help my friends are in the cenote and…" she stopped running and stared as Mike jumped out of the back of the truck grinning. Immediately, he realized a smile was not what she wanted to see.

"You scared me to death. What did you do? Did you plan this to scare me? What sort of person would do something like that?" she started yelling at him as she got closer.

When she could reach him, Alivia hit Mike in the chest several times. He simply pulled her close to stop her from hitting him. He knew she was just scared. After a moment she calmed down.

"I'm sorry. I didn't plan for any of this to happen. The Grandfather was waiting on us on the other side of the cenote and we talked for a while. Time just got away from us. I'm sorry," Mike said, doing his best to calm Alivia down. "We are all perfectly fine."

After a minute, Alivia pulled away from Mike and wiped a tear from her face. "Where did you come from? How did you get out? And who is Grandfather?"

As she asked the last question, the Grandfather stepped out of his truck and came walking slowly toward Mike and Alivia. Alivia stood still and open-mouthed.

"It is good to see you, Dr. White. I apologize for upsetting you. That was not my intention," Grandfather said.

"Wait. You know each other?" Mike asked looking back and forth between the Grandfather of the Maya and Alivia.

CHAPTER 36

Marcus Montero paced the floor as he waited for his lieutenants to arrive. He hoped they brought him good news…for once. The search for the statue, for the heart stone, was taking too long. Everything else was in place. His men were ready. His soldiers were ready. His people were ready for him to rise and lead them to their proper place on the world stage. The Maya would not be overlooked or turned into a road-side attraction any longer. It was time.

He knew, though, that no matter how much money he collected, how much personal power he amassed, without a powerful symbol, he was dead in the water. The heart stone was that symbol. He knew the story all too well. He was raised on it from the time he was a child. Back then, he had thought it was mere superstition and legend. As he got older he studied and saw things that most people, even some of his own people, would not believe. The stories were true. He knew they were.

It wasn't until life took him away from the Mayan world that he learned to appreciate it. While he was in prison he learned about a different way of life. He already knew drugs and gangs and violence. Those things were easy to come by. Anyone could be a gangster with a gun. Until someone better shot him down in the street like a dog. In prison, he learned about organization. He learned about violence without ever raising your hand, or at least not until you had to. Sometimes, demonstrating that the boss was willing and able to do violence was necessary and served a bigger purpose.

He also learned of people that collected Mayan relics for their own purposes. They weren't priests or elders, but men of power in the "world" who liked to keep the things to show off to their friends. He had already investigated several places where he thought the heart stone might be, but with no success.

The heart stone was just one Mayan symbol. It wasn't the only one out there. Montero didn't really believe it had the power to influence his efforts. He knew he had everything already in place to destroy the Spanish who had taken over his country. He knew how to turn them into his servants, into his slaves and to have them serve his people as they did to the Maya so many years ago when they invaded the Mayan world, killing with sword and with disease. Montero knew he could have other sources of power, but something about the story of the heart stone stuck in his mind. He believed that its power as a symbol was what he needed to get them to rise up.

He had enough of the Spanish and their arrogance and the white North Americans coming to his land and turning it into their playground. Mayan Riviera; an insult to his people. Why should they compare themselves to a playground for the rich and indulgent on the European continent? He would throw them out, too. Unless they paid for the privilege. He did like their money. And that money allowed him to buy influence with the weaker-minded people in his country. Montero had extended his influence into the police and the courts so he could avoid spending time in jail again.

Montero knew the power of the heart stone lay in the legend behind it. One man of legend used it to found a remarkable Mayan city. When another man of legend took it away from Tulum, the city collapsed. For Montero, the man who returned it to Mexico would become a man of legend as well and by doing so, he would return his people to greatness. Not a city, but an entire country.

Staring out the window of his office, Montero saw two cars coming up the long road to his house. Few of the villagers nearby had cars of their own so he knew it was his men coming to report. One would be there momentarily. The other was still a few minutes out. Montero had just learned that the man he sent to the United States had been arrested. It was probably insignificant as the chances of the statue being in West Virginia were slim, but he had to check it out. He would take care of the man, one way or the other. If he could not be freed, Montero would make sure he was comfortable in the American prison until he served his time.

Montero settled himself into his high-backed leather chair and lit a Cuban cigar. He knew he needed to project power to his men, as well as the people on the street. He wanted them to look at him like a ruler. Their belief was half the battle. As the two men from the first car entered his office, Montero knew they were not going to tell him what he wanted to hear. They walked like men afraid. Inwardly, he smiled at their attitude even though he was disappointed. Fear was a powerful motivator. Proper application of that emotion could teach an important lesson.

The men quickly described their efforts to find the heart stone, but finally admitted, haltingly, that they were unsuccessful. Montero stared at them quietly for a minute and exhaled the sweet smoke into the air.

"I am disappointed in you both," Montero finally said.

"But sir, it could not be helped. The man did not have what we were sent for. We applied pressure. He will never be able to write his own name again," the man said, nearly begging.

Montero could see them applying "pressure" in his mind, breaking fingers one-by-one as the man screamed in pain. That made him smile. His men were ready and willing to do whatever was necessary to please him. He didn't relax his glare, but he decided to accept that their failure was not their fault.

"I trust that you left the man ready to give us information whenever we need it?"

"Si, si!" both men said together. "He understands that he will work for us. His very survival depends on it."

"That is good. Both of you. I believe that you did what you could to find the heart stone, but the man I sent to you was the wrong one. It is not your fault," Montero said.

The two men visibly relaxed.

"It will be best for everyone, though, if Carlos had more success than you. I would hate to apply more force."

That open statement put both men back on edge. They silently said prayers that the other man found what they were all looking for as they stole looks at each other. They knew their boss' calm demeanor was simply a mask that could be broken in an instant.

Before anyone else could speak, the office door opened and Carlos strode into the room. Tall for a Mayan man, he clearly had some element of the hated Spanish in his blood, but Montero chose to overlook the man's mixed heritage because he was so good at his job. He rose up on the streets of Mexico City as a gang leader and the two men met in prison. They supported each other. Montero recognized the man's ruthless power and saw how it would augment his own plans.

"Were you successful?" Montero asked without preamble. He was tired of waiting. That made it all the more infuriating for him when Carlos didn't answer him immediately.

"It is good to see you, nohchil," Carlos said, using the Mayan word for Chief. "I trust you are well." Carlos stepped inside the double office doors and walked to the side, quickly greeting the other two men. He had a smirk on his face while Montero watched him.

"Out with it, Carlos. I don't feel like waiting any longer," Montero growled. "You constantly test my patience and some day it will be your undoing."

Carlos looked at Montero, feigning to be hurt by his boss' attitude.

"I have the news you have been asking for since we first met. I do not have the heart stone, but I do know where the statue is. It is within your grasp, my nohchil," Carlos said with a bow and a flourish.

"Where is it? Tell me now!"

"It is close by in the hands of a collector. He keeps it in his private collection. I have not seen it yet, but two different sources confirmed it to me. In the man's arrogance, he showed it to both of them."

"Then we will take it from him. Gather the men. We will take it using whatever means we have to use. If he won't give it up freely, we will destroy him and take it from him. I want it in my hands by nightfall!"

CHAPTER 37

"Mike, remember, my Ph.D. is in native cultures and indigenous peoples. I have spoken to the Grandfather many times. He gets out and around quite a bit," Alivia explained in reaction to Mike's question of how they knew each other. "I just wasn't expecting to see him step out of the truck that brought you back from a dive. I expected you to resurface in the middle of the cenote in front of me. I thought you had drowned!"

Alivia's frustration at the situation returned quickly after she caught her emotional balance. Seeing the Grandfather had shaken her up for a moment, but she quickly returned to anger and that was directed at Mike. It made him smile. She wouldn't be this upset if she didn't care.

"I am sorry, Alivia. We found the Grandfather on the far end of the cenote, where it comes back to the surface and started talking. I didn't plan on being gone so long. I know you were worried and I apologize," Mike said.

"I wasn't worried about you," she said, deflecting her emotions and letting Mike know where he stood. "I didn't know how to get home or where Hector put the keys to his truck. I didn't want to tell Loretta that you had gone and gotten her husband killed either."

"Well, I, ummm, I…" Mike stumbled.

"It is my fault, Miss Alivia," Hector said, trying to divert the anger directed at Mike. "Michael did not know the Grandfather would meet us there. I take full responsibility for making us late. I wanted Michael to see something in the cenote and then I wanted the Grandfather to explain what it all meant."

Hector quickly caught Alivia up on what they saw underwater and the explanation offered by the Grandfather about how the room of lights played into the legend of Red Bird and the heart of the Maya. He also explained that the Grandfather was going to introduce them to a collector nearby who might have an idea about the location of the statue.

The three men talked about the cenote and how it fit into the legend, with Alivia asking questions, allowing time to pass for her to calm down and accept that everyone was all right. She still looked crossly at Mike whenever she got the chance and Mike knew enough to keep his distance. Mike and Hector moved their gear back into Hector's truck before returning Mike's borrowed gear to the Tres Chicas dive shop on their way back to the main road. While there, Mike, Alivia and Hector changed back into street clothes. They debated going back home and cleaning up, but Grandfather suggested they go ahead and meet with the collector. He didn't say why he felt it was important that they do it immediately, but by his actions and tone, Mike realized Grandfather believed they needed to go there that afternoon.

Hector followed Grandfather to his home so he could drop off his truck. The small home was simple stucco covered block with wide windows and doors designed to allow air to flow and baked tile used to accent the house and give it color. Two children, a boy and a girl but obviously twins, played on swings beside the house. After the old man spoke to the children for a moment, he placed his truck keys inside his house and then got in the second row of seats in the truck beside Alivia.

"We are close to Tulum. I would like you to see the ruins if you have a moment," Grandfather said when he was settled.

"Grandfather, if you think we need to see Tulum then we can certainly visit the site, but I got the feeling you wanted us to visit the collector. Did I misunderstand?" Mike asked.

"It is urgent, Michael," Grandfather said. "But we have a few minutes before we must be there and I believe it will do you good to see the site."

After that, the old man remained silent. Mike turned to look at him, but Grandfather didn't say anything else. Hector broke the silence.

"Michael, you must understand that Grandfather senses and knows things that we are not in tune with. Long ago I learned to accept what he tells me to do without questioning it. In my experience, it will all become apparent soon," Hector said with a wry grin. "If you don't accept it, you will beat your head against a wall and still not learn anything new."

Mike chuckled and glanced back at Grandfather again. He saw the old man hadn't taken any offense at Hector's comments. Rather, he looked proud at the lesson the younger man had learned. Mike got the feeling that there had been many discussions between them on this very point. He decided to accept the lesson as something he couldn't change.

Not planning to dive on this trip, Mike hadn't brought the underwater housing for his camera along with him. He regretted that after the light show in the "vision room" in the cenote. He knew he could have gotten some amazing photographs if he had been prepared. Even though he couldn't dive with his camera, he did have his camera bag. As an international news photographer, he really never went anywhere without it. While they rode toward the Mayan ruins at Tulum, Mike pulled his camera out and checked it over quickly to make sure everything was ready. He didn't know what Grandfather wanted to show him, but he wanted to be ready just in case.

Mike had visited the Mayan ruins at Tulum before, but entering the grounds with Grandfather felt somehow different. The guards and tour guides immediately recognized the old man, greeted him but also allowed gave him a respectful distance. They smiled at the threesome accompanying the old man, but none of them moved to intercept them, offer to guide them around the grounds or direct them to a vendor selling souvenirs. It was obvious they were not simple tourists and the locals treated them as honored guests.

Aside from those feeling he got from the people, Mike thought he felt a difference in the grounds themselves. He knew that was silly, but he couldn't shake the feeling anyway. He could sense a tension in the air that he had never felt before...at least not here. He felt it at other places revered and considered holy. He had felt it in ancient churches or temples, along with holy grounds or sacred mountains. There was an unmistakable aura to those places. A place like Tulum was a tourist destination. Entering the grounds with Grandfather changed that. Did the site know he was there? Was there an ancient power waiting on him to visit? Was it Mike's imagination? He didn't know, but when he looked at Alivia, he knew she felt it, too.

Tulum stood on a bluff above the Caribbean Sea, facing east and the sunrise. Mike knew it may have been called Zama at one time, meaning "City of Dawn", but all records currently available referred to it has Tulum. It was a walled fort and important trade hub for the Yucatan Maya, especially in obsidian. The site was similar to the much-larger and close-by Chichen Itza in its architectural style. There were three main structures on the grounds: El Castillo, the Temple of the Frescoes and the Temple of the Descending God. Tulum survived until the time of the Spanish invasion at the beginning of the

16th century. By the end of that century, from war, disease and famine, the city was deserted.

Grandfather stood still for a moment surveying the site. Tourist groups moved around the walkways, taking photos, laughing and talking. At that moment, Mike realized "still" meant more than just standing in one place. Grandfather was a spot of calm in the vacationers. He seemed to be standing in one place while everything swirled around him at triple speed. Mike imagined Grandfather saw the once-thriving city as it had been, not as it was now.

Mike assumed Grandfather would take them the El Castillo or one of the other major structures on the grounds, but then Grandfather motioned toward the clear blue Caribbean waters and began walking. Mike, Alivia and Hector followed the man, unsure of his intentions, but trusting him.

They walked toward a smaller structure near the water, on a bluff standing 40 feet above the small sandy beach and turquoise blue water. It would have been hot and nearly unbearable if not for the gentle breeze that blew off the ocean in their face, cooling them against the harsh afternoon sun.

They approached the small outpost looking over the water. Mike and Alivia walked inside and Mike took a few photos of the building with the water in the background. Hector and Grandfather found seats on rocks outside the building and waited. When Mike and Alivia were done looking the building over, they rejoined the two men and sat down to listen.

"This is the Tempe Dios del Viento or the Temple of the God of the Winds," Grandfather began. "It guarded Tulum's entrance by the bay and protected the people from invasion from the sea. It was also where the king kept the statue of Two Wolves. Legend has it that when Red Bird was sent back to the world by the Lords of the Xibalba, his purpose was to take the statue from this very spot and remove it away from here to protect it. He didn't know why or what he was protecting it from, but he made his way back inside the city, through the walls and stole the statue from here. Legend says that the Lords disguised him or that they covered the eyes of Tulum's people so they would not recognize him. I don't know if that is true, or if he was just very good at skulking around, but, either way, he managed to do it. Leaving the city, just after he found the statue, the legend says he climbed to the top of a temple to condemn the people of the city and then the sun was swallowed whole by Kulkulkan, the Mayan snake god. He made his final escape in the darkness and fear the eclipse brought on. The city was never the same again. It rallied, but never regained its former glory."

Realizing why Grandfather brought them to this spot, Mike stood back up and surveyed the area. It was a strategic spot for the city, but it was also open to view from three sides. The fourth was a 40 foot drop to the water. He doubted Red Bird climbed those bluffs to steal the statue. He shook his head at the difficulty of the task. There was no easy way to steal and hide the statue that would have surely been guarded.

"Thank you for bringing us here, Grandfather," Alivia said. "It has given me a much better appreciation for the legend of Red Bird."

"My daughter, it is a legend, of course, but I am here to tell you that the story is true. I cannot say whether the Lords of Xibalba resurrected Red Bird and sent him to steal the statue or not. That is beyond my understanding. But a statue did once stand here and it was stolen and taken away. Following that theft, the city did collapse."

"Isn't that the case with most legends—some grain of truth to them that people then fashioned into stories to explain what happened?" Mike asked.

"That is true, Michael. We will probably never know what really happened," Grandfather continued. "I wanted to share one more story with you, in this very place, before we go to visit the collector. It is said when Red Bird survived the sacrifice, or returned to the land of the living, twins rescued him from the water and nursed him back to health. The twins were a boy and a girl, but they were identical and opposite at the same time. They complemented each other perfectly. The story of those twins shows back up many times in the lore of the Yucatan, but the part that is important today is that a lesser known part of the story says that when the statue and the heartstone is brought back together with the twins, it will signal the dawn of a new age for the Mayan people."

CHAPTER 38

Hector, Grandfather, Mike and Alivia drove another half an hour south from Tulum along the coast to get to the home of the antiquities collector. They had to leave the main highway and take smaller roads. Obviously, the collector had pull with the local authorities since many small roads in the area quickly deteriorated to gravel, if they were ever paved at all, but his were still clean, neat and smooth. They could see the house on a bluff above the water from more than a mile away. The compound was surrounded by a high wall with razor wire on top. It appeared to Mike that the collector didn't like unexpected visitors.

"This guy takes his security pretty seriously," Mike observed as they drove around to the main gate.

"Rumors in the Mayan community have said for years that he has one of the largest collections of antiquities from our people in the world. He maintains a small, but very well done, museum not far from here for tourists. But he keeps most of the best pieces for himself at his home," Grandfather said.

"That's terrible. Those artifacts shouldn't be in the hands of a private collector. They're the legacy of your people. Why haven't you called the authorities and tried to get them back?" Alivia asked.

"Do you see this road we are driving on?" Hector asked.

"Umm, yes. I see it. It is a nice, smooth road," Alivia answered, confused at the change in the conversation.

"Americans are used to good roads and good water and all the other things you take for granted. It is not that way in most of the rest of the world. To make sure there are good roads and all those other conveniences, there has to be money, or power, or both. In towns like Playa del Carmen, we have good roads and water because tourists bring money to the local government and the people with power. Here, we are far away from the tourists. So, what do you think brings money to the government that they would want to pave and care for a road that only leads to one house?"Hector asked.

"And if this collector has that sort of power, there would be no one willing to force him to give up his private collection," Alivia finished, understanding the dilemma.

"Hector is correct and so are you, but there is another reason we have not attempted to get the antiquities of our people back from the collector. He takes care of them," Grandfather explained.

"I don't understand. He is caring for them for you?"

"It is not exactly the way you are thinking, but he is providing my people with a service without knowing it," Grandfather said patiently. "My people are mostly poor and uneducated. Once we were a proud people and we built temples and cities. We traveled, we made art, and we studied the heavens. Today, most Mayans live in poverty, struggling to care for themselves in small remote villages. We do not have the resources to care for treasures of our past. It takes money and resources to preserve them, care for them and protect them. For now, those items are in a safe place. The collector, his name is Julio Sanchez, preserves those items. We have talked many times and he does support the Mayan people to a degree. I am not saying he is a friend to our people, but he is helping us out, knowingly or otherwise. For now, that will suffice."

"Guys, I think we have a problem," Mike said, speaking for the first time. He had been listening to the conversation, but staying out of it. His travels had shown him many of the problems Hector and Grandfather were explaining to Alivia. She might have specialized in native cultures, but as an academic, she didn't always understand how the world really worked. "It seems like someone isn't satisfied with the service Senor Sanchez is providing."

Hector pulled the truck to a stop in front of the main gate to Sanchez's compound. It was wrecked. The steel gate itself was torn from its hinges and lay to one side of the drive leading to the house. The road that led to the house wound up the grounds surrounding the house.

Mike started to get out of the truck to investigate when he heard the sound of gun shots followed by tires squealing. He quickly shut the passenger door.

"Hector, we need to get out of here. Go on down the road a little ways and turn around. I want to be ready in case whoever did this comes our way," Mike said, gesturing toward a small bend in the road where it led to the water's edge. "I don't think we want to face whoever is paying a visit to Senor Sanchez."

Hector quickly put the truck into drive and moved down the hill. He turned around to face the entrance to the compound and waited to see who came out. They didn't have to wait long before a heavy moving truck, an SUV and a car came out of the road and turned north back toward town. All three vehicles were crowded with armed men. They were intent on leaving and didn't look further along the road to see if anyone else was around.

"This is not good," Grandfather said, but he wouldn't elaborate any further.

"It sounds like the trouble is gone," Mike said. "I don't hear anyone else coming out of there. Let's go take a look and see if we can help out. Hector, you should probably call the authorities as well."

Mike had covered several war zones over the years and while he never got used to seeing dead bodies, he wasn't surprised by what he saw. Judging from the uniforms the bodies wore, Mike could tell the collector's security men fought against the invaders, but they were overmatched by speed and sheer firepower. The security men fought well and killed several of their attackers, but in the end they were outgunned. The attackers simply left the dead behind where they fell.

Hector pulled his truck to a stop in front of the house to see the double front doors broken in. Eight men lay dead near the door. Three were dressed in uniforms consistent with the home they were guarding. The remaining five wore clothes you would expect to see worn by villagers. They checked all the men to see if they were still breathing, but there were no signs of life. The foursome entered the house carefully, looking to make sure there weren't any attackers still hanging around or any security men who might shoot them thinking they were looters. Nothing and no one moved.

"Grandfather, do you know where Senor Sanchez kept his collection? I'm afraid whoever attacked the compound decided they didn't want to wait any longer and didn't think Sanchez was providing a service to the people," Mike said.

"What makes you think it was a Mayan and not just criminals?" Alivia asked.

"The people who attacked this place were clearly Mayan locals. They weren't professionals. They were given guns and told to attack, but they weren't particularly skilled fighters. They simply overwhelmed the security with sheer numbers," Mike said, looking at the bodies at his feet. They wore worn street clothes and looked like farmers or local craftsmen.

"He never showed it to me, but I 'knew' where he kept his private collection," Grandfather said, speaking for the first time since he saw the men leave the compound after the attack. "It is over this way."

Grandfather guided them down a hall and into a small room. The room didn't look like much more than a small sitting room, or wouldn't have under normal circumstances, but there was a hidden door against one wall that was broken open and shoved to one side. The invaders had simply broken through Sanchez's defenses with brute force.

Past the broken door was another small entry room. On the floor was a body beside a vault door that stood open. Behind the vault door, Mike could see a museum of antiquities in glass cases. At first glance, it looked largely undisturbed. Mike leaned down to check the pulse of the man lying on the floor at the vault entrance although he was certain the man was dead judging from the amount of blood on the floor. He was surprised when the man moved and spoke.

"I don't know what he is saying," Mike said. "Hector, Grandfather, I need your help."

They rolled the man over to see his face. Alivia grabbed some towels to stop the man's bleeding. Grandfather confirmed what Mike suspected. It was Julio Sanchez, the collector. Grandfather leaned close so he could hear what the man said. Grandfather didn't stir while the man spoke. It didn't last long before Sanchez lost consciousness again. A moment later, he stopped breathing.

"Should we do CPR?" Alivia asked.

"I count no less than four bullet holes in him and most of his blood is on the floor around him. He's gone," Mike said.

"What did he say to you Grandfather?" Hector asked.

"What he told me confirmed my worst fear," Grandfather said. "The men who came were only here for one thing and they took it away after killing everyone at home. They took the statue of Two Wolves."

CHAPTER 39

Grandfather would say no more inside the house so the foursome moved back outside to wait for the authorities to arrive. It took a while for the police to get everything settled. They took statements from Mike, Alivia and Hector about their reasons for being there. For whatever reason, they left Grandfather alone and didn't question him. He didn't say anything to the police about Sanchez's dying words either.

Once everything was settled, they loaded back into Hector's truck and headed back to Playa del Carmen. Grandfather said he wanted to go back to Hector's hotel with them to discuss what was happening. He said he would answer their questions from inside the safe walls and away from prying ears and eyes. The sun was setting by the time they pulled back into the sea-side resort town. Getting out of Hector's truck and smelling the food Loretta prepared for them, they all realized they were hungry. They hadn't eaten all day.

Once everyone was settled and had their fill of the simple, but warm and tasty food, they grew quiet. Hector lit a small fire in the courtyard to keep the bugs away and give more light for them as they relaxed with an after-dinner drink. Grandfather stared into the fire for a few moments before he began speaking. His voice was far away, almost in a trance.

"Julio Sanchez used his dying words to tell me that the thieves definitely stole the statue of Two Wolves. They left everything else alone. That was the only thing they were looking for. And I know why.

"I know the leader of the group that stole the statue. At one time he was my protégé. He is full-blooded Mayan and he wanted deeply to support our people and guide them back to their place in the world. But he was impatient and strong-willed. He studied at first, but then became angry with me because he felt as if nothing was happening. I am afraid that evil spirits took his heart from him.

"His name is Marcus Montero. He came to me as child on the streets. I took him in and fed him, clothed him and taught him. But he always had the streets in his blood and mind. He decided the best way to bring the Maya to the attention of the world was with money and power. Not power given by the gods, but the power of the streets. He began selling drugs to Spanish-bloods. He wouldn't sell to our people. When he made the mistake of selling to the tourists, and one of them died, the policia tracked him down. He had stopped coming to me for advice or guidance by that time, but I was still hurt when they arrested him. He spouted anger, hatred and confusion from the court room, twisting Mayan legend into his own beliefs and making himself out as a martyr. The authorities sent him away for 12 years, but I understand he never stopped believing his twisted beliefs in prison. The time away just made him stronger and more focused.

"Since he was released from prison, he has been building followers and making himself respectable. He donates money to the community, builds schools and hospitals. He is taking good care of the people and they love him for it. I haven't done anything about him, but I can feel his intentions are not pure or for the good of our people.

"There is one part of the legend of the statue of Two Wolves and Red Bird that you have not heard. The stories tell of a time when the lost statue and the heartstone will be brought back together in the land of the Maya and a leader will come forward to restore the city of Tulum to its former glory. Marcus always loved that story and he dreamed that one day the gods would choose him to be that leader. I believe he is trying to make it happen.

"And now, it seems like everything is coming together at one time. The gods have decided to bring the statue back to the world and Marcus plans to rule the Maya with it. To make it happen, though, Marcus needs to offer a sacrifice to the gods in the Holy Cenote and bring the statue back to Tulum. I do not know if he can make this happen or not, but I do know that he is not the stable leader the Maya need and he will certainly bring evil and ruin on my people.

"I saw him in the car that came racing out of the entrance to the collector's home. I don't know if he saw me there or not, but I am sure he could feel my presence as I felt his. We have always had a very strong bond."

When Grandfather was finished, everyone sat silently for a moment considering their options.

"Grandfather, what does Montero need to make this happen?" Mike asked.

"He will need to offer a sacrifice and he will need to prepare himself. In the days of Mayan glory, most sacrifices were war captives taken from other cities. There is no way to know who that will be now. He could already have the sacrifice or he may need to take someone. There is also a version of the legend that says the Twins who saved Red Bird from the cenote have to be there for the power to return."

Mike mulled things in his mind for a moment.

"Okay, so we need to have someone protect the cenote and make sure he doesn't kill anyone there. What about the twins we saw at your house? You don't think he will try to use them, do you? Can you call someone to move them to a safe place? I think we need to notify the authorities of your suspicions, as well," Mike said.

"I had hoped you would not see the twins, but I didn't want to hide them from you, either. They are actually Montero's children, although I do not believe he knows it. He fathered them on a young village girl just before he went to jail. If he knows about them, they will certainly be a target for him. I will call my neighbor and have them moved elsewhere," Grandfather said as he headed toward a phone in the hotel office. "You are right. I should have done something earlier."

"While he calls his neighbor and gets those children protected, we need to get a plan in place. Hector, would Montero do this sacrifice at night? Do we need to go out to the cenote right now?" Mike asked.

"No, I don't think so. I do not believe he will attempt to perform the ritual until tomorrow morning at the earliest. He will probably be there at dawn to begin the process," Hector said. "I don't believe he will wait, though. He will want to perform the ceremony as quickly as possible."

"So we have a few hours, but that's about it," Mike said. "I think we need to go visit the police in person. I can't imagine they will believe this story over the phone."

Before Hector could agree or disagree, Grandfather came back to the fire looking visibly shaken.

"We are too late. He has already taken the twins. He seems to be several steps ahead of me," Grandfather said. "I underestimated how quickly he would act."

CHAPTER 40

Hector took Grandfather home to begin looking for the Twins. Mike volunteered to go along and so did Loretta. Mike had experience with investigations and seeing things other people might miss and Loretta knew the women of the community and could get them organized. Alivia decided to stay at the hotel. It was the low season and no one else was staying there, so she wanted to keep an eye on things in case anyone stopped by. She wanted to use the time to dig into some of her resources and see if she could find out anything about Montero's plans, from the perspective of the ancient Maya. As an anthropologist, she knew how to research and dig through arcane information.

Mike's other reason for going along with Hector and Grandfather was that he felt guilty that he had kept Grandfather away on the search for the statue when he could have been at home. Of course, Mike also realized that Montero's men probably came straight from the collector's home, armed to the teeth, and it is likely Grandfather would have been killed if he had been there and tried to protect the children. They were all probably better off that Grandfather was away. He would know where Montero would take them and they would have a better chance of getting the children back with Grandfather alive. Knowing that intellectually didn't help any of them when they thought about the children being taken away from home by armed men, though.

Arriving at Grandfather's home, everything was in an uproar. Everyone in the neighborhood was still outside, standing around and talking about what they saw. Mike spoke little Spanish and no Mayan. Many of Grandfather's neighbors still opted to use the older language so Mike got left out of the conversation quickly. Realizing he was going to be on his own, he decided to snoop around. Mike grabbed his camera and began walking around the outside of the house looking for signs of what happened.

Grandfather's wife died years before and the old man lived alone most of the time. He often had visitors and people staying with him, taking in travelers needing a place to stay. The people in the neighborhood watched out for the old man and helped him.

The twins had come to live with him just recently after Montero was released from prison. Their mother was afraid he would realize they were his and try to take them from her. She didn't know anything about Montero's aspirations to god-hood or the legendary aspects of them being twins. She simply loved her children and wanted to keep them away from an evil man.

Mike looked at the broken window on the back of the house. The men who came for the children knew which room they slept in. Only a neighbor woman had been there when they came in. One man came to the front door to distract her while two more entered through the back of the house. By the time the woman knew what was going on, the children were bound, gagged and being carried out through the front door. The old woman was roughed up, but would be fine.

Mike took some photographs of the scene with his flash in the dark of the night, not knowing if it would help out or not. He saw police out front when he arrived and realized they had probably already taken photographs and looked the area over. He was just floundering and wanted to do something.

He continued photographing the scene, thinking about the two children taken in the night by strangers, ripped from their beds, scared and apart from everyone they knew but each other. He thought of Sophia and how she was taken captive a few days before. He had been terrified for her and she was an adult, or close to one. These were two children. They probably hadn't traveled very far from their home village. Of course, they saw the world through a completely skewed perspective on television and the internet, but seeing it on TV and experiencing it in person were two different things. While he knew he had nothing to do with the situation the kids were in, seeing children in trouble always hit him harder. Adults, to a degree, could choose what they got involved in, but kids rarely got that choice.

"We've got to find out where they went after they left here," Mike said out loud as he stalked toward the front of the house.

"What was that, Michael?" It was Loretta. She was talking to a small Mayan woman as he walked past.

"Oh, I'm sorry, Loretta. I was just talking to myself. I said we need to find out where they went after they left here. I was thinking that would help us figure out what Montero is up to and maybe it will give us a clue to where he took the twins," Mike explained. "I doubt Montero took the children back to his home, so it would sure be nice to know if they said something about what they were going to do next."

"Let me ask," Loretta said as she turned to the small woman. She had a bruise on her face and her hair was messed up some, but she still carried herself with great dignity.

"I doubt they would say anything out loud like that. I was just being rhetorical..." Mike began, when Loretta signaled for him to be quiet. After a minute, the older woman stopped speaking to Loretta and she turned back to face Mike.

"It seems they did say something. They wanted to know if Grandfather was still with Hector. They saw them together earlier today and wanted to know if that was where the Grandfather was. Does that help?"

"It does, actually," Mike said. "If they knew Grandfather was with Hector and wanted to find him, maybe they went to the hotel to look for him. Oh no!"

"Miss Alivia is there by herself! We must get there before the bandidos do!"

CHAPTER 41

Everything happened so quickly when Montero and his men entered the small boutique hotel where Mike and Alivia were staying, Alivia didn't have a chance to react. Not that there was much she could have done. Montero's men were on a mission and she was alone.

Alivia was sitting in the courtyard with her laptop on her lap, connected to the outside world through the hotel's wifi. She wasn't finding much about rituals designed to bring about the new Mayan age, but she knew it would be out there somewhere. She just had to find the right combination of search terms or the right archive that would lead her where she wanted to go.

Alivia looked up, startled by the sound of the door to the street being thrown open. She expected Mike and Hector to come in, and was thrown off-balance when she saw men coming through the door she didn't recognize. Carrying guns. It took her a moment to make the mental leap to what was happening and by then it was already too late. Two men grabbed her.

"Where is the old man? Where is the Grandfather?" Montero barked at her as he approached. "I know you know who I'm talking about. You were with him at the house. Tell me where he is. I want him to be there to see the sacrifice. I want him to be there to be a part of it when I restore the Maya to their rightful place with the gods!"

"I don't know who you're talking about. My grandfather died years ago…" Alivia tried anyway. She knew it wasn't going to help, but she really didn't like to be told what to do, guns or not.

Montero's reaction was swift. He backhanded her across the mouth. Alivia's head lolled to the side for a moment before she regained her composure. With her tongue, she licked at the dribble of blood leaking from her cracked lip.

"You American women are so proud. So full of yourself. You have no respect for our culture or the men who lead this world. That will all change in the new age, I promise you," Montero growled at her moving his face within a few inches of hers.

"If this is your idea of a new age, where men can beat women and threaten them, I think it is a very old age, or at least one that we should have long since moved beyond," Alivia said, glaring back at Montero. Her nose was inches from his, but she didn't back down. "If you have to rule over people with threats and violence, I want no part of your world and I promise you it won't last very long. Tyrants have tried it before, but their people usually learn the lessons you teach them all too well and then you're the one being beaten for information."

Montero flinched. He tried to cover his discomfort at her prediction by standing up and backing away. Alivia knew what she said got to him.

"I will let you walk away from all this if you just tell me what you know. This is not your world and not your fight. Just tell me where the Grandfather is and we will leave. It is none of your concern."

"I'll tell you, because you are already too late. Grandfather knows what's going on and is already moving to stop you. He knows what you took from the collector's house, too," Alivia said. "You have already lost."

"That is unfortunate. I hoped to talk to Grandfather before he made it home or knew of my movements, but I guess it cannot be helped. If we had been able to move faster, we could have avoided much bloodshed. I didn't mind killing the men who worked for that pig Sanchez. He was of the Spanish blood that has defiled this land. The gods will smile on me for removing him from the world. But I do not want this movement to come to hurt Mayans, especially men like Grandfather. We could rule together and lead our people. The people will follow him without hesitation. If he were still here, I would have given him the statue and taken him to the place for the sacrifice. It would have been glorious if I could have convinced him to join me…"

Montero's voice trailed off. Alivia realized the man was talking to himself more than he was to her. She just hoped the voices in his head weren't answering him back.

"Why don't you just let me go? Tell your men to release me. There is nothing else you need here since Grandfather is gone. I'm sure he is with the authorities by now so you can't reach him," Alivia said, trying to sound reasonable.

Montero ignored her for a minute while he stared at the sky, his eyes fixed on an object only he could see. Alivia thought for a moment he was going to do what she suggested. He slowly turned and looked at her and had a smile on his face. He seemed relaxed and confident. And then, slowly, his smile turned into something more ominous.

"The gods have spoken to me and told me what to do," Montero said.

"Oh great, the voices in his head are speaking to him. Just what I need," Alivia said, shaking her head with disgust.

"The voices in my head are from my gods, the Mayan gods that ruled this world long before your Christian god made himself known. They are the true creators and they will rule again," Montero said flaring with anger at her insult. "And you are going to help me make that happen."

"I don't know what you think is going to happen, but I'm not going to help you do anything, especially if it involves your half-baked plan to take over the world," Alivia said, putting as much scorn into her voice as she could muster while being held by two men. They stood her up and at 5'10" that made her several inches taller than any of the men around her.

"Don't worry, nothing about your life could help me the way your death could. You are going to be my sacrifice to the Gods. I will envoke the spirit of Red Bird and Two Wolves with the statue and the heart stone. Your sacrifice into the cenote will close the circle and bring about the new age!"

"You're going to kill me and throw me into the cenote?" she asked, shocked at how Montero's mind was working. She knew he was making things up as he went without a solid plan.

"No. I'm going to throw you into the cenote and watch you drown, just as the king tried to do to Red Bird. You represent everything that is wrong in the Mayan world. Your American attitudes and your blonde hair symbolize the decaying world. It is my destiny to destroy what you represent and restore my people!"

Montero was working himself into a fevered pitch again. Alivia doubted she could escape, at least for long, but she had to try to do something. She pretended to faint, allowing her knees to buckle. The men holding her were more interested in Montero's speech than what she was doing and they had relaxed their hold. When she dropped, they lost their grip and she was free. Alivia lunged forward, grabbing her laptop from the table. She ran for a dark corner of the courtyard.

"Stop! You cannot escape from here!" Montero screamed. His men ran after her.

Just as quickly as it began, Montero's men dragged her back to Montero. One of them had punched her as soon as he caught her and she was nearly unconscious.

"That was foolish," Montero gloated standing above her. He slapped her again. "You should spend your last few hours on this earth making peace with your god. Or better yet, you should ask the Lords of Xibalba for their mercy. You will be meeting them soon."

CHAPTER 42

Mike and Hector raced back to the hotel in Playa del Carmen from Grandfather's home, but without saying so, they both knew they were going to be too late. They had spent too much time taking Grandfather home and then looking around for clues about where Montero took the twins.

Hector slid his truck to a stop in front of the front gate that led to the hotel's courtyard. They saw the gate standing open and rushed through it without thinking about what could be on the other side.

Inside, everything was quiet.

Mike ran to Alivia's room and pounded on the door, but there was no response. A moment later, Hector came running up with his hotel pass key. As soon as Hector opened the door, Mike barged inside, afraid of what he might find. Nothing. No one was there.

"She's gone, Hector," Mike said. "Why do you think they would take her?"

"I do not know, Michael," Hector said. "This entire night is a mystery and a bad dream."

Mike walked to the center of the courtyard where he last saw Alivia sitting by a table. She had been sipping on a cold watermelon juice drink while she searched the internet.

"Hector, do you see Alivia's laptop anywhere? She was using it here at the table, but I didn't see it in her room."

"Maybe she took it with her wherever she went," Hector said.

"It's possible, but I want to make sure."

Hector began looking around the courtyard area. He noticed a bush in one corner that had been torn up and pushed over. Walking behind it, he found what Mike was looking for: Alivia's laptop.

"That's really strange," Mike said when Hector handed it to him. "How did it get over there?"

Mike touched the laptop mouse pad and the screen came on. It hadn't gone completely into hibernation mode, telling him that whatever happened had been recent.

Mike stood still when he looked at the screen.

"Alivia left us a message," Mike said.

"What does it say?"

MM sacrifice me cenote tomorrow dawn.

Mike read the message three times before he allowed himself to breathe.

"We don't have much time."

CHAPTER 43

Mike and Hector drove back to Grandfather's house. It was still dark, but they knew they weren't going to get any sleep that night. They needed to make a plan.

Hector and Grandfather both advised against calling the local police to stop Montero and his planned sacrifice. The villagers had called in the police to investigate the disappearance of the children from Grandfather's home, but this was an entirely different matter. Montero had connections with the local police. Not every cop was on his payroll and most of them were honest, both men agreed to that, but if they spoke to the wrong one or the wrong person found out and tipped Montero off, it might go badly for Alivia and the twins. Having spent much of his career in the Third World, Mike understood the possibility for corruption in local police departments. In the few hours they had left until dawn broke, there was no chance the Policía Federal could get there in time to help.

Grandfather also felt that this was an internal matter, at least at first. He was fine with the police getting involved eventually, but he knew the Mayan people needed to take care of one of their own for causing trouble.

They were a team of three.

"How many men can you get together?" Mike asked as he paced the floor in Grandfather's home. "Can you get guns? I'm sure Montero is going to have an army with him. He is going to want as many of his close followers with him as he can so they can witness everything. We've seen what they can do. They aren't exactly trained soldiers, but there will be lots of them and they will be armed."

"It is for that reason that I will be going in without men or guns. I do not want this to turn into a war among my people. Those men and woman who are with Montero, they are not to blame. Or at least they do not deserve to die because evil has taken over his life. We will do this without violence and bloodshed," Grandfather said slowly and quietly. "I will go alone and unarmed."

"You can't be serious!" Hector shouted. "Montero will shoot you down!"

"Hector, Hector, please be calm. If it is my day to die, then so be it. But I do not think it is."

"Grandfather, with all due respect, Alivia is my friend. I am not going to sit here on my hands while you walk into the hornet's nest alone. I'm going along to stop this madman and save her," Mike said. "I will go with you and we can work together or I will go on my own. But I am going."

Grandfather stood and walked toward Mike. There was no heat in his movements. He was almost prayerful. Grandfather stepped close and reached out his wrinkled hand. Mike's instincts told him to step back or grab the old man's hand, thinking for a moment that Grandfather was going to strike him.

"Michael, don't," Hector said quietly.

Mike stood still while the old man, his eyes shut, touched Mike's forehead. Mike could feel the rough skin of the man's finger tips. He could feel the strength in his fingers from years of working in the fields, scraping out a living in the harsh climate of the Yucatan. Later, Mike would describe that moment as feeling as if it lasted for years. He felt as if he was tumbling down a hole without a bottom, but he wasn't afraid.

Grandfather removed his hand and opened his eyes. Mike looked down at the smaller man and he saw a depth there he hadn't imagined. Grandfather held Mike in his gaze for another moment and then he smiled, releasing his hold.

"Michael, it is not often I am wrong about these things, but this time I am and I will freely admit it," Grandfather said.

"We're going to take a group with us and stop Montero?" Mike asked hopefully, although he doubted that was the change.

"No, Michael. It will be a group, but not a group going to war. You will come along. And so will Hector. I see a fourth person there, but I am not sure who it is. It feels feminine, but her appearance and identity are hidden from me for now," Grandfather said. "Now, we must leave. Already the sky is beginning to lighten. Dawn will be here soon."

Mike and Hector both asked Grandfather if he saw the outcome of the rescue, but Grandfather simply smiled at them. Whether he did or didn't, he wasn't about to answer that question.

Since they were going in unarmed, there wasn't much to get together. Soon, they had a plan and were piling into Hector's truck to face Montero and his people. Mike just hoped they were in time.

CHAPTER 44

Knowing Montero would have access to the Holy Cenote guarded, Hector took a different route that would bring them out near the second, smaller cenote opening where Hector and Mike had surfaced to meet the Grandfather for the first time.

Was that just the day before? Less than 24 hours ago? Mike thought to himself. *Amazing how quickly things can change.*

Hector stopped his truck 100 yards away from the entrance, pulling it off the rocky, bumpy road into a space between some trees. They would walk the rest of the way in. The walk from the smaller cenote opening to the larger one was another two hundred yards above ground although the terrain was going to be rough. The local Mayan community kept the location of the smaller entrance secret and there was no path between the two. Still, it couldn't be helped. They didn't want to tip off Montero that Grandfather was there before they were ready. Hector and Grandfather knew the area, though, so Mike simply followed along. He didn't know if Grandfather had some special otherworldly guidance or had visions like he had at the hotel when he agreed to bring Mike and Hector along. But he hoped the man was getting help from above right at the moment so none of them twisted an ankle or broke a leg and failed to even get close to Montero and his followers. They had to save Alivia.

Mike wasn't sure what role the twins were supposed to play. He didn't know if they were actually in danger, or whether they were just to there for the ceremony. Regardless, he didn't want to two 12-year-olds to be involved in a murder just because they were born twins and could fulfill a legend in the twisted mind of a Mexican drug dealer.

The sky continued to lighten as the threesome crept through the woods. They began to hear noise ahead of them. Montero was making no secret about what was going on. He had invited all of his followers to witness the sacrifice. When Mike got close enough to see the edge of the cenote, his jaw dropped. He saw more than 100 Mayans gathered around the upper edge. When Mike and Hector entered the water the day before, they had done so through a series of steps built into the lower side of the opening where the limestone had collapsed over the years.

Montero had staked out the higher side of the cenote like a stage. He wanted to be the center of attention and make sure everyone could see him.

The drug dealer turned wanna-be Mayan leader and resurrectionist stood quietly at the top of the hill. He was wrapped in a robe covered in traditional designs and colors portraying ancient gods and symbols of leaders from long past. Grandfather snorted when he saw the younger man.

"A shawl we make for tourists," was all he said.

Montero spoke to his followers to get their attention and Mike immediately knew he was going to have a problem. Montero was speaking in Mayan. His grasp on Spanish wasn't very strong, but Mayan was completely alien to him. There was no way Hector would be able to translate for him to keep him up to speed with what was going on either. He wasn't going to be much help here.

"My friends, the time has come. Everyone come together! The time has come to begin the Fourth Age of the Mayan people and to reclaim our lost glory," Montero said, his face exultant at the situation as if he truly believed he was about to receive blessing from the gods.

Mike stared for a moment, trying to decide what to do. His eyes searched the crowd and the cenote for some way to help. Grandfather was right about the armed men. Throughout the crowd, Mike could see Montero's soldiers armed with handguns and submachine guns, rifles and shotguns. They were spread out among the common people. Mike guessed they were there to encourage people to be supportive and cheer or pray at the appropriate times as well as to keep anyone from protesting what was going on. It was a good strategy, but it told Mike that not everyone there in the audience was a die-hard participant. That was a good thing.

Mike made eye contact with Hector and Grandfather and he realized they had come to the same conclusion. They hadn't planned out how they were going to stop the sacrifice. At least Mike and Hector didn't know what Grandfather planned or saw in his vision. He wasn't sharing. The realization that some of the people in the audience might be swayed to see reason and not follow Montero was what the old mystic needed to see to make his decision. Mike saw that in Grandfather's eyes.

"Tell me about the sacrifice," Mike whispered. "Will they cut her before they throw her in the cenote? Or just throw her in to drown?"

Grandfather was quiet for a moment, considering his answer.

"The legend says that when Red Bird was sacrificed in the cenote, he was thrown into the water without being cut or having his blood let out. I believe Montero will attempt to duplicate that same ceremony here today. He wants to make a strong connection to the legend of Red Bird and the statue of Two Wolves before he shows them that he possesses the statue. I believe he will attempt to drown her in the holy waters by throwing her in from above."

Mike considered the drop and the fall. And then he thought about the armed men and the crowd above and made his decision. He wasn't going to be much use to Grandfather and Hector in dealing with Montero, but he had an idea how he could save Alivia. He hoped he wouldn't be needed, but it was better than sitting here and doing nothing.

As quickly as he could he explained his plans to Hector and Grandfather.

"It is as I have seen, Michael," Grandfather said. "Everything is becoming clear."

"I don't know about that, but it's time for me to go," Mike said.

As quietly as he could, Mike turned and began moving back toward Hector's truck leaving the two men to face Montero alone. As soon as he felt safe, Mike stood up and began running toward the truck. He knew he didn't have much time to save Alivia.

CHAPTER 45

Marcus Montero was in his element. He was a drug dealer and a criminal, but he was also a visionary and a showman. Having an audience and followers put him on top of the world. He was right where he wanted to be. In just a few moments, he was going to solidify his position as the leader of the Maya. He knew his people would follow him and protect him. They would kill or die for him. The life of a single gringa, with the statue of Two Wolves in his hand, was all he needed to make it happen.

Once the sacrifice was done, no one would stop him and no law could touch him. The Mexican government would press charges for murdering a white woman, but they would never take him into custody. His people would see to that. The Federales would not want a riot on their hands. He was so confident in the outcome of the morning, he had men stationed around the cenote with video cameras. He was going to record the sacrifice and share it with Mayans throughout Central America to show them he was not afraid of the governments of the world. He was standing up for them. It would be online by lunch time.

"The time has come!" Montero said again, as he raised his arms over his head and stepped to the edge of the cenote. The water was more than 40 feet below him. "Today we will reclaim our lost glory."

The crowd quieted down and moved closer to Montero to hear him. They didn't have to, though. Montero had a hidden microphone in his robe with speakers placed around the grounds. His voice boomed out from everywhere. He had planned this moment down to the last detail.

"Nearly 500 years ago, the Spanish came to our shores. They invaded and killed with spears and swords. They killed even more with the diseases they brought with them, intentionally wiping out our people by the millions. They took our women and raped them. They beat our men into submission and killed our children to make room for their own offspring. Our people became a bastard race of half-breeds," Monterro shouted to the crowd.

"The gods were displeased with us and they brought this evil upon us to teach us a lesson. We had lost their blessing," he continued, quietly this time, drawing the people in like a revival preacher. He was stirring them up and enlisting them into his cause.

"But now, we have the chance to bring our people back from this desolation. We have a chance to restore our people to the glory of old and to rule all of our lands again like kings while the gringos and the halfbreeds bow down before us. We have a chance to set everything right."

The crowd stirred and moved still closer. For too long, many of them had starved and struggled, watching their own children and families die in poverty. They were looking for an answer to their misery and Montero seemed to be giving it to them.

"You all know the story of Red Bird," Montero said, shifting gears again. "He was a warrior and a priest in the ancient city of Tulum not far from here. The gods were unhappy with Tulum's king and sent a drought to oppress the city. I am here to tell you that they foresaw what would come when the Spanish arrived and wanted to protect something even more valuable. We will never understand the ways of the gods. They could have simply told Red Bird what to do, but I think they understood what was to come and had to make sure what happened next was put into action. They saw a difficult time was coming for our people and that we would be here today. The gods saw us here today 1000 years ago and knew what we would need. One thousand years is a blink of an eye in the world of the gods and they saw me standing before you. They chose me to be here and to lead you back to your chosen place in this world."

As he concluded, he was shouting again, his voice ringing through the woods around them. Montero gestured for his men. They immediately moved forward, bringing the twins to the edge of the cenote to stand beside Montero. They were both dressed in pure white robes with simple rope belts tied around their waists.

"The legend of Red Bird tells us that the great warrior and priest was sacrificed by the king into this very cenote. He died and saw the gods in the water. They gave him a mission and then returned him to the world. A boy and a girl, twins, saved him from the water and gave him the aid he needed to do what the gods told him to do when he was in Xibalba, in the underworld. I can now present to you this set of Mayan twins. While some of you may recognize them, today is the first time that I can tell you that they are my children!"

The crowd gasped as they stared at the two children. Montero was painting himself as Red Bird reborn and doing it well. Even the skeptics in the crowd were beginning to believe.

"They are my children," he repeated quietly. "The gods sent the twins to help Red Bird and they have sent them again to help me finish the task they set before Red Bird."

Montero had planned every moment of this show and he smiled inwardly at how well it was coming together.

"You know that the gods sent Red Bird to take the statue of Two Wolves from the Temple of the Winds in Tulum and move it far away, out of the reach of our people. They knew the days of suffering for our people were coming and they knew the statue could not fall into those evil hands. The twins gave him aid and he saved the statue, coming into the city he once defended, like a ghost, and then going out of the reach of the people. The legend tells that the statue and the magic that went with it was taken away and Tulum fell soon afterward. Until today. The statue is back in my hands and its power has returned to our people!"

Carlos, Montero's gang leader, came forward, dressed in white robe like the twins, carrying the statue covered in a white sheet. He bowed as he handed the statue to Montero and then stepped back, taking the sheet with him. It all went exactly as Montero had rehearsed with him. Montero stood with one hand on the boy twin's shoulder and lifted the statue into the air with his other hand, its weight negligible in Montero's present state of euphoria. He didn't say a word and he didn't have to. All the people cheered.

Montero reveled in the cheering and adulation for a few minutes and then he gestured for his audience, his congregation, to quiet back down. It was time to introduce them to the final act in his performance and to solidify his place as the leader of the Maya. He was the only one to bring all these symbols together and he had the guts to do what needed to be done.

"The legend of Red Bird began with his sacrifice into the Holy Cenote. The gods have told me that they do not expect regular human sacrifices like they asked for from our ancestors. They ask that their people sacrifice in other ways that shows their support and worshipfulness," Montero said, reminding the people that personal sacrifices were important and ordained by the gods, and reminding them that they would owe him when it was all done. He would let them figure out on their own how much, in terms of pesos, the equivalent of a human sacrifice would be. After all, it took a lot of money to rule in today's world.

"There are times like this one, that a human sacrifice is required to show the gods that we are with them and to appease their desires," Montero continued. He paused for a moment, making eye contact with everyone around him. "I know that each and every one of you would be willing to sacrifice yourselves for the good of our people, but that is not necessary today."

Montero gestured once again for Carlos and the man brought forward the sacrifice, also wrapped in a white robe. Her hands were tied together in front of her and there was a hood over her head. The rope belt used to tie the robe around her had lead weights on it. There were more weights around her ankles.

"Today we will sacrifice this gringa, one of the *Norte Americanos* who have brought misery upon our people in the modern age, studying us as if we are a thing of the past while ignoring our plight," Montero said as he pulled a hood off of Alivia's head, revealing her blonde hair and fair skin. Alivia appeared to be half asleep; the affects of the drug Montero gave her to keep her quiet and pliant before the ceremony. "With her sacrifice, we will bring the statue back to the Maya and return our people to their rightful place."

"Stop!" Grandfather commanded as he walked from the woods toward Montero and his spectacle. "You do not represent the Maya and you do not speak for the gods. You only represent yourself and have twisted the legend of Red Bird to suit your own wishes."

Grandfather didn't have a microphone connected to speakers like Montero, but his voice was strong and commanding. It seemed to come from the very trees and grass and the earth itself. Everyone on the hill stopped at stared at the old man as Hector helped him move forward. A few of the people in the front row, close to Montero, were shamed by the sight of Grandfather who had long been their leader and had supported their people for years. They began to realize they were being manipulated.

"You are not going to sacrifice this woman to the cenote to satisfy the desires of the gods. You are going to commit murder to justify yourself!"

CHAPTER 46

Mike had run to Hector's truck and started it. As he did, he tried to remember exactly where he needed to go. The sun was coming up, so that would help, but as best as he could remember, the road to Tres Chicas wasn't marked, or at least not any way he could determine. It was just a small dirt road off of another dirt road. Mike forced himself to drive slowly and look around every bend. He had to watch for the road he needed and avoid running into any of Montero's people at the same time.

Leaving the cenote was a tough decision. He knew he wasn't going to be much help there, but walking away, or running away in this case, was not something he was happy about. For all he knew he might be too late to help Alivia, but he had to try.

Mike nearly missed the turn, but he slammed the truck's brakes to the floor as he passed the turn off. He could just see the dive shop around a turn in the road. He backed the truck up and then put it into Drive. Now that his destination was in sight, he punched the accelerator and spun gravel and dirt as he rushed the last 50 yards to the dive shop. He barely had the truck stopped in front of the dive shop, when he was opening his door and jumping out. Beverly, one of the Tres Chicas, heard his approach and came out to see what was going on. She started to yell at him for stirring up all the dust the look on his face told her something was wrong.

"What's going on, Mike?" she asked.

"I need some gear. I'm going to have to go into the cenote and hopefully stop a murder," Mike said. While they grabbed the gear Mike would need, he caught her up on the events of the last 24 hours since he and Hector made their dive. Beverly listened, but she also grabbed her dive gear and started piling it into the bed of the truck.

"What do you think you're doing?"

"I'm going with you. You've been in that cave system once. I've been in there a dozen times with Hector. Nobody dives and dies alone on my watch."

"Fair enough. Thanks. I'm sure I'll need the help," Mike agreed after a moment. He had a bad habit of trying to protect others from danger while facing it by himself. In this situation it would be best if he had backup.

Taking Beverly along with him helped out in an unexpected way. She knew how to get back to the entrance to the small cenote without creeping along and looking for it. They were able to get to the water quickly.

"How do you want to play this?" Beverly asked while she donned her dive gear and pulled her curly brown hair into a pony tail.

"I'm hoping we're just backup. Grandfather and Hector were going to try to stop Montero before he throws Alivia into the water. If he can't do that, I want to be in the water to grab her and swim her to safety. I swim over, catch her and then bring her back into the caves and out of there."

"I understand that you just came up with this plan, but there is an awful lot that can go wrong with it," Beverly said shaking her head.

"I know. I'm just praying it will all work out."

"I've made dives on a wing and a prayer before, Mike. My money is on the Grandfather, but if he can't pull it off, we'll be there to save her."

*****

"The Grandfather of the Maya has decided to join us for this momentous event," Montero said, asking the question of Grandfather, but addressing the crowd. "Are you here to bless this sacrifice, too? Or are you just going to tell us to be patient and not cause problems like you have been doing for years while our people go hungry and die?"

The crowd murmured at the situation. Montero excited them with his promises, but the Grandfather had been their leader for a long time and they trusted him. The people didn't know which way to go. The younger ones wanted to believe Montero's promises, but the older ones had grown up with Grandfather watching over them.

"Marcus, I taught you. You sat on my lap at my home and I taught you the very legend you are now trying to pervert. You know the gods are not asking us to do the things you say they are asking. This is about you. Maybe it is about you and me, but it is definitely about you. Please let the woman go and let the twins go as well. None of them has done anything to hurt you. If you let them go, I will stand on your behalf to the authorities."

As Grandfather spoke, he and Hector moved closer to Montero, making their way slowly up the hill.

"Grandfather, once again you are worried about everyone else but your own people. You are seeking to protect a white woman. What about the women behind me who want their children to grow up and have the opportunities this woman had? What about your own people, Grandfather?" Montero said. "I have brought all the symbols together and her sacrifice will pave the way for our people to regain their rightful place!"

"Marcus, do you really believe what you are saying? Have you been saying it over and over so long that you have convinced yourself it is the truth? It can't be the truth and you know it. You refer to the things you have in front of you as symbols. That is all they are. They aren't magic. They aren't the gods themselves."

Montero grabbed Alivia by the hair and brought her to the edge of the cenote. She was starting to wake up from the drug, much as Red Bird had just before he was thrown into the water below. Montero held the statue of Two Wolves that Red Bird took from Tulum over his head with his other hand.

"It is all going to happen now, just as I foretold. You can't stop me Grandfather!"

"Marcus, my boy," Grandfather said, trying to get through the misguided man. "You are talking about how you are going to do this. Not the gods. Do you realize that? That is a sign this is about you, not anything from a higher power."

"I am going to do this Grandfather. I am going to sacrifice this woman in the cenote and the gods will smile on me. I know it!"

"Marcus, the statue is beautiful and it belongs to our people. You have done a good thing by taking it from the collector and bringing it back to the Maya. Maybe I made a mistake of not doing it sooner. I have made many mistakes in my years. I am sure when I go to Xibalba, I will pay for those mistakes. But there is a problem with what you believe is a powerful symbol. It is not there."

"What are you talking about old man? I have the statue right here. It is the real one. There can be no other."

Grandfather moved still closer, hoping to do something to save Alivia. He didn't know where Mike was or if the big American had a chance to put his plan into action.

"Marcus, let the woman go and I will show you. The statue you are holding is the ancient statue of Two Wolves, but it does not contain the heart stone. I can tell from here, without even touching it, that the stone is missing from the statue. Without it, you cannot save our people as you imagine."

"You are lying, Grandfather. He is lying!" Montero said turning to the people around him. His quick turn caught Alivia off balance. Her foot slipped and she almost fell.

"Marcus, let me help you. Spare the woman. This is not right. This will not accomplish what you want!" Grandfather said, raising his voice for the first time.

"I will prove it to you," Montero said. "I had planned for this to be more of a ceremony, but I know that not all sacrifices go as planned. Sometimes the offering wakes up or screams and yells. Sometimes they don't die immediately. The bloodthirsty gods don't care. They just want their offering. And so it will be today!"

Monterro turned with his hand still in Alivia's hair and pushed her off the edge. She fell 40 feet below into the cool clear water's off the cenote below her. The weights tied to her waist and ankles guaranteed she would sink to the bottom.

CHAPTER 47

Everything was a blur for Alivia. The last thing she really remembered was Montero and his men grabbing her at the hotel. She remembered sounds and strange visions, but nothing made sense. She felt separated from her body. Nothing seemed right.

She heard loud voices around her and then she couldn't see. The white covering over her eyes was removed. Then there was pain. It was the first time she felt pain in days, or years, or minutes. She couldn't be sure exactly how fast time was passing. Or how slow. But the pain was there. On the back of her head. Someone was pulling her hair.

The pain gave her something to focus on. There were voices. One of the voices seemed familiar. That voice was calm and controlled. It was trying to convince and persuade. The other voice was shrill and angry. It wasn't being persuaded at all.

She heard the voices argue back and forth and she tried to focus on what they were saying. Something about a sacrifice. And the heart stone. And the statue. Alivia knew what they were talking about, but she just couldn't put it together. Not yet. Things were becoming clearer and things were making more sense, but not quite yet.

And then there was the feeling like she was falling. She had felt that way since the hotel, but this was different. The earlier falling never ended, but this time she heard herself scream and then felt her feet hit the water below her. The cool water in her face shocked Alivia the rest of the way back to the here and now. She hadn't had a chance to grab a breath before she hit the water but now her mouth was clamped tight.

Alivia struggled against the ropes holding her wrists, but they wouldn't come lose. She tried to kick with her feet and swim back to the surface, but that wasn't much use either. She was sinking fast.

Alivia's lungs screamed in pain. She wanted to breathe badly. Her mind was fully awake and yet it was quickly approaching her final thoughts. She was starting to lose consciousness again. This time it was different, though. The drugs Montero gave her, now she remembered him doing it, were some sort of hallucinogen. She had drifted off and imagined a world of pink ponies and a Technicolor sky. But this time, her loss of consciousness was anything but cartoonish or pleasant. It was ugly, painful and terrifying. Her arms and legs didn't work. She struggled and struggled, but her actions began to slow.

It was almost over. She couldn't hold on any longer. Everything went dark.

And then there was a touch. Then the taste of sweet air. At first it didn't make sense. Where did it come from. She felt lips on hers. And air. Air. Air!

She greedily inhaled the air and her eyes flew open. She couldn't see clearly. Everything swam before her. Again a kiss. And more air.

And then she felt something being shoved against her mouth. Not lips this time, but a mouthpiece. She took it and felt a blast of air in her mouth as Mike hit the purge button and cleared the water from the regulator. She inhaled. She could breathe!

She felt hands on her head and something being lowered over her eyes. A finger poked her in the nose and she exhaled through it. The water from in front of her eyes drained away. She was wearing a scuba mask. Mike was there in front of her. He had saved her life.

Mike gave Alivia an OK signal by placing his hand right in front of her mask. She nodded yes. Mike held up his hand in front of her face to tell her to stop. Alivia thought that was unnecessary. She wasn't going anywhere but where the regulator was, although she would have liked to swim to the surface. Mike pulled a small knife off of his borrowed scuba unit and cut the ropes tying Alivia's hands and feet and then cut off the weights Montero had tied to her waist to drag her down to the bottom for the sacrifice.

Her hands free, Alivia started swimming and attempted to pull to the surface, but Mike shook his head and pointed in the direction where she should swim. They entered the tunnel off the side of the cenote where Beverly was waiting. She helped Mike swim Alivia back to the "vision room."

Mike asked Alivia again if she okay with the same hand signal and again she replied she was with a nod of her head. Through a series of hand gestures,

Mike indicated he wanted Beverly to stay there with Alivia. He wanted to go see if he could find out what was happening with Hector and Grandfather. It took a moment for Alivia to understand that Mike wanted her to give up her air supply, but Beverly showed her she also had a second regulator Alivia could breathe from and finally Alivia accepted it and switched over. After nearly drowning, she wasn't happy about giving up her source of air, and less happy about staying underwater in the cave, but she accepted it for the moment when she remembered that Montero was above and would probably just try to kill her again to complete his sacrifice.

As quickly as he could, Mike swam back to the Holy Cenote to find out what happened after Alivia hit the water. Surfacing, Mike stayed close to the edge to avoid being seen. As soon as he got his head out of the water, he heard shouts and anger from above. He couldn't understand what they were saying, but he knew they weren't happy.

"What have you done?!" Mike recognized that voice was Grandfather.

"I have done what the gods told me to do. Our people will rise up again, old man. We will not wait and be patient any longer. It is time for the Maya to take the lead and take control of their own lives again!"

"You have killed a woman for your vanity. The gods did not ordain this. This is all about you!" Grandfather sounded both angry and devastated by the situation. He knew how the outside world would react to what happened there. He knew how it would look for the Maya. "You have doomed us all."

Without knowing exactly what was being said, Mike quickly decided he needed to defuse the situation. He realized he needed to produce Alivia and show everyone that she was still alive. It would deflate Montero and help Grandfather to gain control of the situation. They would just have to keep her alive when he did.

He submerged and swam back into the tunnel to get Alivia.

Mike was able to move quickly through the cave system. The line that Hector left in the cave was still in place. With the events of the last 24 hours, he had not had a chance to remove it. Mike approached the chamber where he left Alivia with Beverly and saw that the lights were filtering down through the holes in the ceiling. He hesitated for a moment, taking in the spectacle of the lights, but he knew he didn't have time to waste. As he approached Alivia, he saw that she was staring into the lights. It appeared for a moment that she was crying behind her mask, but Mike assumed she was just enjoying the sights and the water on her face was there from when she was tossed into the water before Mike got to her.

As Mike touched Alivia's shoulder, the lights ended and the gloom returned to the cave. Mike and Beverly brought lights into the cave with them when they began the dive so they weren't in total darkness. Mike signaled to Beverly and Alivia to follow him back to the main cenote. In just a moment, they were swimming back to the surface.

Breaking the surface again, Mike could tell things hadn't gotten any better in the few minutes he was gone. He couldn't make out specific voices anymore, but there was still a lot of anger and yelling. He decided it was time to make his presence known.

"Grandfather! Grandfather! Hector! I am here and Alivia is safe. She is not dead!" he shouted from the water as he swam to the middle to make himself, and the two women in the water with him, seen from the side. As soon as Alivia got her head above water, she spit out Beverly's extra regulator and began stroking for the beach. She was not a diver and was not happy about breathing underwater. She was less happy about being drugged and thrown in the cenote to drown. All in all, she just wanted out of the water.

"Michael? Michael, is that you? You were successful?" Hector shouted back in English.

"I got to her in time, Hector. She is alive."

Grandfather and Montero stepped to the edge of the cenote to look down into the water.

"What have you done?" That was Montero, speaking in English.

"Michael, you have saved your friend and saved us all," Grandfather said.

"No! He has doomed us all! You were behind this. You have denied the gods of Xibalba, the lords of the underworld, their due!" Montero said, turning on Grandfather. "You have doomed us all! Take him! There must be blood!"

Everything on the hill above them exploded into chaos. Mike followed Alivia and reached the small beach area. He quickly dropped his dive gear. People were shouting, pushing and fighting. Grandfather and Hector were alone among Montero's followers. He saw a man he didn't recognize grab Grandfather. Hector tried to get in between them, but he was struck from behind and knocked down. Montero lunged forward toward Grandfather and the man who held him. It was his chief lieutenant Carlos. Mike saw a flash of steel and then a sound he had heard too many times before. A gunshot.

Mike took off running. By the time he got to the top of the hill, everyone was standing still, staring in shock at what had happened. Hector was holding Grandfather and the old man was bleeding.

Montero was shouting at the sky, waving the gun around and screaming.

"You demanded blood and I have provided it for you! I have given you the blood you asked for on this holy ground! Save my people and make me their king! Make me the lord of the Maya! I deserve it!"

Montero's followers weren't rushing to him joyously. Many looked afraid but they didn't try to interfere since he was still holding the gun.

Mike had seen crazy men with guns before and wasn't impressed. He knelt down beside Hector and tried to put pressure on Grandfather's wound, but one look told him that it was not going to work out well. A young, healthy man might survive it, but Grandfather didn't have the reserves. Mike heard sirens arriving and knew that the police were there. Beverly had called them while they were heading back to the cenote and given them directions. He hoped they brought an ambulance.

"Grandfather, hold on just a little longer. Help is on the way," Mike said, trying to give the man hope.

"Michael, my time is finished. I know that. Thank you for saving my people," Grandfather said and then he turned to Hector. "My friend, you have been a blessing to me and the Maya for many years. I ask one last favor of you."

"Anything Grandfather. I will do whatever I can."

"Look after the twins. They will need guidance and support, but they will lead the Maya after me. I have seen it and they will do good things for our people. Montero didn't understand, but he has brought about the Fourth Age. Just not the way he expected it to happen," Grandfather said.

All three of them turned when they heard Montero screaming. The police were approaching and his supporters were abandoning him quickly, melting into the woods when they could to get away. Mike could see from the look in Montero's eyes that he had lost it. Montero continued to wave his gun around over his head. Mike expected the police to shoot him any moment.

"This cannot happen! NO! I will lead my people! I will rise! The gods have said it was so!"

Mike heard the police order Montero to stop and to drop his weapon, but he could tell Montero didn't hear them. He was lost in his delusion. The man had finally lost all connection with reality. Mike heard a strange noise and looked down at the ground to see where it was coming from.

Without warning the ground beneath Montero's feet opened up and Montero disappeared into the earth below them. He was gone in the blink of an eye without even a chance to scream. The earth around the opening fell in around him covering up the spot where he stood, leaving a hole 10 feet deep.

Montero was gone.

"It is as the gods have shown me. It is over," Grandfather said, closing his eyes. Mike and Hector both held their breath for a moment until they realized the man was still breathing.

"He's just gone," Hector said looking at the hole in the ground. "I've never seen anything like that in my life."

"The ground around these cenotes can be unstable at times…"Mike said, not really believing what he was saying.

"Or maybe the gods got their vengeance," Hector said.

Mike didn't know if Hector was right or not, but he was sure that was exactly what the legend would say.

"Michael, there is one last thing I must tell you," Grandfather said, rousing himself.

"Anything you need, Grandfather. Tell me."

"The statue the collector had and that Montero took was incomplete. The heart stone was not in it. I could feel its source of power was elsewhere and safe. The statue was a symbol, but men would have fought over it without gaining the real power that it once possessed," Grandfather said.

"I understand, Grandfather. But what does that have to do with me?"

"To find the heart stone for my people, you must go home. Red Bird took it with him, but he kept it separate from the statue. He knew that men would envy and desire the statue without understanding its true power. He took it with him to his death."

"Grandfather, I don't understand," Mike said, but the old man once again closed his eyes. Mike and Hector moved back as medics arrived and began caring for the Grandfather of the Maya.

Mike and Hector gave their statements to the Policía Federal and the medics took Alivia to the hospital to examine her to make sure there were no side effects from the drug Montero gave her. The police began making plans to excavate the sink hole where Montero disappeared, but they weren't moving quickly. No one expected anyone could survive a collapse like that. Several people commented that it was amazing that the hole had opened exactly where he was standing, but no one offered any explanation of how that could happen.

CHAPTER 48

The rest of that day and most of the next, Mike and Alivia spent dealing with the police and the aftermath of the attempted murder/sacrifice. The authorities were rounding up the remaining members of Montero's gang and tying up the loose ends of the assault on the collector's home. They found a treasure trove of antiquities in the hidden "special" room the collector kept for himself. If he had lived through the attack, he would have been in trouble, as well. Since he didn't, there wasn't much left to do but call in archeologists and anthropologists from Mexico City to begin cataloging everything. Alivia assumed her mantel as "Dr. White from Marshall University" and was given access to everything. Since she nearly died in the process of regaining the artifacts, the Mexican authorities invited her to be involved as much as she wanted. Mike could tell something was bothering her, though.

Mike called his *First Account Magazine* editor in New York and told her what was going on. It took her a few minutes to understand that he wasn't in West Virginia any more since that was where she last heard from him. He hadn't checked in since he filed a story and photos about the burial site underneath the Adena mound. When she learned the intrigue in Mexico was related to the other set of stories in West Virginia, she definitely wanted more. Mike grabbed his cameras and began photographing everything he could so he could send it to the magazine's Mexican bureau. In the same way that the Mexican anthropologists gave Alivia unlimited access, everyone opened their doors to Mike. They weren't exactly sure what his role in the whole affair was, but most of the group saw Grandfather talking to Mike and that was good enough for them.

The authorities were looking for Montero's body, but they hadn't been able to find it yet. Someone said it seemed as if the earth swallowed him up. Many of the people there agreed that was exactly what had happened.

As it turned out, Grandfather's words to Mike were his last. He never regained consciousness in the hospital. According to Grandfather's wishes, his body was cremated and his ashes were thrown into the sea from the Temple of the Winds at the Tulum ruins. Mike and Alivia joined Hector and Loretta, along with the twins, and a number of friends and members of Grandfather's extended family for the quiet ceremony to pay tribute to the man.

The sun was high in the sky when everyone made it to the site. A gentle ocean breeze blew in off the ocean. Everything seemed perfect. The authorities didn't want to close off the grounds of the entire ruin, but they did put up ropes to give those visiting the site for Grandfather some privacy.

Most of what the speakers said was in Mayan or Spanish so Mike couldn't follow the memories people shared about the old man, but he knew they were speaking from the heart. He and Alivia stood off to the side watching everyone pay their respects. He also realized the twins were assuming the role of leadership for the Mayan people as Grandfather wished. They stood at the front of the crowd, looking wiser than their years. There would be elders around to guide them and teach them as they grew to adulthood, but the people took Grandfather's intentions for the children seriously, regardless of who their father was.

After everyone had a chance to speak, the twins held the urn up to the wind released the old Mayan's ashes. A strong wind gust blew in off the water and lifted the ashes straight into the sky. Everyone present smiled at the sight.

Afterward, the twins greeted everyone in a receiving line. Mike and Alivia brought up the rear.

"It is good to see you, Michael. You too, Alivia. I hope you have recovered from your experience in the cenote," the boy said to Alivia in English.

"I'm feeling…well, I will be fine. Thank you for asking," Alivia said.

"Michael, you would have been free to speak about the Grandfather if you wanted to," the girl told Mike.

"Thank you, but I only met Grandfather a few days ago. I didn't know him well enough to speak about him. It's funny, though. I know I'll miss him, anyway," Mike said. "I'm sure it has been a difficult time for the two of you."

"We will miss the Grandfather, but he instructed us well in the time we were with him," the boy said. "He told us that you have one more mission."

"What do you mean?"

"We know his last words to you. That he told you to go home to finish the quest. We look forward to hearing from you when you have found what you are looking for," the girl said.

Mike was momentarily stunned and couldn't answer the girl. How would they know what Grandfather told him? They were nowhere near when Grandfather spoke his last words. Hector heard him, but the twins could not have. The twins quickly moved on to say their final goodbyes to the other people and head home. Mike walked to the edge of the bluff overlooking the water and looked out at the aquamarine Caribbean Sea with the Temple of the Winds to his right. For a moment, he could imagine he was standing there in the time of the Maya, in the days of Red Bird and the statue.

"Mike, did you hear me?" It was Alivia.

"Sorry. No. What did you say?" Mike asked, turning to face her.

"I said, now that Grandfather's ceremony is over, I think it is time for us to go home."

"Really? With all of the stuff they found in the collector's house and Montero's cult, I would think this was an anthropologist's dream. You want to go home?"

"There is so much to do back in West Virginia. We have the mound to wrap up and I have to take over from Dr. Rowe. This has been an amazing adventure, but I need to get back," Alivia said, looking away from Mike, staring out at the water where Mike had been looking just moments before.

"Ummm, sure. I'll call the airline and get us seats back home tomorrow. A big advantage of all the travel I've done is I get extra attention from them when I call."

"Thanks, Mike."

Alivia walked away without another word. Mike watched her go and shook his head. He had no idea what was going on there. Near-death experiences affected different people in different ways, of course. He would give her some time.

They rode back to the hotel with Hector and Loretta and as soon as they got there, Alivia went to bed.

Mike made the arrangements for the next day and then went back to the courtyard to relax.

"Michael, I know you like beer, and in Mexico we are known for our tequila, but I would like to have a drink with you. It was the Grandfather's favorite, a miel beer. He gave me the recipe himself, but he said it was passed down from the days of the Maya."

"We had a few of these the first night I was here…wow, that seems like a long time ago."

"That beer was based on Grandfather's recipe. He was a homebrewer and liked to recreate the drinks of the ancients. That beer was good, but this miel was made by Grandfather's own hands. He would give me some from time to time and he taught me how to make it, but unfortunately once these are gone, there will be no more," Hector said as he poured Mike drink.

"I am honored you would share it with me," Mike said with a smile and a toast to his friend, and to Grandfather.

The two men stared at the stars for a while, sipping the ancient recipe.

"Hector," Mike said finally breaking the silence. "Something I've been wondering about. When I got back to Alivia in the cenote, the lights were reflecting down from the ceiling, just like when you and I were in there. But I only thought that happened at midday. How was it happening at that time of the morning?"

Hector was quiet for a while, continuing to stare at the night sky.

"Mike, legend says that is the room where the gods gave Red Bird his vision to take the statue away from Tulum. I have heard of others having visions in the chamber as well. It seems as if there are times the lights appear when the gods want them to, not always because of the position of the sun in the sky."

"I have one more question for you, Hector. Did you tell the twins what Grandfather said to me just before he died?"

"No, Michael. I have talked to the twins about many things, but that hasn't come up. I wasn't sure what he meant. I believed it was something between the two of you," Hector said. "Why do you ask?"

"Oh, nothing. Just something that occurred to me. How about one more drink and then it is time to hit the sack? I've got a long travel day tomorrow."

CHAPTER 49

After landing in West Virginia, Mike stopped to see his parents. With everything going on, he hadn't spent nearly as much time with them as he had planned…the story of his life; they were used to it. Alivia barely spoke on the plane ride home and she went on to Huntington alone. After the one night in the hotel, their relationship had cooled off considerably. Mike just shrugged his shoulders. In his 40s now, he knew he was too old to worry about those things. He liked Alivia, but if she was going to run hot and then cold, he would move on.

After talking to his mom for a while, Mike called Rich and Gardner and got them organized for a dive the next day. The quiet plane trip gave him a lot of time to think and he had an idea. He needed to make another dive in the cave beneath the burial mound.

Mike drove straight to the Adena mound the next morning. Rich and Gardner were already there and had most of the gear set up. They were ready and waiting on him. It took Mike a while to catch them up on everything that had happened in the last couple days, though.

"Damnitman," was all Gardner had to say as he shook his head. Mike wasn't sure if that meant he was sorry he missed it, glad he missed it or just a generalization.

"That's awesome, Mike. It sounds like you wrapped everything up," Rich said when Mike was done.

"Not everything. And that's why I asked you guys to come out this morning. We found the statue and made the connection that the skeleton down below is Red Bird, even if we didn't prove it without a shadow of a doubt. I mean, we know something was stolen from here, but we don't have anything to connect the two places. Maybe."

"What do you mean, maybe?" Rich asked.

"Just before Grandfather died, he said 'To find the heart stone for my people, you must go home. Red Bird took it with him, but he kept it separate from the statue. He knew that men would envy and desire the statue without understanding its true power. He took it with him to his death.' I think the heart stone is down below with his skeleton."

"So the answer to this puzzle, or at least the thing everyone really wanted, was down there all along?" Rich said.

"Damnitman…" Gardner grunted in reply. Then the diver began climbing down the ladder into the lower room beneath the burial mound to get the equipment ready. They had already agreed that Gardner would serve as topside support and as the safety diver, like before. Mike and Rich were going to make the dive into the cave wearing their closed circuit helmet cameras, with Mike carrying his camera back in its housing.

It had only been a few days since Mike and Rich last dived into the chamber, when they found the submerged plaque with the clues that led Mike to Mexico, but with everything that had happened to Mike along the way, he felt like it had been years. Both divers donned their diving helmets and tested out the air supply and communications. Gardner was at the controls and confirmed he could hear them loud and clear. Mike and Rich could hear each other, too.

Holding the air hoses, Mike and Rich walked out into the cool spring water on the boards Gardner and Rich laid down to keep the silt down. Mike shivered when he stepped into the water. He was wearing the DUI drysuit again, but the water was still 30 degrees colder than the water in the Mexican cenote. It took him a moment to adjust. When they were floating, supported by their own gear, they simply nodded to each other and let the air out of their buoyancy jackets and slipped below the surface.

Gardner turned on the underwater lights and lit up the room as Mike and Rich slipped into the cave. This time there was no looking around or inspecting anything. They did a quick check to make sure everything looked the way it did before Mike left, and it did, so they moved right to the smaller chamber off to the side where they found and recovered Red Bird's skull.

Mike was carrying his camera so he gestured for Rich to go in first.

"Rich, as gently as you can, clear away some of the sediment in what would be Red Bird's chest."

"Roger that, Mike. You think he was that literal?"

"It's called the heart stone for a reason. I think he knew he was going to die and he lay down on top of the stone. He knew the Adena wouldn't disturb his body. They just closed him off and left him there out of respect. So, yep, I think the stone is going to be right under his chest."

Rich began moving sediment away from the skeleton as gently as he could. He was still worried about stirring up the fine silt, and he knew Mike wanted to get photographs of the moment of discovery if they found the stone. Mike took a few photographs of Rich as his friend worked as methodically as he could. Both men, and Gardner, too, were barely breathing as they watched.

Rich paused for a moment.

"Hmmmm," he said.

"Nothing there?" Mike asked.

"No, I'm just wondering how you are always right all the time," Rich said. "It's here. I found it. Are you ready?"

"Pick it up," Mike said as he tapped the shutter button on the camera housing to make sure the digital camera inside was focused on the scene.

Rich lifted the smooth stone from the silt between Red Bird's rib cage and the ground. They had been calling the skeleton Red Bird ever since Mike got back, but it looked like they had confirmation of that, too.

The stone was rounded, vaguely oblong, and smooth like a river stone. It was a light pink with veins of a darker red running through it. They had found the heart stone, 'del corazón de piedra'.

"Let's get it back to the surface and call Alivia. She is going to flip," Mike said.

"You know, every time you say her name, there is something different now that you spent several days in Mexico with her. Anything you want to talk about, Mike?" Rich asked as they slowly swam to the surface.

"Ummmm, no, not really," Mike said with a laugh. He wasn't sure what there was to tell, but he did think she would be excited to hear the news.

Out of the water, Mike took a few more photos of the stone, and of Gardner and Rich holding it. Rich said something about making it his new profile photo and Gardner asked him to tag him in it.

As soon as the men were out of their dive gear, they headed up the ladder to the surface. Mike wanted to call Alivia and then he assumed she would want to call for another press conference to talk about what they found. This time he was actually looking forward to it.

And he couldn't have been more wrong.

CHAPTER 50

Reaching the top of the ladder, they heard sobbing. No one had bothered to turn on any of the lights on the upper level and the only light in the chamber was the morning light streaming in through the open door. It took Mike's eyes a moment to adjust. Finally he saw a person huddled against the cold earth wall of the inside of the mound. Walking over, he realized it was Alivia.

"Alivia, what's wrong? Are you okay?" he asked.

"I'm sorry, I'm so sorry," she said.

"What are you sorry for? What's wrong?"

Mike reached his hand out and touched her on the shoulder. She jumped backward and screamed. The sound from her throat rang with the most basic, the most primal scream imaginable. Mike resisted the urge to move closer to her.

"Alivia, it's okay. Whatever happened, whatever scared you, it's gone now."

"No, no, no. He's still here!" She pointed into the darkness on the other side of the chamber.

Mike looked at Rich and Gardner and then around the room. They couldn't see anything.

"Erick, I am so sorry," Alivia said through her tears. "I didn't mean to. I swear. I'm so sorry."

"Erick? You see Erick here? What did you do?" Mike asked.

Alivia continued crying for a moment, and then Mike could tell she was beginning to calm down. The hysterical tone to her voice was leaving. Gardner went outside to his truck and brought back a bottle of water. When he approached, she looked up and accepted it from him with a simple "Thank you."

"Alivia, are you back with us now? I need you to tell me what's going on. Did something scare you?" Mike asked.

Alivia stared at the wall for minute, but her breathing was easy and Mike knew she wasn't about to lose control again. She was just thinking of how to begin.

"It all started in Mexico. Or it all started 25 years ago, but I'll get to that," Alivia began, her voice flat and broken. "Montero drugged me and I saw all sorts of weird things that night while he kept me. Grandfather would probably call them visions, and he would probably be right. I saw Erick. I saw the Mayan who came here. I saw things I can never explain. I was starting to come out of it when Montero threw me off the edge of the cenote and I was drowning. I was so afraid Mike. I saw more visions. I saw the statue and the heart stone and the Mayans. And then you were there. You brought me back from the dead."

"I don't think you were dead yet," Mike said, trying to lighten up the discussion, but a look from Alivia told him that she didn't feel like joking.

"You brought me back from the dead and I thought everything I saw in my visions was wrong. None of it was going to happen. Then we swam to the chamber and you turned me over to Beverly. While we waited on you, I saw the Mayan gods. I saw Red Bird and I saw Erick there, too."

"The lights were shining into the chamber, but it wasn't the right time of the day for them," Mike said, remembering the scene.

"That was the Mayan gods talking to me," Alivia said. "They told me I had to ask forgiveness for my sins. I had to admit to what I did."

At this point, Mike knew better than to interrupt. He remained quiet. Rich and Gardner shifted uneasily, but they just listened as well.

"I came here this morning knowing you would be here. I knew you were going to follow up on what Grandfather told you. When I got here, he was…he was here waiting on me. It was Erick and it was Red Bird. I'm not sure which one it was. Or maybe it was both of them, maybe they are the same person."

"You saw Erick here? Today?"

"I saw him today and I saw him here the day he died. Dr. Rowe didn't kill him. He took the statue later and sold it to the collector, but he didn't kill Erick. I did."

"You killed Erick?"

"He invited me along to help him. He was so excited about the plaque that he found. He kept talking about how his parents were going to be so excited and how it was going to open up so many doors," Alivia said. "I knew it was going to be an important find. It was a career maker. At the time, we didn't know what was down below. All we knew was there was a plaque there just below the surface of the water that had Mayan and Adena markings mixed together. When he told me what he saw, I couldn't believe it. I just snapped. I couldn't let him be the one. It was just jealousy. Pure greed came over me. Not for money, but for recognition. He turned his back to me and I hit him with a rock. I've thought about it every day since then and I still don't know what came over me, but I did it. And then I put him in the dive gear and put him in the water. I found out later that they found water in his lungs. That meant he was still alive at that time. I knocked him unconscious and then I killed him when I put him in the water."

Following Alivia's admission of guilt, things happened quickly. She insisted Mike call the police and the university. The police responded to the site of the burial mound and arrested her and took statements from Mike, Rich and Gardner. Then the media and several university officials showed up and had an impromptu press conference on the same spot where just a few days before Alivia spoke to the national media about the tremendous finds beneath the burial mound. Mike and the two divers hung around and tried to stay out of the way. They had their dive gear and didn't want to leave it in case sightseers tromped in. They didn't want to carry it out with all the commotion outside. So they waited.

Mike was sitting inside the upper chamber staring at the walls, thinking about everything that had happened in the last few days. And what happened 25 years ago. He felt profoundly sad for Erick's death. He was a promising young man and a friend. His death influenced Mike's career in several ways, a few of which he was just realizing. Mike had long sought to right wrongs and get to the bottom of mysteries. He knew that came out of the situation around Erick's death. And Erick's death by scuba, or at least that was how he thought about it at the time, definitely influenced his decision to become a diver after he graduated from Marshall. It also crossed his mind that he had been seduced by a murderer—something that sat uneasy on his conscience.

He glanced up and saw movement in the room, but couldn't tell who was there.

"Hello?"

The person came closer, but didn't get any clearer.

"Erick? Is that you?"

Mike saw his old friend smile. And then the image shifted from Erick to something, or someone, slightly different. Mike guessed it was Red Bird. He looked young and strong, dressed in the finery of a priest. The ancient Mayan smiled at Mike, too. And then the vision disappeared.

"They say thank you."

"What? Who? What?"

"Easy, Mike. It's just me," Sophia said as she entered the burial chamber. "You saw Erick and the other one. They're just saying thank you for what you have done."

"You saw them?"

"Of course," the college student said with a smile. "Erick saved me the night when Dr. Rowe held me captive. His presence here scared Rowe so badly he stepped backward and fell down the hole."

"And you didn't tell me?"

"Would you have believed me if I told you I saw the ghost of my uncle who died before I was even born?"

"Well, no, probably not," Mike agreed.

Sophia came over and sat on the floor beside Mike.

"Hey, I have something to show you," Mike said. He pulled the heart stone out of his jacket pocket.

"Is that what I think it is?"

"We found it today with Red Bird's skeleton."

"It needs to go to the university or back to Mexico," Sophia said.

"You're right, but I think your parents should see it, and probably Anvil Blackwell. It's been missing a thousand years. Another day or two isn't going to hurt anything. You can give it to whoever takes over the anthropology department with my blessing. If they want to know how we found it, tell them I have plenty of photos and video when they are ready."

"Funny you should mention Anvil. He's outside and wants to talk to you," Sophia said with a grin.

"What's your connection to him, anyway? I could tell you knew him the night he appeared, but there wasn't time to ask."

"He's one of those uncles that aren't really related, but you call them family anyway. He knew my grandparents in Mexico, before they moved here. They helped him when he was a young researcher and became close," Sophia explained.

"It seems like everyone involved in this mess knew each other and knew what was going on long before I got involved," Mike said with a chagrinned laugh.

"Yes and no. Uncle Anvil will explain. We talked about this while you were gone. We all knew parts of the story, or thought we did, but it took someone like you with a fresh perspective to bring it all together—and unravel it all at the same time."

"Nice mixed metaphor," Mike said, teasing the young student. "I hope you don't write that way or I have to take all those nice things I said to my editor about you."

"Hey now…" Sophia started to argue and then let it drop. She knew Mike was playing. And then more quietly she said "Anvil is waiting on you."

Mike stood up from the hard stone floor and walked outside the Adena burial mound.

The sun was beginning to set, turning the sky pink, and a light breeze blew across the farm where the ancient mound stood. Mike could almost imagine the lives of the people who lived there and built the structure by hand, carrying small baskets of dirt, one at a time, to the hill and lovingly, or reverentially, shaping the mound to memorialize their elders.

After a moment's daydreaming, Mike glanced around to find Anvil. He didn't see the mountain man, but there was a stranger in a suit leaning against an old truck. And then it clicked.

"Anvil?"

Well, you should probably call me Theophilus, or Theo if that's easier," the older man said with a chuckle.

The man's voice hadn't changed from the night Mike first met him, but everything else had, or so it seemed. Theophilus was clean shaven with a haircut. The suit was a few years old, and fit a little tighter than would be comfortable, but it still looked good on the man.

"I'm coming back to the world for a while, so I thought I should fit the part. It's been a while since I wore a suit," Theophilus/Anvil said with a smirk. "The university called and they want me to take over the Anthropology Department now that Dr. White's status has changed. It will be an interim position."

"That's great news," Mike said. "I was wondering what was going to happen. Losing two senior people in just a matter of days has to have things in an uproar."

"That's what they said to me when they called and asked me to come in. They said they wanted some "stability" for a while. I asked them if they had seen me recently…"

Mike smiled at the thought of the big mountain man walking into a classroom full of college freshmen. Both men were quiet for a moment as they looked out across the field in front of them.

"I imagine you have some questions about all this," Theophilus said finally.

"I've seen some things the last few days that I don't understand," Mike began. "But I'm sort of used to that. I know there are a lot of things in this world that I can't explain and it is probably better if I don't even try. But can you tell me more about the heart stone? What is it?"

"I'm glad that's what you're asking. If you were going to ask me about the 'meaning of life' I was going to be stumped," Anvil began.

Mike quickly looked at the older man, surprised by the answer. And then he realized Theophilus was teasing him. Mike simply shook his head.

"The stone that you found with Red Bird's skeleton originally came from here, in the mountains not far from here, actually," Theophilus said.

"How do you know about…nevermind."

"Yeah, there are things you probably never will understand," Theophilus said with a totally serious look on his face. "Like I said, the stone came from the mountains not far from here. I'm not a geologist, but they tell me the Appalachians are an ancient mountain chain, dating all the way back to Pangea when all the land on earth was one big continent. They were originally as tall as the Rockies or the Alps, but they have been weathered down over the millennia. That weathering has revealed the very heart— the very core— of the mountains themselves. And that's where the heart stones come from."

"Heart stones?"

"They show up in legend from time to time. There have been heart stones in just about every culture, but they all seem to have some connection back to this place, back to these mountains," Anvil explained, gesturing at the hills above them. "They have been around since the beginning of the world; since God formed this world. I've heard theories that the heart stones were left by the angels, but of course those are just stories."

Mike pulled the heart stone from his pocket. Sophia had insisted he keep it when he left the mound to speak to Theophilus. Now he understood why.

"There is no way to be sure, of course," Theophilus continued, "since all we have to go on is legends, but that stone came from here, went to Tulum to found the great city and then returned here to be buried in that cave."

"I've never heard of a connection between the Adena and the Maya before," Mike said.

"And you probably won't. Or if you do, you'll hear people throw in alien civilizations and that sort of thing. Who knows? They may just be right," Theophilus said with a laugh. "The Adena were actually a tall race of people, taller than just about anyone else on earth at the time. Two Wolves was described as a giant when he arrived in Tulum. Between that and the heart stone, he was easily able to organize the people and found the city."

"But then Red Bird was told to take the heart stone away and bring it back here."

"That's what the legends say. Why? I have no idea. Maybe he did have a vision. Again, who knows? That is the frustrating part of anthropology. Some things we will probably never have answers to."

"Seems pretty frustrating to me," Mike said.

"It is, but then again, whenever you ask the 'why' questions, it's tougher to understand. People do things that make sense to them at the moment, but hindsight rarely makes those reasons clear to us."

"You've got that right," Mike said, thinking back to Alivia killing Erick. It still didn't make sense to him, but he knew it was a rash act.

After a moment, Theophilus asked, "What are you going to do next, Mike? Do you already have your next story assignment?"

"I don't know. I've enjoyed hanging around here and reconnecting with some old friends. I'm not going to give up my house on the Outer Banks and not going to quit the road, but I might see if the School of Journalism needs a little help for a while," Mike said. "When I was talking to my mom yesterday, she reminded me of an old saying. 'Don't get above your raisin'. It means you can go wherever you want, but that you should never be too proud to go home. I think I'll stay around a while."

Of course, Mike needed to let his editor know about the latest events at the mound. He knew she would want an update…both about Alivia and the heart stone. And then he was going to have to break the news that he was thinking about staying in West Virginia for a while. He wasn't sure how that would go.

ABOUT THE AUTHOR

Eric Douglas spent his childhood Sunday nights watching "The Undersea World of Jacques Cousteau" and dreamed of diving alongside the Captain. He became a diver, and then a dive instructor, meeting his goals and pursuing a life of adventure and travel.

Through his fictional works, Eric takes readers on adventures of their own. His stories have everything thriller junkies crave; action, adventure and intrigue, set against a backdrop of beautiful locations, the ocean and the environment, and scuba diving. The fast-paced stories are exciting, but Eric also hopes to inspire future generations of explorers and adventurers like Cousteau did for him.

After completing a program at the Center for Documentary Studies at Duke University, Eric jumped into documentary work, creating nonfiction works on lobster divers, war veterans, and cancer survivors.

Mike Scott Adventures

Cayman Cowboys

Flooding Hollywood

Guardians' Keep

Wreck of the Huron

Heart of the Maya

Return to Cayman: Paradise Held Hostage

Oil and Water

The 3rd Key: Sharks in the Water

Withrow Key Short Stories

The complete Withrow Key Collection: Tales from Withrow Key

Going Down with the Ship

Bait and Switch

Put It Back

Frog Head Key

Queen Conch

Sea Monster

Caesar's Gold

Life Under the Sea

Lyin' Fish

Children's Books
Sea Turtle Rescue and Other Stories

Other books by Eric Douglas:
River Town

Non-fiction
Heart Survivor: Recovery from Open Heart Surgery
Capturing Memories: How to Record Oral Histories
Keep on, Keepin' on: A Breast Cancer Survivor Story
Common Valor: Companion to the multimedia documentary West Virginia Voices of War
Russia: The New Age
Scuba Diving Safety

Made in United States
North Haven, CT
04 February 2022

15679811R00122